by the same author

Lullaby
Adèle
Sex and Lies
The Country of Others

WATCH US DANCE

LEÏLA SLIMANI

Watch Us Dance

*Translated from the French
by Sam Taylor*

VOLUME TWO

faber

First published in the UK in 2023
by Faber & Faber Ltd
The Bindery, 51 Hatton Garden
London, EC1N 8HN

First published in France in 2022 by Éditions Gallimard
under the title *Regardez-nous danser*

Typeset by Typo•glyphix, Burton-on-Trent DE14 3HE
Printed and bound by CPI Group (UK) Ltd, Croydon CRO 4YY

A CIP record for this book
is available from the British Library

ISBN 978–0–571–37606–3

2 4 6 8 10 9 7 5 3 1

To Bounty,
without whom nothing would be possible.

Dramatis Personae

Mathilde Belhaj: Born in Alsace in 1926, she met Amine Belhaj in 1944 while his regiment was stationed in her village. She married him in 1945 and, a year or so later, joined him in Meknes, Morocco. After three years at the family house in the medina, they moved to a remote farm where Mathilde gave birth to two children, first Aïcha and then Selim. While her husband worked furiously to make the farm a success, she turned her home into a clinic to care for the health of the peasants from the surrounding area. She learned the Arabic and Berber languages and, despite many difficulties and her opposition to certain traditions, particularly those concerning the status of women, she grew to love Morocco.

Amine Belhaj: Born in 1917, the eldest son of Kadour Belhaj, an interpreter in the colonial army, and Mouilala, Amine became head of the family after his father's death in 1939. He inherited Kadour's lands but, when the Second World War broke out, chose to enrol in a Spahi Regiment. Along with his aide-de-camp, Mourad, he was sent to a POW camp in Germany, but managed to escape. In 1944 he met Mathilde, and they were married at a church in Alsace in 1945. In the 1950s, while Morocco was in turmoil, he devoted himself to the farm, which he dreamed of turning into a prosperous, modern business. He developed new varieties of olive and citrus fruit trees and, after years of setbacks, his partnership with the Hungarian doctor Dragan Palosi finally enabled him to start making a profit.

Aïcha Belhaj: Born in 1947, Aïcha is Mathilde and Amine's only daughter. She went to a convent school, where she finished top of the class. A shy, mystical child, she is her parents' pride and joy.

Selim Belhaj: Born in 1951, Selim is Mathilde and Amine's only son. Spoiled by his mother, he too went to a colonial school.

Omar Belhaj: Born in 1927, Omar is one of Amine's brothers. As a child and as a teenager he felt a complex mix of admiration and hate for his elder sibling. He resented the fact that Amine fought for the French army and that he was their mother's favourite. An impulsive young man, he joined the nationalists during the war. In the 1950s he became a leader in the anti-colonialist rebellion and was involved in the violence that preceded Moroccan independence.

Jalil Belhaj: Born in 1932, Jalil was the youngest of Amine's brothers. Suffering from mental illness, he lived his life alone in his bedroom, staring endlessly into a mirror. When his sick mother moved to Amine and Mathilde's farm, Jalil was sent to stay with an uncle in Ifrane. After refusing to eat, he died of starvation in 1959.

Mouilala Belhaj: Born at the start of the twentieth century, Mouilala married Kadour Belhaj. Though her family was middle class, she never learned to read or write. Many of her ancestors were mentally ill and would run naked through the streets or talk to ghosts. She gave birth to seven children, four of whom survived: Amine, Omar, Jalil and Selma. A courageous, loving mother, she adored her eldest son and admired his French wife, Mathilde, for her freedom and education. Around 1955, starting to show the first symptoms of dementia, she left her house in the medina to live out the rest of her life at Amine and Mathilde's farm. She died a few months before her son Jalil, in 1959.

Selma Belhaj: Born in 1937, Selma is the sister of Amine, Omar and Jalil. Cosseted by her mother, this radiantly beautiful girl was jealously guarded by her brothers and regularly beaten by Omar. An inattentive student, she frequently played truant from school, and in the spring of 1955 she met the young French pilot Alain Crozières and became pregnant by him. To avoid scandal and dishonour, Amine forced her to marry his former aide-de-camp, Mourad. In 1956 she gave birth to her daughter, Sabah.

Mourad: Born in 1920, Mourad is from a small village eighty kilometres from Meknes. In 1939 he joined the army and was sent to the front, where he became Amine's aide-de-camp before being promoted. Secretly in love with Amine, he was jealous of Mathilde. When the war ended he went to Indochina with a Moroccan regiment. Sickened by the violence, he deserted and found his way back to Morocco, where he took refuge with Amine. Given the job of foreman on the farm, he carried out his duties so zealously that his underlings hated him. He married Selma in 1955.

Monette Bart: Born in 1946, Monette Bart is the daughter of Émile Bart, an aviator at the base in Meknes. A student at the convent school, she became close friends with Aïcha. Her father died in 1957.

Tamo: The daughter of Ito and Ba Miloud, two workers living in the douar near the farm, Tamo was hired as a servant by Mathilde. Although treated harshly by the Frenchwoman, she found her place within the Belhaj family and worked for them until the end of her life.

Dragan Palosi: A Hungarian gynaecologist of Jewish origin, he took refuge in Morocco with his wife, Corinne, during the Second World War. After a bad experience at a clinic in Casablanca, he decided to move to Meknes, where he opened his own practice. In 1954 he persuaded Amine to go into business with him, exporting oranges to Europe. He became friends with Mathilde and helped her when she felt overwhelmed by the responsibility of caring for the health of the local peasants. He took young Aïcha under his wing, giving her books to help quench her thirst for knowledge.

Corinne Palosi: A Frenchwoman from Dunkirk, Corinne is Dragan's wife. Her voluptuous body provoked lust in men and suspicion in women. She suffered from her inability to have children and lived a somewhat solitary life in Meknes.

I

The times pay no heed to what I am. They impose
whatever they wish upon me.
Allow me to ignore the times.

Boris Pasternak

Mathilde stood at the window, looking out at the garden. Her opulent, chaotic, almost vulgar garden. Her vengeance against the austerity that her husband imposed upon her in every aspect of life. It was very early in the morning and the sun peeped shyly through the leafy treetops. A jacaranda, its mauve flowers not yet open. The sole weeping willow and the two avocado trees sagging under the weight of fruit that no one ate and that fell to the ground to rot. The garden was never as beautiful as at this time of year. It was early April 1968, and Mathilde thought it was not by chance that Amine had chosen this moment. The roses, which she had brought in from Marrakech, had bloomed a few days earlier and their sweet, fresh scent pervaded the garden. Beneath the trees lay agapanthus, dahlias, lavender and rosemary bushes. Anything could grow here, Mathilde always said. For flowers, this soil was blessed.

Already she could hear the songs of starlings and she spotted two blackbirds hopping in the grass, their orange beaks pecking at the earth. One of them had white feathers on its head and Mathilde wondered if the other blackbirds made fun of it or if, on the contrary, its uniqueness made it stand out, earned it the respect of its peers. Who knows how blackbirds live, she thought wistfully.

She heard men's voices, the roar of an engine. A huge yellow monster appeared suddenly on the path that led to the garden.

3

First she saw its metal arms and then, at the end of those arms, the enormous shovel. The mechanical digger was so wide that it could hardly pass between the rows of olive trees, and the men yelled instructions at the driver as branches were ripped from the trees. At last the machine came to a halt and peace returned.

This garden had been her lair, her refuge, her pride. She had played here with her children. They had napped beneath the weeping willow and picnicked in the shade of the Brazilian rubber tree. She had taught them to flush out the animals that hid in the trees and bushes. The owl and the bats, the chameleons that they kept in cardboard boxes and sometimes left to die under their beds. And when her children had grown up, when they had tired of her games and her tenderness, she had come here to forget her loneliness. She had planted, pruned, sown, replanted. She had learned to recognise the different bird songs audible at every hour of the day. How could she dream now of chaos and devastation? How could she wish for the destruction of what she had loved?

The workmen entered the garden and hammered stakes into the ground to form a rectangle twenty metres long and five metres wide. They were careful as they moved around not to crush the flowers with their rubber boots and Mathilde was touched by this pointless consideration. They gestured to the driver of the mechanical digger, who tossed his cigarette out the window and started the engine. Startled, Mathilde closed her eyes. When she opened them again, the gigantic metal claw was sinking into the ground. A giant's hand penetrated the black earth, releasing a smell of moss and humus. It tore up everything in its path and, as the hours passed, built a hill where shrubs and decapitated flowers lay lifeless amid the soil and rocks.

That iron hand was Amine's. Or so Mathilde thought that morning as she stood statuesque behind the living room window. She was surprised that her husband hadn't wanted to watch it happening, to see her plants and trees torn out one after another. He had told her the hole had to be there. That they had to dig it next to the house, in the sunniest part of their land. Yes, in the place where the lilacs grew. Where the lemange tree had once stood.

He had said no at first. No, because they couldn't afford it. Because water was a rare and precious commodity that could not be used for mere leisure. He had yelled no, no, no, because he hated the idea of displaying such indecency before the eyes of the poor farmworkers. What would they think of the way he was educating his son, of his attitude towards his wife, when they saw her, half-naked, in a swimming pool? He would be no better, then, than the old colonists or those decadent bourgeois families that proliferated all over the country, shamelessly showing off their glittering success.

But Mathilde did not give up. She swept aside his protests. Year after year she tried again. Every summer when the chergui howled and the sweltering heat frayed their nerves, she brought up the idea of the swimming pool that so repulsed her husband. He could not understand, she thought, this man who did not know how to swim, who was afraid of water. She spoke to him softly, sweetly, imploringly. There was no shame in displaying their success. They weren't hurting anyone. They had the right to enjoy life, didn't they, after dedicating their best years to the war and then to this farm? She wanted that swimming pool; she wanted it as a reward for her sacrifices, her loneliness, her lost youth. They were over forty now and had nothing to prove to anyone. All the farmers in the area, at least those with modern lifestyles, had swimming pools. Would he prefer it if she flaunted herself at the municipal pool?

She flattered him. She praised the success he had enjoyed experimenting with olive tree varieties and exporting citrus fruit. She thought she could persuade him by standing there in front of him, her cheeks pink and hot, hair glued to her temples with sweat, varicose veins bulging from her calves. She reminded him that everything they owned was down to their hard work and tenacity. 'I'm the one who did all the work,' he corrected her. 'I'm the one who decides what to do with the money.'

Mathilde did not cry or get angry when he said that. She smiled inwardly, thinking of all that she did for him, for the farm, for the workers and their families. She thought about all the time she'd spent raising their children, taking them to dance and music classes, helping them with their homework. And for the past few years Amine had entrusted the farm's bookkeeping to her. She wrote invoices, paid wages and bills. And sometimes – yes, sometimes – she would falsify the accounts. She would alter an amount, invent an extra farmhand or an order that had never been made. And, in a drawer for which she possessed the only key, she kept rolls of banknotes held together with beige elastic bands. She had been doing this for so many years that she no longer felt any shame or even any fear at the idea of it being discovered. The nest egg kept growing and she believed she had earned it; it was a tax for all the humiliations she had suffered. It was her revenge.

Mathilde had aged. It was true that she looked older than her years, and that was almost certainly his fault. The skin of her face, constantly exposed to the sun and the wind, was coarser. Her forehead and the corners of her mouth were wrinkled. Even her green eyes had lost their sparkle, like a dress worn too many times. She had put on weight. One day in the middle of a heatwave, to provoke her husband, she had grabbed hold of the garden hosepipe and, watched by the maid and some of the farmworkers, sprayed water all over herself. Her clothes stuck to her body, revealing her erect nipples and her pubic hair. That day the workers prayed to the Lord, rubbing their tongues between their blackened teeth, not to let Amine go insane. Why would a grown woman do such a thing? People might spray water at their children sometimes, it was true, when the sun blazed down so hard that they were on the verge of fainting. But they always told them to hold their noses and shut their mouths because the water from the well could make you sick or even kill you. Mathilde was like a child herself. And, like a child, she never grew tired of begging. She'd talked about the happiness of days gone by, the holidays they'd spent by the sea in Mehdia, at Dragan's beach hut. Talking of Dragan, hadn't he had a swimming pool built at their townhouse? 'Why should Corinne have something that I can't have?' she'd asked.

She was sure it was this argument that had finally made Amine surrender. She had delivered that line with the cruel confidence of a blackmailer. Her husband, she thought, had had an affair with Corinne the previous year, an affair that had lasted several months. She was convinced of this despite never having found any clues other than a hint of perfume on his shirts, a trace of lipstick – those mundane, disgusting clues that are a housewife's bane. No, she had no proof and he had never admitted it, but it had been so obvious, like a fire burning between their two bodies, a fire that did not last but had to be endured. Mathilde had tried once, clumsily, to talk to Dragan about it. But the doctor, who had grown even more debonair and philosophical with age, had pretended not to understand what she meant. He had refused to take her side, to lower himself to such pettiness, to join the impassioned Mathilde in fighting what he considered to be a futile war. Mathilde never knew how much time Amine had spent in that woman's arms. She didn't know if it was love, if they had spoken words of tenderness to each other or if – and this would perhaps be worse – their passion had been silent, purely physical.

Amine's handsomeness had only intensified over the years. The hair at his temples had turned white and he had grown a thin salt-and-pepper moustache that made him look like Omar Sharif. Like a film star, he wore sunglasses even indoors. But it wasn't only his bronzed face, his square jaw, the white teeth that he flashed on the rare occasions when he smiled . . . It wasn't only this that made him handsome. His manliness had matured like a fine wine. His movements were smoother now, his voice deeper. His emotional stiffness had come to seem like self-control, and his humourless face made him look like some wild beast, slumped in the sand, apparently listless, but which can, with a single bound, descend upon its prey. He was not entirely aware of his seductive powers; he discovered them little by little as they took effect on woman after woman, as if they did not really belong to him. And this sense of being almost surprised by himself probably explained much of his success with women.

Amine had grown in self-confidence and in wealth. He no longer spent endless nights staring at the ceiling as he calculated his debts. He no longer ruminated over his imminent ruin, his children's degradation, the humiliations they would be forced to suffer. Amine slept well now. The nightmares had left him and in town he had become a respected man. These days he was invited to parties; people wanted to meet him, to be seen with him. In 1965 he'd been asked to join the Rotary Club, and Mathilde knew that he, not she, was the reason for this, and that the members' wives probably had something to do with it too. Although silent and reserved, Amine was the centre of attention. Women asked him to dance, they pressed their cheeks against his, drew his hand to their hips; and even if he didn't know what to say, even if he didn't know how to dance, he would sometimes think that this life was possible, a life as light as the champagne he smelled on their breath. Mathilde hated herself at these parties. She always thought she talked too much, drank too much, and afterwards she would spend days regretting her behaviour. She imagined she was being judged, that the others considered her stupid and useless, a coward for closing her eyes to her husband's infidelities.

But another reason why the Rotary members were so insistent, so welcoming and attentive toward Amine was that he was Moroccan and the club wished to prove, by increasing its number of Arab members, that the era of colonisation, the era of parallel lives, was over. Of course, many of them had fled the country during the autumn of 1956 when the angry mob had invaded the streets and abandoned itself to a crazed bloodlust. The brickworks had gone up in flames, people had been killed in the streets and the foreigners had realised that this was no longer their home. Some of them had packed up and left, abandoning apartments where the furniture gathered dust before being bought up by Moroccan families. Landowners gave up their estates and the years of work they had put into them. Amine wondered if it was the most fearful or the most clear-eyed who went back to France. But that wave of departures was only an interlude. A readjustment before life returned to its normal course. Ten years after independence, Mathilde had to admit that Meknes had not changed all that much. Nobody had learned the new Arabic street names, and when they arranged to meet someone it was still on Avenue Paul Doumer or Rue de Rennes opposite Monsieur André's pharmacy. The notary had remained, and so had the haberdasher, the hairdresser and his wife, the owners of the fashion boutique on the avenue, the dentist, the doctors. They might show more discretion now, more restraint, but they all wanted to keep enjoying the pleasures of this chic, flower-filled city. No, there had not been a revolution, only a change in the atmosphere, a reticence, an illusion of harmony and equality. During those Rotary dinners, at tables where bourgeois Moroccans mingled with members of the European community, it appeared that colonisation had never been anything more than a misunderstanding, a faux pas that the French now repented and the Moroccans pre-tended to forget. Some came out and said that they had never been racist, and that they had found the whole thing terribly embarrassing. They swore that they were relieved now, that things were clearer and they too could breathe more easily since the city had rid itself of the rotten apples. The foreigners were more careful about what they said. If they hadn't left, it was because they did not want to precipitate the ruin of a country that needed them. Of course, one day they would vacate their place, they would leave, and the town's pharmacist, dentist, doctor and notary would all be Moroccans. But in the meantime they would stay and make themselves useful. And anyway, were they really so different from the Moroccans who sat beside them at their tables? Those elegant, open-minded men, those colonels or senior officials whose wives had short hair and wore Western dresses? No, they weren't so different from those bourgeois Moroccans who, without any qualms, let barefoot children carry their shopping home from the central market. Who refused to give in to the pleas of beggars 'because they're like dogs that you feed under the table. They get used to it and lose what little motivation they have to get off their arses and work.' The French would never have dared say anything about the people's propensity for begging and complaining. Unlike the Moroccans, they would never have dared accuse maids of dishonesty, gardeners of laziness, the working classes of stupidity. And they laughed, a little too loudly, when their brown-skinned friends despaired of ever constructing a modern country with a population of illiterates. Yes, deep down, these Moroccans were just like them. They spoke the same language, saw the world in the same way, and it was difficult to believe that they might one day not belong to the same side, might consider each other enemies.

To start with, Amine had appeared mistrustful. 'They're hypocrites,' he'd told Mathilde. 'Before, I was the dirty Arab, the *crouille*, and now it's all Monsieur Belhaj we would so like the pleasure of your company blah blah blah.' Mathilde had realised he was right one night during a dinner dance at the hacienda. Monique, the hairdresser's wife, had had too much to drink and in the middle of a conversation let slip the word '*bicot*'. She raised her hands to her lips as if to push that abhorrent word back into her mouth, then sighed 'Ohhhh', eyes wide, cheeks crimson. Mathilde was the only person who'd heard, but Monique couldn't stop apologising. 'Honestly, that's not what I meant to say,' she repeated. 'I don't know what got into me.'

Mathilde never knew with any certainty what it was that convinced Amine. But in April 1968 he announced that the swimming pool would be built. After the excavation they had to pour in the concrete walls then install a plumbing and filtration system; Amine supervised the work with an air of authority. He had a row of red bricks laid alongside the edge of the pool, and Mathilde had to admit that they gave it a certain elegance. They were both there when the pool was filled with water. Mathilde sat on the hot bricks and watched the water level rise, waiting as impatiently as a child for it to reach her ankles.

Yes, Amine gave in. When it came down to it, he was the boss, the one who put food on the farmhands' tables, and it was none of their business how he chose to live his life. Before independence the best lands had still been in the hands of the French, and most Moroccan peasants had lived in poverty. Since the protectorate, which had enabled immense progress in terms of healthcare, the country's demographic curve had shot up. In the ten years since independence, the peasants' plots of land had been divided up so many times that they were now too small to provide a living. In 1962 Amine had bought part of the Mariani domain as well as the lands belonging to the Mercier widow, who moved to a squalid apartment in town near Place Poeymirau. He had picked up her machines, livestock and grain reserves for a modest price, and he'd rented out plots of land to a few farming families, who irrigated them with seguias. Amine had a reputation locally as a tough, stubborn, short-tempered boss, but nobody ever questioned his integrity or his sense of justice. In 1964 he had received a considerable grant from the government to irrigate part of his farm and to buy modern equipment. Amine told Mathilde many times: 'Hassan II understands that we are first and foremost a rural country, and that he must support our agriculture.'

When the swimming pool was ready, Mathilde decided to celebrate with their new Rotary Club friends. She spent a week organising what she called, in English, her 'garden party'. She hired waiters and went to a caterer in Meknes to rent silver platters, Limoges porcelain tableware and champagne flutes. She had tables set up in the garden and arranged bouquets of wildflowers in small vases: the farmworkers were sent into the fields the morning of the party to pick poppies, marigolds and buttercups. The guests were all very complimentary. The women kept repeating that they thought it all 'charming, quite simply charming'. And the men slapped Amine on the back as they admired the pool. 'This is it, Belhaj, this is success!' When the barbecued lamb was presented, there was a round of applause, and Mathilde insisted that everyone should eat it 'Moroccan-style' – with their hands. They all gathered round and dug in, sinking their fingers into the creature's flesh, picking off the grilled skin and tearing out pieces of the tender, fatty meat which they dipped in salt and cumin.

The meal went on until mid-afternoon, by which point the guests were all drowsy from alcohol, the heat, the soft lapping of water against the sides of the pool. Dragan, eyes half-closed, nodded gently. A swarm of red dragonflies hovered over the surface of the water.

'This place is a real paradise,' Michel Cournaud told Amine. 'But watch yourself, my friend. You'd better hope the king doesn't come out here. Do you know what I heard the other day?'

Cournaud had a belly as big as a pregnant woman's and he always sat with his legs spread and his hands resting on his paunch. His face, flushed bright red, was extremely expressive, and there was still some spark of childhood in his green eyes: a mischievousness, a curiosity that made people warm to him. Beneath the orange parasol, Cournaud's skin looked even redder than usual, and as Amine stared at his round face the thought occurred to him that his new friend was about to explode. Cournaud worked for the Chamber of Commerce and knew many people in the business world. He divided his time between Meknes and the capital, and at the Rotary Club he was famed for his sense of humour and above all for the entertaining stories he told about intrigues at the Court. He handed out gossip like sweets to starving children. Nothing much ever happened in Meknes, so the smart set there felt cut off from the world, stuck in a dull, provincial backwater. They knew nothing of what was really going on in the major coastal cities, where the country's future was being decided. The Meknes elite had to make do with official communiqués and rumours of conspiracies, riots and the mysterious disappearances of opposition leaders such as Mehdi Ben Barka and others whose names were never spoken out loud. Most of them were not even aware that for the past three years the country had been under martial law, with Parliament suspended and the constitution ignored. Of course, they all knew that the beginning of Hassan II's reign had been difficult and that he'd had to face up to an increasingly radical opposition. But who could claim to know the whole truth? The heart of power lay in a distant, veiled place, a place that provoked in these wealthy provincials a mixture of fear and fascination. The women in particular loved to hear stories about the king's harem of almost thirty concubines. They imagined that behind the walls of the mechouar the Prophet's descendant presided over parties straight out of a Hollywood epic, with champagne and whisky flowing like water. This was the kind of tale with which Cournaud liked to tantalise them.

He tried to lean closer to the table and began speaking in a conspiratorial tone. The other guests listened in, all except Dragan who had fallen asleep, his lips vibrating softly. 'So . . . I was told that a few weeks ago the king was being driven in a car and they passed a beautiful property. In the Gharb, I think . . . Well, actually, I'm not sure about that, but anyway, the point is: he liked this place. He said he wanted to visit the farm, to meet the landowner. And in no time at all he bought the place for an amount that he himself decided on the spot. The poor owner couldn't do a thing!'

The other guests laughed, but Amine didn't. He didn't like it when people spread rumours, when they said bad things about this monarch who, since inheriting the throne in 1961, had made the development of agriculture the country's first priority.

'That's just malicious gossip,' he said. 'The king is being smeared by the lies of jealous people. The truth is that Hassan II is the only one who understands that Morocco is capable of

17

becoming a new California. Instead of badmouthing him those people should be praising his policies: the dams, the irrigation project that will enable all the country's farmers to make a living from their work.'

'You're deluding yourself,' Cournaud cut in. 'From what I've heard, the king is far more interested in playing golf and having all-night parties at the palace. I hate to disappoint you, my dear Amine, but all that stuff about him caring about fellahs is pure propaganda. If he really cared about them he would already have launched real agrarian reform. He'd have given land to the millions of peasants who have nothing. But in Rabat they know the reality: there will never be enough land for everyone.'

'What do you expect?' Amine demanded angrily. 'You expect the government to nationalise all the colonial properties over-night and ruin the country? If you understood anything about my work you'd know that the palace is right to do it bit by bit. What do they know about it in Rabat? Our agricultural poten-tial is immense. Cereal production just keeps rising. I myself am exporting twice as much fruit as I was ten years ago.'

'You'd better watch out, then. They might come here soon and take your land off you so they can give it to poor fellahs.'

'I have no problem with helping the poor. But not at the expense of people like me who spent years and years building viable businesses. The king knows that. The peasants are and always will be the most loyal defenders of the throne.'

'I admire your optimism, my friend,' Cournaud said with a smile. 'But if you want my opinion, this king only cares about his own little schemes. He leaves the country's economy in the hands of the wealthy bourgeoisie who get even richer and thank him by telling anyone who will listen that the king is in charge of everything.'

Amine cleared his throat. For a few seconds he stared at his guest's ruddy face, at his hairy hands, and he imagined how it would feel to button his shirt all the way up to the collar and watch him suffocate.

'You should be careful what you say. You could be deported for saying things like that.'

Cournaud stretched out his legs. He looked as though he was about to slide off his chair and collapse to the ground. He forced his lips into a weak smile.

'I didn't mean to offend you,' he said.

'You didn't offend me. I'm telling you this for your sake. You keep saying that you know this country, that this is your home. So you should know that, here in Morocco, you can't speak freely.'

The next day, Amine hung a photograph in a gilt frame on the wall of his office. It was a black-and-white picture of Hassan II in a flannel suit, gazing solemnly at the horizon. He hung it between a plate from an agronomy textbook about the pruning of vines and a newspaper article about his farm that described Amine as a pioneer in the cultivation of olive trees. Amine thought it would impress the clients and suppliers who came to visit him here, and the farmworkers who came to complain. They were always moaning, those peasants, with their filthy hands resting on his desk, their craggy faces wet with tears. They would complain about their poverty while looking outside, through the glass door, their eyes insinuating that Amine was one of the lucky few. That he could not understand what it was like to be a simple farmhand, a poor yokel with no means of feeding his family beyond an arid patch of land and a couple of hens. They would ask for an advance, a favour, credit, and Amine would refuse. He would tell them to pull themselves together and show some guts, just as he had done when he took over this farm. 'Where do you think I got all this?' he would ask, sweeping his arm across the vista. 'You think I was lucky? Luck has nothing to do with it.' He glanced at the photograph of the king and thought that the people of this country expected too much from the makhzen – the state and its agents, and more specifically the king and his entourage. What the king wanted were workers, strong peasants, Moroccans who were proud of their hard-won independence.

His farm was growing and he had to hire men to work in the greenhouses and harvest the olives. He sent Mourad into the neighbouring douars and even as far afield as Azrou and Ifrane. The foreman returned accompanied by a gang of malnourished boys who had grown up in the onion fields and could not find any work. Amine questioned the boys about their abilities. He took them to visit the greenhouses, the warehouses, showed them how to use the press. The boys followed him, silent and docile. The only questions they asked were about their wages. Two of them requested an advance, and the others, emboldened by their colleagues' courage, said they would need an advance too. Amine never had any complaints about the application of these young men who turned up at dawn and worked themselves into the ground come rain or burning sun. But after a few months some of them began to disappear. Once they'd received their wages, they were never seen again. They had no desire to move to the farm permanently, to start a family, to impress their boss enough to earn a raise. They only had one idea in mind: to earn a bit of cash then leave behind the countryside and its poverty. To leave behind the shacks, the smell of chicken shit, the anxiety of winters without rain and women who died in childbirth. During the days they spent under olive trees, shaking the branches to make the olives fall into their nets, they would whisper their dreams of going to the shanty towns around Casablanca or Rabat where each of them had an uncle, a cousin, a big brother who had gone off to make his fortune and who never wrote home.

Amine watched them. In their eyes he sensed an impatience, a rage he had never seen before, and it scared him. These boys cursed the soil that they dug. They hated the work they did, even as they did it well. And Amine decided his mission in life was no longer just to grow trees or harvest fruit, but to keep the boys here. At that time, all of them wanted to live in a city. The city was an abstract, obsessive thought that filled their minds, something of which, very often, they knew nothing at all. The city kept moving closer, like a slouching beast, a growing threat. Every week its lights seemed brighter, eating up the darkness of the countryside. The city was alive. It twitched and quivered, creeping forward, bringing with it distant noises and disquieting dreams. Sometimes it seemed to Amine that a world was vanishing, or at least a way of seeing the world. Even the farmers wanted to be bourgeois. The new landowners, the ones who had acquired their properties after independence, talked about money like industrialists. They knew nothing of mud or ice, of violet dawns spent walking between rows of blossoming almond trees where the joy of living within nature seemed as obvious as breathing. They knew nothing of the disappointments meted out by the elements, or the obstinacy and optimism needed to keep trusting the seasons. No, they were content to roam around their domains by car, showing them off to visitors, boasting of their merits but learning nothing. Amine felt the purest contempt for these phoney farmers who hired foremen to do their work and preferred to live in the city, surrounded by people. In this country that for centuries had known nothing but farms and war, all the talk these days was of cities and progress.

Amine had started to hate the city. Its yellow lights, its dirty streets, its stale-smelling shops and its broad avenues where boys strolled aimlessly, hands in their pockets to hide their erections. The city and its cafés whose open mouths devoured the virtue of young women and the desire for work in men. The city where young people wasted whole nights dancing. Since when had men needed to dance? How stupid it was, how ridiculous, thought Amine, this hunger for pleasure that had taken hold of everyone! In reality Amine knew nothing of the big cities and the last time he'd been to Casablanca the country had still been ruled by the French. He understood very little of politics and did not waste his time reading newspapers. Everything he knew came from his brother Omar, who lived in Casablanca now and worked for the intelligence services. Omar would sometimes come to spend Sunday at the farm, where everyone – from the employees to Mathilde and Selim – feared him. He was even thinner these days, and his health was poor. His face and arms were covered in blotches. And his Adam's apple slid up and down his long, scrawny neck as if he couldn't swallow his own saliva. Omar, whose sight was too bad for him to drive, would be dropped at the entrance to the property by Brahim, his chauffeur. The workers would crowd around his luxury car and Brahim would have to yell at them and shove them away. Omar was an important man now, but he didn't like to talk about his work. He never went into any detail about his missions, although he did once let slip that he collaborated with Mossad and had been to Israel, where, he told his brother, 'The orange plantations are every bit as good as yours.' To Amine's questions Omar offered only vague replies. Yes, he had prevented plots against the

23

king and arrested dozens of people. Yes, the shanty towns and universities and seething medinas of this country were home to thousands of fanatics and murderers calling for revolution. 'Marx or Nitcha,' he breathed, referring to Nietzsche and the father of communism. Omar waxed nostalgic about the days of the struggle for independence, when everyone was united by a single ideal and driven by a nationalism which, he believed, ought to be rekindled. Omar confirmed Amine in his own beliefs: cities were dangerous places full of dangerous people, and the king was right to prefer the peasantry to the proletariat.

In May 1968 Amine listened to the radio every night for news of what was happening in France. He was worried about his daughter, whom he had not seen for more than four years and who was studying medicine in Strasbourg. He didn't fear that she might be influenced by her fellow students because Aïcha was like him, fully focused on her work, a quiet, relentless toiler. But he feared for her safety, his little girl, his pride and joy, lost amid the chaos. He never told anyone this, but Aïcha was the reason he had agreed to build the swimming pool. He wanted to make her proud of him. So she, the future doctor, would not be ashamed to invite her friends to the farm one day. He never boasted about his daughter's success. To Mathilde he said coldly: 'You don't realise how jealous people are. They would pluck out their own eye if it made the others blind.' Through his daughter, through his child, he became someone else. She elevated him, she lifted him out of poverty and mediocrity. When he thought about her he was gripped by an intense emotion, a burning inside his chest that made him gasp for breath. Aïcha was the first member of their family to go to university. You could search as far back through their ancestors as you liked, you would not find anyone who knew more than she did. They had all lived in ignorance, in a sort of darkness and submission to other people or to the elements. All they had ever known was a life of immediacy, a life to be observed and endured. They had knelt before kings and imams, before bosses and colonels. It seemed to him that, ever since the birth of the first Belhaj, the family tree could be traced all the way back to its roots without finding a single existence of any depth, a single person with any knowledge beyond old wives' tales and worn platitudes. Certainly none of them would have known the things found in the books that Aïcha read. Until their lives' ends, they would never have learned anything that did not come from their experience of the world.

He asked Mathilde to write to their daughter, begging her to come home as soon as possible. Her exams had been post-poned so she had no reason to stay there any longer, in that country where everything was collapsing. When Aïcha was here again he would walk with her through the plantations of peach trees, between the rows of almond trees. As a child she had been able to point out the trees that gave bitter fruit, and she had never been wrong. Amine had always refused to cut down those trees, to get rid of them. He said they had to be given another chance, that he should wait for the next bloom, continue to hope. That little girl with her thick, unruly hair had become a doctor. She had a passport, she spoke English. Whatever happened, she would be better than her mother; she wouldn't have to spend her life begging favours. Aïcha would build swimming pools for her own children. She would under-stand the value of hard-earned money.

When classes ended, Selim ran out of school and rode his moped to the sailing club. He went into the changing rooms and saw a group of naked boys playfully whipping one another with their towels. He recognised a few of them; they had been with him at the Jesuit school. He greeted them, headed towards his locker and slowly undressed. He rolled his socks into a ball. He folded his trousers and his shirt. He hung his belt on a coat hanger. Then, standing there in his underwear, he noticed his reflection in the mirror on the inside of his locker's door. For some time now he had felt that his body was no longer really his. He had been transported into a stranger's body. His chest, legs and feet were covered with blond hair. His pectorals had grown bigger from swimming, which he practised assiduously. He looked more and more like his mother, whom he now towered over by almost four inches. From her he had inherited his blondness, his broad shoulders and his love of physical activity. This resemblance embarrassed him; it felt like wearing a too-tight shirt whose buttons he could not undo. In the mirror he recognised his mother's smile, the shape of her chin, and it was almost as if Mathilde had taken possession of him, was haunting him. Now he would never be free of her.

It was not only his body's appearance that had changed. It forced on him now so many desires, urges and aches whose existence he had never even guessed at before. His dreams were utterly different from the serene nocturnal fantasies of his childhood; they were like poison, penetrating his veins and intoxicating him for days on end. Yes, he was tall and strong now, but this man's body had come at the cost of his tranquillity. A constant anxiety gnawed at him. His body went haywire over nothing. His hands turned clammy, chills ran up and down his neck, his penis grew hard. For Selim, his physical development was not a triumph but a devastation.

Long ago the farmworkers used to make fun of him. They would run after him in the fields, laughing at his skinny calves, his white skin that burned so easily. They called him 'the kid', 'the weakling', sometimes even 'the German' just to annoy him. Selim was a kid like any other and he tried to blend seamlessly into the crowd. He got nits from rubbing his blond hair against the dark manes of the Berber children. He caught scabies, he was bitten by a dog and he played obscene games with the local kids. The farmworkers and their wives let him share their meals, never worrying that the food they ate wasn't good enough for the boss's son. All a child needed to grow was bread, olive oil and hot sweet tea. The women would pinch his cheeks and go into ecstasies over his beauty. 'You could be a Berber. A real Rif boy with your green eyes and your freckles!' A child that wasn't from here, in other words: that was what Selim understood.

A few months before this, for the first time, one of the farmworkers had called him 'Sidi', showing him a deference he wasn't expecting. Selim had been shocked by this. At the time he hadn't known whether what he felt was pride or its opposite: shame, the feeling of being an imposter. One day you were a child. And then you became a man. People said: 'A man would not do that' or 'You're a man now, behave like one.' He had been a child and now he wasn't, and it had happened so suddenly, with no explanation. He had been expelled from the world of hugs and sweet nothings, from the world of indulgence, and thrown unceremoniously, without warning, into the world of men. In this country, adolescence did not exist. There wasn't time, there wasn't space for the hesitations and delays of that hazy, in-between age. This society hated all forms of ambiguity and it regarded these adults-in-progress with suspicion, confusing them with those frightening fauns of mythology, with their goat legs and human torsos.

In the changing room, alone at last, he took off his underpants and reached into his bag for the sky-blue swimming trunks his mother had given him. As he put them on, the thought occurred to him that he had never seen his father's penis. This thought made him blush and his face grew hot. What did his father look like naked? When Selim was a child, his father used to take the family to the seaside sometimes, to the beach hut belonging to Dr Palosi and his wife Corinne. Over time he had got into the habit of merely dropping them there and coming back to fetch them two or three weeks later. He never ventured onto the beach himself and he never wore trunks. He claimed he had too much work and that the holidays were a luxury he could not afford. But Selim had heard Mathilde saying that Amine was afraid of the water and that the reason he did not join in with their summer fun was that he couldn't swim.

Fun. Holidays. Just as he had no idea what his father's penis looked like, Selim could not remember ever seeing him relax, play, laugh or take a nap. His father would constantly rail against all those shirkers, idlers and lazy good-for-nothings who did not understand the value of work and instead wasted their time whining. He found Selim's passion for sport ridiculous: not only the sailing club but also the football team he played for every weekend. As far back as Selim could remember, his father had always worn a look of disapproval on his face.

His father chilled him, petrified him. As soon as he knew that Amine was there, somewhere nearby, he could no longer be himself. Though, really, the whole of society had this effect on him. The world in which he lived wore the same expression as his father and he found it impossible to be free. This world was full of fathers who must be shown respect: God, the king, the military, the heroes of independence, the workers. Always, when a stranger approached you, they did not ask you your name but: 'Whose son are you?'

With the passing years, as it had become more and more obvious that he would not become, like his father, a farmer, Selim had felt less and less like Amine's son. Sometimes he would think of those artisans in the alleys of the medina and of the young apprentices they trained in their basement workshops. The young boilermakers, weavers, embroiderers and carpenters who forged relationships full of deference and gratitude with their masters. This was how the world worked: the old passed on their knowledge to the young; the past continued to infuse the present. This was why he had to kiss his father's shoulder or hand, why he had to bow down in his presence, signalling his total submission. No one was free of this debt until the day he himself became a father and could in turn dominate someone else. Life was like that ceremony of allegiance, where all the dignitaries of the kingdom, all the tribal chiefs, all the proud handsome men in their white djellabas, in their burnouses, lined up to kiss the king's palm.

At the club, his coach always told him he could become a great champion if he showed absolute dedication. But Selim had no idea what kind of man he could be. He didn't like school. His teachers, the Jesuits, castigated him for his laziness. He did not misbehave, did not talk back to adults, and he lowered his head when they threw his mediocre homework assignments at his face. He had the feeling that he was not in the right place, that he had somehow been born into the wrong world. As if someone had made a mistake and accidentally dropped him in this stupid, boring town, surrounded by the narrow-minded denizens of the petit bourgeois. School was torture for Selim. He always found it hard to concentrate on his books. His mind was drawn elsewhere, towards the trees in the courtyard, the dust motes dancing in a beam of sunlight, a girl's face smiling at him through a window. As a child he had dreaded maths lessons. He never understood a thing his teacher said. All the numbers and symbols swirled in a shapeless muddle that made him want to scream. The teacher would question him and Selim would stammer something in reply, his voice soon drowned out by his classmates' laughter. His mother had read books about his speech impediment. She'd wanted to take him to a doctor. Selim had always felt tense, constrained, restricted. He felt as if his whole life had been spent in one of those torture devices where the prisoner can neither stand up straight nor lie down flat.

In the pool, when he swam, he found a certain serenity. He had to exhaust his body. In the water, when his only goal was to breathe and move fast, he was able to gather his thoughts. As if finally he could find the right beat, the right rhythm to create a kind of harmony between his body and his soul. That day, while he swam lengths under the supervision of his coach, his mind drifted. He wondered if his parents loved each other. He had never heard them exchange words of affection or seen them kiss. Sometimes they would go whole days without speaking to each other and Selim could detect a torrent of hate and resentment flowing between them. When Mathilde became angry or sad she lost all sense of modesty and reserve. She used vulgar expressions, she shouted, and Amine had to order her to shut up. She threw all his betrayals and infidelities back in his face, and Selim, now he was a teenager, understood that his father had affairs with other women and that his mother, whose eyes were permanently red, suffered as a result. The image of Amine's penis surged into his mind again, so shocking that Selim lost his rhythm, and he heard the voice of his coach berating him from the edge of the pool.

Amine did not care about his son's bad marks at school. The day before, a teacher had summoned Mathilde to his office to tell her that Selim was a waster who would never pass his baccalauréat. Amine hadn't passed it either. 'And it didn't do me any harm,' he told his son. Amine had taken him on a tour of the farm. In the humid warmth of the greenhouses, in the overheated warehouses where plants were loaded onto trucks, his father had listed all the things that would soon be his. As he did this he appeared to be watching his son's face for signs of pride, even vanity, at the idea of one day being the lord of this domain. But Selim had not been able to hide his boredom. While his father was telling him about new irrigation techniques that they ought to invest in, Selim spotted a plastic bottle lying on the floor. Without thinking he gave it a kick, sending it flying towards a boy leaning against a wall, who laughed. Amine slapped the back of his son's head. 'Can't you see these people are working?' He started cursing then, loudly bemoaning the fact that Selim lacked the seriousness of his sister, whose only fault was that she was a woman.

Aïcha, Aïcha. His sister's name alone was enough to send him into a rage. When she'd left for France four years earlier, Selim had felt an enormous sense of relief. The tree that cast him in shadow had been cut down and, bathed at last in full sunlight, he could grow normally again. But tonight, Aïcha was coming home.

In September 1964 Aïcha moved to the capital of Alsace. Before that, she had never imagined that winter could come so early, ruining October with its solemn cortège of ashen skies and rain-soaked days. During her childhood she had listened attentively to her mother's stories about Alsace, but she had never thought that this place was hers too, that it was a part of her. In truth, she had always had the impression that the tales her mother told concerned an imaginary land, a fairy-tale kingdom where people ate plum tarts in little wooden houses. When she came here she was struck by Strasbourg's beauty, by the wealth of its inhabitants, its cobbled streets, its dark wooden beams, and by the grandiosity of its monuments, foremost among them the cathedral, which would have towered over the highest mosque and where, in her first months, she often took refuge. She rented a small room in a soulless new housing estate on the edge of the city. The landlady, Madame Muller, greeted her with steely, unsmiling eyes. She had received a tearful letter from Aïcha's mother explaining that she, Mathilde, was Alsatian and that she was entrusting her daughter to Madame Muller's capable hands. But as soon as Madame Muller saw her new tenant standing in the lobby of the apartment building, with her frizzy hair and her golden skin, she felt cheated, betrayed. She didn't like the French and she didn't like foreigners. It made her uncomfortable to speak anything other than Alsatian, and the idea of welcoming into her studio flat a girl like this was repulsive. As she showed the new tenant around the flat, as she demonstrated the workings of the kitchen equipment, she asked her: 'So, you're Alsatian?'

'Yes . . . Well, my mother's from here,' Aïcha replied.

'From Strasbourg?'

'No, from another town.'

'Which one?'

The girl's face blushed darkly then and she stammered: 'I . . . I don't remember.'

Mme Muller was given no cause to complain about this tenant whom she privately dubbed 'the African'. It had to be admitted that the girl was studious and hard-working. During the four years she spent in Strasbourg, Aïcha never once brought anyone back to her room and she very rarely went out at night. Her life consisted of attending lectures at the medical school during the days and swotting over her books at the kitchen table in the evenings. She only ever went out for a walk when she was so exhausted by her studies that she needed some fresh air or she had to buy food from the supermarket. In those moments she had the feeling that she was invisible, and she was always surprised when someone spoke a word to her or even looked at her. She couldn't get over the idea that people could actually see her. In Strasbourg she had to learn everything from scratch: how to live in a city, how to live alone, how to cook and clean. Some nights she had so much work that she didn't sleep at all. Gradually the colour of her skin changed, becoming dull and earthy. Bluish rings appeared under her big, dark eyes.

34

She worked harder than she had ever worked in her life, to the point of exhaustion, sometimes even to the point of madness. She lost all notion of time. She got so little sleep and drank so much coffee that her hands shook and she felt constantly nauseous. She passed her exams at the first attempt and wrote to her parents to tell them she would not be coming home that summer. She had found a job running the office in a clinic. As careful as an old lady, she was already saving her money.

* * *

In their third year the students were taken to a vast, windowed hall in which a dozen corpses were laid out on high, black tables. On the sides of these tables there were iron wings to support the dead bodies' outstretched arms. Deep trenches ran along the tables' edges to trap fluids and other waste products. When they saw all this, the students gave little cries of disgust or hilarity. Some of them made tasteless jokes, others said they couldn't do it, that they were going to faint. The lecturer, an old Alsatian man with grey eyes, was used to these puerile reactions. He ordered the class to be silent. Then he organised them into groups, each of which would dissect a different body part.

Aïcha felt no fear or revulsion. The corpses, preserved in formaldehyde, did not have too bad a smell and she knew it would be several weeks before it became unbearable. Throughout her youth she had been fascinated by anatomy and even now, if she closed her eyes, she could visualise the plates that Dr Palosi had given her when she was young. She had seen the innards of animals thousands of times at the farm. A cow dead in a field, its belly exploded in the hot sun. She still remembered that stench, an odour so strong and repugnant that the farm-workers had stuffed mint leaves into their nostrils before they burned the animal.

Aïcha walked over to the corpse she had been assigned. Its skin had turned a greyish colour and its facial features were deformed, as if a sculptor had tried to mould a face in a block of clay but had given up before he could finish. It was above this cold, naked body with blackened genitals that she first met David. Unlike the other students, he wasn't laughing. His expression was serious, almost reverent, as he examined the corpse's left shoulder, which he had been told to dissect. He did not immediately pick up his scalpel, but joined his hands beneath the table. He appeared to enter inside himself. He looked at the guinea pig in front of him as if it were not a stranger but his father, his brother, perhaps even himself. When he glanced up, he noticed that Aïcha was waiting for him. She had joined his prayer and she seemed to understand that, before slicing open this man's flesh, before stripping away his nerves, he needed to offer his apologies. In that moment David felt no fascination for the complexity of human anatomy or for the magnitude of medical knowledge accumulated by mankind over centuries. On the contrary, he was filled with a heavy, melancholic feeling of powerlessness. This corpse had once lived, it had had a name, it had been loved. Where his classmates saw a body, David saw the incarnation of a mystery.

He picked up his scalpel and began. Across the table, Aïcha's movements were assured and precise, and when the lecturer approached her he made a sort of grunt that David interpreted as an expression of admiration. David asked her if she had done this before. And Aïcha, whose shyness usually prevented her from speaking, told him, with her eyes fixed on the corpse's empty blood vessels, about her memories of Eid al-Adha at the farm, how she had sunk her fingers into the aortas and carotids of sheep.

David became her friend. Aïcha thought he was sweet, with his curly hair, his thick eyebrows and his plump cheeks that made him look like a sixteen-year-old boy. David was part of Strasbourg's Jewish community and his father taught at the theology faculty. Later he explained to Aïcha that he belonged to an ancient lineage of Alsatian scholars. The two of them would meet in the evenings to revise at the library and sit next to each other in the lecture hall. During the winter of 1968 he often took her to have dinner at a kosher restaurant run by a woman with such an enormous bottom that she could barely walk between the tables. She treated the students who came to her restaurant like her own children, insisting they finish their plates to give them strength for all their studies. She thought Aïcha too skinny and after every meal she would hand her an aluminium box full of leftovers. A bowl of *baeckeoffe*, vol-au-vents with mushrooms, gefilte fish with rice. Aïcha loved that restaurant, the noisiness of it and the cigarette smoke behind which the customers' faces disappeared. And she loved watching David, who ate with an extraordinary appetite. There was never the slightest ambiguity in their friendship, never a single awkward moment. Aïcha was convinced of her own ugliness in any case, and she could never believe that a boy might be interested in her. She also knew that her friend was deeply attached to his family and to his religion, which he practised with a devotion she found quite moving. She often asked him to tell her about Judaism, its rites and its prayers. About the place that God occupied in his life. She confided in him too, telling him about her love for the Virgin Mary and the comfort she had found, long ago, in the freezing chapel of her boarding school.

That winter David introduced her to his old schoolfriends whom he still saw from time to time and who were now studying philosophy, theatre or economics. Aïcha was surprised by the warmth of these young Alsatians, by all the questions they asked her and the admiration in their eyes when she told them about her childhood at the farm. Sometimes she was slightly embarrassed by the way they treated her and she had the impression that she was lying to them, leading them astray. For them, she represented a sort of ideal. She was a woman from the Third World, a farmer's daughter, a native with frizzy hair and olive skin who had succeeded in overcoming her disadvantages. Their discussions often revolved around politics. They asked her whom she had voted for. She said: 'I have never voted. Nor have my parents.' They questioned her about the condition of women and wanted to know if Simone de Beauvoir was famous in Morocco. Aïcha replied that she had never heard of her.

They forgave her for not understanding their theories and for staring wide-eyed when they talked about historical materialism. Aïcha was shy and uncultured. Once, she admitted that she had never taken part in a protest march and that in her parents' home no one read newspapers. She felt ill at ease during their discussions about class conflict, anti-imperialism, the Vietnam War, and she prayed they wouldn't ask her what she thought. The girls made fun of her because she blushed at the slightest provocation and bit the insides of her cheeks when they talked about sex or contraception. For these students, Aïcha was beyond mere theory: she was the revolution incarnate. She was living proof that women could escape their oppression through education and achieve emancipation. One day David's friends dragged her to a café near the cathedral. Joseph, who was wearing khaki canvas trousers and an American shirt, asked her what she thought about Algeria's independence and the Moroccan workers who came to work in factories in the north of France. Everyone fell silent, waiting for her answer. Aïcha felt scared. She thought she was going to be accused of something, that they had conspired against her and were going to reveal their hand in this noisy café where they had forced her to order a beer. She stammered that she knew nothing about it. In a high-pitched voice she added that she had nothing to do with Moroccans like that. She looked at her watch and made her excuses. She had to go and revise.

At the medical school she was known as the brightest student in her year and, ever her father's daughter, she worried about the jealousies this might arouse. Her classmates made fun of her rabbit-in-the-headlights appearance, the way she always walked so quickly through the corridors of the university, books under her arms, her hair sticking up. They said she was uptight, timid, overly deferential to authority in the form of her lecturers. During classes she concentrated so hard that she seemed to forget the presence of the others. She chewed her biro and spat little bits of plastic into her hand. Her lips were often ink-stained. But what annoyed her classmates most was the habit she had of pulling out hairs from her forehead one by one. She did it without realising and at the end of each class her desk would be covered in hair.

Medicine was the only thing that interested Aïcha. She couldn't have cared less about the Israeli–Palestinian conflict, the fate of de Gaulle or the situation of Black people in America. No, what fascinated her, what thrilled her more than anything, was the incredible, complex functioning of life. The fact that, when we eat, each piece of food is assimilated, each element going exactly where it is supposed to go. What astonished her was the tenacity and intelligence of a disease when it entered a healthy body, intent on destruction. The only newspaper articles she read were about science, and she eagerly followed news of the first heart transplant in South Africa. Her memory was phenomenal and whenever David worked with her he kept saying: 'I can't keep up, you're too fast for me!' She impressed him with her capacity for concentration and the ease with which she absorbed the lessons of clinical cases. One day, as they were leaving the library, he asked her where her passion for medicine came from. Aïcha put her hands in her jacket pockets and, after a moment's reflection, replied: 'Unlike your friends, I don't believe we can change the world. But if we can heal the sick, at least that's something.'

Aïcha was baffled by the events of May '68. That spring she prepared for her exams with her usual focus, and spent whole days and nights at the hospital where she was on call as often as she was asked. Of course she noticed that something was happening: a change, an agitation. People would hand her pamphlets and she would take them with a shy smile before dumping them in the dustbin outside her apartment building.

It felt as if an enormous party was being readied all around her, an orgiastic celebration in which she could play no part. David and his friends took her to the literature faculty, where thousands of students were sitting on the lawns. A boy yelled at them through a megaphone to rise up. She was amazed that they felt so free to say whatever they wanted. Her father had always warned her to be careful with her words. She looked at the girls around her, in short skirts and thigh-high socks, their breasts wobbling under their blouses. One of David's female friends told her how groups of young people were travelling on a bus to Kathmandu to lose themselves in clouds of opium smoke. But Aïcha would never be one of them. The megaphone was passed from hand to hand and Aïcha started to feel bored. She didn't dare tell David that she thought his friends were hysterical, sometimes even ridiculous. All these big words, all these concepts, struck her as meaningless. Where had they found this fervour? Where did this wide-eyed idealism come from? And, most mysterious of all, why weren't they afraid? Just then, she thought of an Arabic expression that her father often used: 'When God wishes to punish an ant, he gives it wings.' Aïcha was an ant, hard-working and obedient. And she had no intention of flying anywhere.

The day before her return to the farm, Aïcha went to a hairdresser's in the centre of Strasbourg. In the four years she had lived there, she must have passed the window of this elegant salon thousands of times on her way to the medical school. She had often looked in at the women sitting in those white leather chairs, their hair covered with strips of aluminium or big blue curlers. She would imagine herself as one of them, her head under a dryer, her manicured hands holding a women's magazine. But something always held her back, prevented her from entering. She would feel guilt at her vanity, wasting money on something so trivial, wasting precious time that could have been spent studying. But the exams had been cancelled now and she had saved enough money to pay for a flight back to Meknes and get herself a new haircut. She pictured her mother's reaction when she saw her little Aïcha with beautiful long smooth hair, like Françoise Hardy. And she opened the door.

Aïcha waited in front of the unattended reception desk. Employees rushed past her wearing grave, anxious expressions, as if they were not merely cutting hair but saving lives in an operating theatre. Sometimes they would cast her a sideways glance, a look that seemed to say 'What does she expect?', and Aïcha almost turned around and left. Nobody offered to take her coat and, standing in that overheated entrance, she began to sweat. Finally the salon's boss – a tall, blonde, voluptuous Alsatian woman – came over to serve her. She was wearing a tweed dress that showed off her curves and, around her plump wrists, some gold bracelets that clinked together when she moved her blemish-covered arms.

'How can I help you, mademoiselle?'

Aïcha said nothing. She stared at the pearlescent lipstick stains on the hairdresser's incisors. Then she noticed a swelling in the woman's thyroid, similar to that of certain species of bird. You should get that looked at, she thought.

'Mademoiselle?' the woman prompted her, annoyed.

Aïcha could only murmur: 'I'm here for my hair . . . Um, to straighten it? Like Françoise Hardy.'

The hairdresser raised her eyebrows and leaned her cheek on her hands, distressed by what she saw. With a clatter of bracelets, her expression betraying something close to repulsion, she reached out to touch Aïcha's hair.

'We don't do this kind of hair usually.'

She rubbed a lock of hair between her fingers and it made the sound of dry leaves being crumbled to dust.

'Follow me,' she said, and led Aïcha towards the back of the salon. It smelled of ammonia and nail polish. A woman with long grey hair was telling off one of the employees: 'I want more hairspray!' Her silver helmet was already frozen in place, like an old wig in a shop window. She could have walked through a tornado without disturbing a single hair on her head, but 'I want more!' she repeated, and the young hairdresser obeyed.

The boss abandoned Aïcha near the shampoo chairs. The walls were covered with large mirrors and every time Aïcha turned around she saw her reflection without really recognising herself. She could not admit that they belonged to her, those enormous bulging eyes and the receding gums that were exposed whenever she smiled. She could not believe that she was beautiful and she refused herself all the little adornments common to girls her age. No make-up, no jewellery, no elaborate chignon. No, when the idea suddenly came to her that she ought to do something – to 'make an effort', as her mother always said – her actions were purely impulsive. One day, in a fury, she had tried to straighten her hair with an iron; she had leaned her face against the table in her attic room and pressed the hot iron to her frizzy hair. Smoke had filled the room, along with the bitter smell of grilled meat. The tips of her hair had been blackened and she had burned her temple. Another time, after reading a magazine, she had shaved off both her eyebrows and tried to redraw them in black pencil, but she could never manage to make them symmetrical. Now, in front of the mirror, under the stark fluorescent lighting, she noticed that one of her eyebrows was thicker than the other and that the black line had run down slightly onto her eyelid.

As she waited, her memory supplied her with all the nicknames her old classmates had invented for her. Poodlehead. Black sheep. Damp squib. Barbary lion. They called her nigger, darkie, bad-hair girl. She waited a long time. Hairdressers shoved past her, carrying pots of dye in their rubber-gloved hands. Aïcha's presence bothered them. She was in the way and she imagined that everyone could smell the acidic odour of her sweat. She was sure that beneath their hairdryers the other customers were whispering about her, mocking her shapeless hair. At last a teenage girl with round cheeks and bored eyes told her to sit down in front of a white enamel sink. Aïcha thought: What wouldn't I do to have hair like hers? Smooth, soft hair that she could run her fingers through.

The hairdresser brutally stabbed a comb into Aïcha's hair. She spoke Alsatian and laughed with her colleagues and the other customers. She yanked so hard that Aïcha yelped.

'Well, what d'you expect, eh? It's not easy untangling this mess.' Exasperated, she barked: 'Jesus, Mary and Joseph, pass me the straightening cream!'

The hairdresser covered her nose with her elbow and dipped the other hand in a large red pot. She applied this cream to Aïcha's scalp. After a few minutes her head started to itch so badly that she had to slide her hands under her bottom to stop herself scratching her scalp. Tears ran down her cheeks and she looked around helplessly. When the boss saw her, she exclaimed: 'Oh, don't be such a wimp! You have to suffer if you want to be beautiful.'

In the aeroplane that took her back to Meknes, Aïcha did not lean her head back against her seat. For the whole of the three-hour flight she kept her neck still and stared down at her hands to avoid damaging her new hairstyle. She suppressed the urge to run her hands through her hair, to wrap a lock of it around her index finger as she so often used to do when she was studying or daydreaming. She could feel the long, smooth hair caressing her neck and her cheeks, and she still couldn't quite believe it.

Aïcha landed at the airport in Rabat in the early afternoon. She walked slowly down the steps to the tarmac, dazed by the brightness of the sky. She looked up and saw on the building's roof, behind red letters spelling out 'AÉROPORT DE RABAT', a few figures moving around, waving their arms and trying to recognise the passengers who were advancing towards them. The arrivals hall was in turmoil. Men were running about, shouting orders that nobody seemed to be following. Porters were carrying in luggage and handing it out to passengers, while policemen checked passports, customs officials opened suitcases, shook magazines, tossed bras and knickers to the floor. Aïcha watched all this through the glass partition separating the passengers from the waiting families. Among the children holding cuddly toys, the women in make-up and the chauffeurs in djellabas, she spotted her father. He was wearing a pair of sunglasses so dark that she could not see his eyes. She was surprised by how elegant he appeared in that brown turtleneck sweater and that new-looking leather jacket. His hair was whiter now and he had grown a moustache. Hands crossed behind his back, he was staring down at the tiled floor, embarrassed by the excitement of the crowd around him. He had that lost, absent air that she knew so well. It really was him, her father, that silent bear, capable of the roughest tenderness and the harshest anger. Moved, she took a step to the side to separate herself from the other passengers standing in line. Amine took off his sunglasses and gazed at her for a few seconds. He raised his eyebrows when he noticed her very short skirt and the brown leather boots that came up to her knees. She was wearing an orange vinyl jacket and a pair of oversized smoked glasses like the ones worn by pop singers in magazines. She thought that it was seeing her there, recognising her, his daughter, that seemed to wake him from his stupor. She assumed that it was his overflowing love for her, his sudden inability to control his own emotion, that led Amine to push past people, to shoulder his way through the crowd to the glass divider. He waved his hand at her and smiled. She stared at his white teeth and realised the truth. It wasn't Aïcha he was looking at. It wasn't her he was smiling at so winningly. He was smiling at a woman, a stranger he thought beautiful and desirable, and who had distracted him from the chore of meeting his daughter at the airport. Perhaps he had been expecting Aïcha to still be the same drab, shy teenager he had seen off four years earlier? Perhaps it never even crossed his mind that those legs he was staring at, those long slim bare legs, could be his own child's. Aïcha touched her hand to her head, stroked her hair. Ah, yes, that was why he didn't recognise her. It was that long straight hair hanging down to her waist. Her stupid Françoise Hardy hairstyle.

Aïcha extricated herself from the queue. She walked towards the glass divider and took off her sunglasses. Amine was still staring at her and for an instant he must have thought she wanted to get to know him, to arrange a date or hand him her telephone number. But abruptly his expression changed. His smile vanished, his eyes darkened and his lips started to quiver. She recognised that look: it was the one he wore before fury took him, before he shouted, before he hit. He made an irritated hand gesture which meant: 'Get back in line, you little idiot.' He tapped his watch. 'Hurry up!' She had lost her place so she went to the back of the line. She was sweating now in this jacket that made an unpleasant creaking sound whenever she moved her arms. The next time she looked at the glass divider, her father had disappeared.

Aïcha waited almost an hour before handing her passport to a policeman who wished her a happy return to her country. She couldn't help turning around, unsure whether she was hoping to see Amine or whether, on the contrary, she was hoping he had vanished, that none of what had happened had actually happened, and that they could start again. She left the airport. A porter grabbed her suitcase from her hand and she didn't dare tell him no. When her father appeared suddenly, she jumped. She acted as if nothing was wrong, laughing as she hugged him. She wrapped him in her arms and held him tight against her in a way that meant: 'I forgive you.' She felt ashamed at having humiliated him. She wanted to remain hanging there from his neck to make him understand that she was still his little girl, but Amine freed himself to pay the porter. In the car park a gang of children were haranguing the tourists, offering to carry their suitcases, take them to a taxi, book them a hotel room. Soon Aïcha was surrounded by little boys in rags who laughed and made obscene suggestions. She didn't need to see her father's face to know that he was furious.

Amine sat behind the wheel and raised a cigarette to his mouth. As he leaned towards the lighter, he shot a furtive glance at his daughter's thighs.

'What on earth do you think you're wearing? You're not in France now, you know.'

Aïcha tugged at the hem of her skirt then draped her jacket over her lap to hide her naked flesh. On the way home they exchanged only a few words. He asked if her studies were going well. She asked about the farm. She remembered that people liked to talk about rain here and she asked if it had rained recently and if the peasants were happy. Then they both withdrew into silence. Occasionally Amine would put his arm through the open window and gesture angrily at other drivers. In the middle of a bend he almost knocked over a cart, pulled by a teenage boy and his donkey, that had abruptly emerged from a field. Amine slammed on the brakes and insulted the boy. He called him an idiot, an ignoramus, a nobody. 'Another little murderer in the making!' And he rolled up his window.

Aïcha gazed out at the landscape and was surprised by the wave of happiness that engulfed her. She was going home, she thought, and there was a sweetness, a comfort in being surrounded by others of her kind. She sank into a reverie as she stared at the vineyards and the rows of olive trees growing among rocks on this dry, yellow earth. At the foot of a hill she spotted a cemetery full of whitewashed gravestones with pale-green cactuses growing between them, their branches covered in prickly pears that had exploded in the heat, exposing their shiny yellow innards. The grass, almost grey, gleamed in the sunlight like an animal's fur. They passed some modest houses with a few hens and a skinny dog running around in front. Aïcha knew exactly what the smell would be like inside those houses, where she had been many times as a child. The smell of damp earth and baking bread. It was of smells, too, that she thought when they saw a car ahead of them packed with a family of eight, all sitting on each other's laps. A little boy, standing on his mother's thighs, waved at Aïcha through the rear windscreen. She waved back at him.

But that feeling of plenitude did not last. As soon as they entered the family estate she started to worry. So much had changed in the four years she'd spent abroad. She was amazed by how noisy it was: the rumbling engine of a combine harvester, the machine-gun crackle of automatic sprinklers. Then she saw, beside the house, the vast swimming pool and its border of red bricks shining in the afternoon sun. Aïcha knew that the farm had become more successful, that her parents were wealthier now. Even so, she was surprised as she entered the house by the bourgeois furnishings, the crocheted doilies, the fake-crystal vases and, on the blue velvet sofas, the piled-up cushions stuffed close to bursting with foam. She walked through the corridor. On a pedestal table she recognised a few knick-knacks dating back to her childhood: a copper candlestick, a porcelain box where Mathilde kept some keys, a small glass vase in which a red rose was wilting. She wanted to caress these objects, hold them in her hands for a moment, thank them for still being here. But already she could hear her mother's voice, tense and high-pitched, giving orders to Tamo. Aïcha went past the living room and contemplated a series of still lifes on the walls. Above the fireplace hung an immense portrait of Amine in his Spahi uniform. Her father's painting did not really resemble him: the artist had exaggerated the olive colour of his complexion and the darkness of his eyes, making him look like a failed copy of Delacroix's warriors. But Aïcha knew it was her father because she remembered that photograph she had seen as a child, with Amine straddling a white charger, his face hooded by a burnous.

Mathilde emerged from the kitchen. She was wearing a blue apron and her hair was tied back. A strand of grey fell over her right eye. She wiped her wet hands on a dish towel then threw herself at her daughter, breathing in her smell. 'Let me look at you,' she said. And for a few moments she gazed at her child's face, her outfit, the orange jacket she was carrying. 'You've changed so much. I wouldn't have recognised you!'

Mathilde had prepared a celebratory dinner in honour of this long-awaited reunion. For days on end this woman who had never got used to Moroccan cuisine cooked an assortment of traditional hors d'oeuvres, tajines and even a pigeon pastilla sprinkled with cinnamon and icing sugar. Selma, Mourad and their daughter, Sabah, who now lived in town, came for aperitifs. Sabah had just turned twelve. Seeing her and Selma together, Aïcha found it hard to believe that they were mother and daughter, so dissimilar did they appear. Sabah had not inherited Selma's smooth brown hair, nor her radiant complexion. She was a thin child with coarse features and bushy eyebrows. She was wearing a black cotton skirt that revealed her thick, hairy ankles.

While Amine poured champagne, Sabah clung to Mourad. She put her arm around her father's shoulders and hid her face behind his neck. Without a word he pulled her towards him, sat her on his lap and whispered a secret into her ear. The child nodded and stayed where she was, in silence, her cheek leaning on Mourad's shoulder. She called him 'Papa' and Mourad could not help feeling ashamed when he heard those two syllables. He felt as if he were lying to her, taking advantage of her innocence, and he worried about the day when she would discover the truth. The hate she felt for him then would be unassuageable. And yet, who else could claim to be her father? Who else would deserve the sweet and tender title of 'Papa'? Were it not for him, she might not even have survived. He had saved her life, he had taken care of her, he had protected her from the madness of her mother. In the weeks following their wedding, Selma had done nothing but cry. She had lain on her side for whole days at a time, one hand on her swollen belly. After the tears came the violent tantrums, the escape attempts, the suicide threats. Selma tried to throw herself under the wheels of a truck. She threatened to drink insecticide. She swore she would stab herself in the belly with a knitting needle. The child was born but that did nothing to dampen Selma's rage. On the contrary, the baby's howls drove her crazy and she would go out to walk in the fields, abandoning her starving child in the storehouse. Some of the things she said in front of Mourad were so violent that they chilled him, and he had lived through war, imprisonment, desertion. She said she might let the baby die then leave its corpse outside Mathilde's front door. 'That way, she'll see what she's done,' Selma reasoned. Mourad was living in a state of constant terror. One day, when Sabah was still only two, he had abruptly left his workers in the middle of a job and started running like mad towards the farm. There, he saw his daughter. She was alone. She was wearing a grey T-shirt that exposed her bare legs and sucking the stones that she held in her little hands. 'Papa!' she cried, and the stones fell to the ground.

What was he doing with these two females? What was he doing in this family where nobody wanted him? Amine had never treated him like a brother-in-law or even like a friend. Amine was a gentleman now, a respectable person who organised poolside parties in his garden decorated with Chinese lanterns. A bourgeois who celebrated New Year's Eve with others of the same class and who was unafraid of ridicule even when wearing a gold-coloured cardboard hat, his shoulders wreathed with paper streamers. Amine was stuffed full of money and vainglory. He wore tailored suits and had learned to dance the waltz and the mambo. He had slept with half the town. For months after Mouilala's death, Mourad's boss had used her old house in the medina to meet his mistresses, screwing them on those mouldy old benches. Sometimes, thinking himself alone, thinking himself invisible, Amine would park his car in a field of sunflowers and lick the breasts of another man's wife. Once, coming home drunk from a party, he drove his car into the trunk of an olive tree. 'I wasn't drunk,' he told people afterwards, 'I was just tired. I yawned and I closed my eyes.' Mourad knew all of this. Just like he knew that, in this country, no one is ever alone. He wanted to warn Amine: 'There's always someone who knows what you've been doing.'

* * *

During the aperitifs, while Mathilde happily made conversation, Aïcha observed her family, their house, the comings and goings of Tamo as she brought dishes from the kitchen. She noticed that the maid was limping slightly, but Tamo refused to let her help. There was no connection, thought Aïcha, between this world and the student world of Strasbourg, no link between her life here and her life back there. These two existences were completely separate. They took place in two parallel dimensions, neither of which had any influence on the other. She even thought that a part of herself was still in

54

Strasbourg, continuing its routine existence. She was seized by a feeling of unreality. She wasn't absolutely sure she had lived through those four years. Maybe she had never left Morocco. Maybe it had all been a dream.

Over dinner Amine did not join in the chorus of praise for the parade of dishes that passed before their eyes. He put his hand on Aïcha's back – 'May God keep you, my daughter' – and asked her how it felt to be the first doctor in the family. Aïcha imagined then that her father had forgiven her, that the unease of her arrival had faded, and she began to tell him what she'd been doing. She described the dissection of bodies. 'Oh no, not when we're eating!' Mathilde interrupted. She talked about her work at the clinic, the things her department head at the hospital said. She did not mention her friendship with David, but said vaguely that she'd made some good friends. While she was speaking, Selma and Selim kept their eyes lowered to their plates. Amine appeared to notice this and he made even clearer his joy at having such a serious, hard-working daughter. 'A respectable daughter who doesn't run around with boys and get into trouble. Who doesn't waste her time skipping school and going to parties.' Aïcha had nothing to do with those communists, those revolutionaries who knew nothing about life and wanted to destroy their elders' heritage. He said this in a mean voice but Aïcha didn't realise he was saying it for the benefit of his sister and his son. He was revelling in his daughter's success and independence to rub salt into Selma's wounds. Rather than attempting to fix an injustice, he seemed to want to highlight it, to make it worse.

When the meal was over, Selma stood up. Nobody asked where she was going. Perhaps she had gone to look after her daughter or wash dishes in the kitchen. Selim, on the other hand, knew exactly where she was. He walked through the living room, went out into the backyard and climbed up onto the roof. Selma was sitting on the edge, feet dangling in the void, waiting for him.

Selim took two cigarettes from his pocket and handed one to his aunt. It was Selma who had initiated him in the habit. Back then, she still lived at the farm, in the hideous storehouse that Mourad had converted. Selim must have been eight at the time and he was playing in the garden. He had surprised his aunt as she leaned against the pebbledash wall, blowing smoke through her nose. She had put a finger to her lips and made him promise to keep the secret. And to seal this pact, this pact against Amine and all the other men, she had added: 'You want to try?' He had moved his lips to the cigarette and sucked. 'Anyone would think you'd been doing it all your life.' And she had laughed. Selim knew all her hiding places. As a child he would pick up the stubs she left in the garden, each bearing traces of the crimson lipstick she wore. He would collect the discarded grey packets too, deciphering the single strange word upon them: 'Marquise'.

Selma lit her cigarette, and Selim saw her face in the gleam from the lighter, her forehead furrowed with irritation. He sat next to her. 'If my father saw me here, he'd kill me.'

Selma laughed sarcastically. 'Fuck your father.'

The phrase was like a punch. The words echoed endlessly inside him. For a few moments he just sat there on the roof of the house, speechless. In the distance the city lights were becoming visible. Tamo's voice reached them from below, as did Mathilde's. Selim noticed that Selma was crying.

'Why did I come? I could have said I was ill. Or that Sabah was. She's always got a stomach ache. I should have found some excuse to stay home. But Mourad would have insisted. He'd have said it was impolite, that it's only because of them that we have a roof over our heads and food on our table. That we should bless them for taking care of us and our kid. God, the way he talks about your father, you'd think he was the one with his face on every banknote in Morocco, not the king! Your father snaps his fingers and Mourad obeys. He's like a dog. And bloody Mathilde, acting like a saint or something, slipping me an envelope on holidays. She always whispers, "For the little one" or, "You're allowed to have some fun too." And she smiles whenever I wear a new dress, because it makes her feel good that everything I wear, everything I eat, even the air I breathe, is thanks to them. One day I'm going to stop eating, I won't talk any more, I'll hold my breath until I collapse. I won't make any more effort at all. I'll stop resisting. It's like if a dog bites you, you shouldn't struggle. If you move, it just tightens its jaws. That's how things are here. You have to submit. They keep saying there's nothing more important than family. Nothing. Just the king and queen in their beautiful house. But you'll see . . . One day I won't be able to take it any more and I'll have enough courage to tell them to go fuck themselves, them and their lies and their hypocrisy and their good manners and their perfect daughter. What the hell does Aïcha know about life? She still looks like a snot-nosed kid. A stupid little girl who worships her father. Ugh, the way she flatters him and adores him . . . But she has no idea what he is. Or she pretends to forget.'

Selma was whispering and, to Selim, it seemed as though she was completely indifferent to his presence, that she was

57

talking to herself, not to him. Abruptly she appeared to notice him there. She stubbed out her cigarette, gestured for another one and went on: 'Ask your sister. Ask her if she remembers the night of the revolver. It must still be there, inside that terracotta vase in the corridor. Take a look if you don't believe me. The revolver he wanted to kill us with – your mother, your sister and me. He says I was lazy, that I didn't work in school. But the truth is that even if I'd been a perfect student, as perfect as little Miss Aïcha, he still wouldn't have let me leave. He'd never have paid for me to go to university. So what's the point, huh? When I was your age I wanted to be a flight attendant. "A flight attendant?" he said. "I'd rather you just became a prostitute." I always loved aeroplanes. And I fell in love with a pilot. He took me to the airfield and explained how it all worked, all the machines and stuff, and he told me how it felt to fly. I wanted to travel, to get away from this place, become somebody. And I thought I had my whole life ahead of me.' Selma sniffed. Big fat tears were rolling down her cheeks now. 'When I got pregnant with Sabah, I begged your mother to help me. Saint Mathilde. She told me that Dragan had agreed to do it, that she would arrange everything. No one would know and I'd be able to get on with my life. You know what I'm talking about, right? You're big enough to know all that. Every day I would ask her when she was going to take me to the abortion clinic and she'd say: "Soon, very soon." And then she got scared. Or she wanted revenge. Or she was jealous. Anyway, she never took me. Your father brought the adoul to the house and they forced me to marry Mourad. And I had the kid over there, in that mouldy old storehouse. Sometimes I think it would have been better if he'd used his revolver. He should have just killed me.'

58

During her first days at home, Aïcha did nothing but sleep. Mathilde worried about her. She thought her daughter might be ill. 'It's like she's been bitten by a tsetse fly,' she told Amine. Whenever she sat down, Aïcha was overwhelmed by exhaustion. She slept in the living room, in the middle of the morning, or on a garden chair. In the afternoons she would close her bedroom shutters and sleep until evening, and she would have no difficulty falling asleep again at night. It was as if, during all those years in Strasbourg, she had never had a moment's rest, like the victim of a witch's curse in some fairy tale. Now the spell had been broken and she abandoned herself to sleep. Or perhaps this endless sleep was the curse. Aïcha didn't know what to think any more.

It took her a week to emerge from this lethargy, and then she was able to enjoy the burgeoning summer and the beauty of nature. In the mornings she would watch her brother swim; she could sit there for hours, her feet in the water, admiring the sleekness of his body and the regular rhythm with which he swam lengths. Selim didn't talk to her very much. He had to take his baccalauréat at the end of June and he was in a sullen mood. Aïcha offered to help him revise but he coldly rejected her, saying that revision wasn't the problem and anyway he was big enough to manage on his own. In the evenings she would put on an old pair of trainers and walk through the

fields, her pockets filled with stones to scare away stray dogs. ✦
She picked barely ripe oranges from the trees, knowing even
before she sniffed them, even before she raised a segment to
her lips, exactly how they would taste. She lay in the grass and
stared up at the sky, at that blueness which had often come
to her in dreams during her Alsatian exile. The sky here was
naked, open, as if a divine hand had stripped away everything
that might cover it, obscure it, diminish its brightness. Birds
flew, sometimes alone, sometimes in flocks, and the branches
of palm trees and olive trees swayed in the wind, awakening
within her a desire for storms.

Several times she invited Monette to spend the day with
her. Her friend still lived in Meknes, where she worked as a
classroom assistant. She envied Aïcha for having been able to
leave this provincial town, meet new friends, learn a profes-
sion. Monette lived with her mother at a house in the hills.
Her mother was so fat that she hardly ever left the house
and she whined constantly about her varicose veins and the
diabetes that was slowly killing her. The day of their reunion,
Monette threw her arms around Aïcha. She kissed her and
began to giggle so happily that Aïcha, too, burst out laughing. Aïcha had barely thought about Monette during the four
years she had spent in Strasbourg; the image of her friend
had been a vague, distant presence in the back of her mind,
like something remembered from a dream. Now Monette
was standing there, before her, her face lit up with a radiant
smile, and Aïcha realised how much she had missed her.

Monette looked like an adult, thought Aïcha. She was
exactly what Mathilde would have liked Aïcha to be. She wore
a loose-fitting knee-length dress and square-toed, low-heeled

shoes. She wore her hair like Brigitte Bardot, in a high bun pierced with pins that forced her to stand very straight. Monette was no longer the insolent, clumsy girl she had been before, whose only ambition had been to humiliate and ridicule adults. She behaved like a woman of the world. She paid Mathilde compliments about the fabric of her sofas or those little glass ornaments in the shapes of animals that Aïcha's mother had decided to collect.

Mathilde enjoyed her presence. When the two girls sunbathed by the side of the pool she would bring them lemonade, making Aïcha feel like a tourist at a luxury hotel. Her mother treated her so respectfully that it was embarrassing. She refused to let Aïcha help clear the table, saying: 'Stay where you are, you must be tired.' Aïcha no longer felt at home. This house where she had grown up was strange to her now, and she sensed a sort of hostility in these walls, these paintings, this new furniture. She missed her independence and even the silence of her attic room in Strasbourg. Here, she had the impression she was becoming a child again, and the regression irritated her.

In the mornings Mathilde came into her bedroom. She drew the curtains and kissed her daughter as she used to when Aïcha had to get ready for school. Her mother encouraged her to eat, to get some fresh air; she warned her about the winter sunlight that caused migraines and the chergui that made your lungs wheeze. Aïcha wanted to tell her that these were just old wives' tales, that there was no scientific evidence for such claims. But she stayed silent. At the end of June, while Monette was busy monitoring the school exams, Aïcha offered to help her mother at the clinic, where a long queue of patients

61

formed every morning. Mathilde agreed without enthusiasm. When Aïcha had been a child, her mother had called her 'my nurse' and had let her disinfect and bandage wounds. Now she asked her to cut out blister packs of pills, but it was always Mathilde who gave the medicine to the peasants, like a priest handing over the sacred Host. She listened to their secrets and, with gentle authority, overrode their prudishness, persuading them to unbutton their blouse or pull down their knickers. She had come to believe in her science, her pseudo-science, the way a preacher might believe his own sermons.

When she had first come to Morocco, in 1946, Mathilde had prided herself on being the only woman in the family to have received a real education. She boasted about reading books, speaking several languages, playing the piano. At first she had been proud of Aïcha's brilliance at school, the nuns' compliments on her intelligence. Then she had begun to anxiously await the day when her daughter knew more than she did. Because then she would be confounded. Aïcha would understand that her mother was an impostor who didn't really know anything. As soon as Aïcha started secondary school, Mathilde realised that she was incapable of helping her with her homework. The numbers swam before her eyes, losing all meaning. The history, geography and – worst of all – philosophy questions were utterly incomprehensible to her, and she wondered how children so young could possibly absorb so much knowledge. She dreaded Aïcha's questions and the way her daughter looked at her. Sitting at her desk, hands resting on a book, she would gaze up with dark eyes at her dumbstruck mother.

Mathilde felt certain that she had been part of the reason Aïcha had chosen to pursue medicine as a career. She had given

her the taste for healing, had let her read the medical magazines lent to her by Dragan even though they were not really
suitable for a girl that age. But Aïcha had overtaken her now.
She was the possessor of an immense, irrefutable reservoir of
knowledge. This shy, skinny girl, barely twenty-one, looked
down on her own mother from humiliating heights. How
pathetic Aïcha must think this little clinic of hers! Her gaze
was probably scanning the walls in search of a diploma from
some foreign university – like the one in Dragan's office – that
granted her mother the power to make decisions about other
people's lives.

One morning Aïcha turned up at the clinic in her baggy
jeans and old trainers. She gave her mother advice about the
patients. 'He needs to see a dentist. That's why he has a fever.
There's nothing we can do to help him.' She made fun of the
remedies her mother prescribed. Warm, salted water to heal a
sprain. Ginger decoctions for sore throats. A spoonful of cumin
to stop diarrhoea and vomiting. Watched by her daughter,
Mathilde didn't dare offer a diagnosis. She lost all her confidence, second-guessed her every move, kept looking to her
own child for approval. Aïcha reacted with cold reticence to
the hugs and kisses that the patients gave her. 'Look how she's
grown! Tabarakallah! May God watch over her,' they told
Mathilde. Their admiration for Aïcha was of the same blissful,
unquestioning nature that the illiterate always feel for the
educated. Aïcha hid in the toilet. And as she was washing her
hands she saw her mother open a drawer, take some cash out,
and hand it to one of the peasant women. 'May God bless you,'
Mathilde whispered. 'And may He protect your children.'

63

One evening in early August, while they were drinking aperitifs by the pool, a farmworker came to ask to see the boss and his wife. He told Tamo it was an emergency and the maid, tortured by curiosity and furious with the man for not telling her what the problem was, went to tell her masters. Mathilde and Amine went to see the farmworker, but he appeared hesitant. First he asked about their family – 'How is your son? And your daughter? And your sister?' – then he began mumbling apologies: he didn't want to disturb them, he knew it was late, he was sorry. Amine, annoyed by all this deferential small talk, cut him short: 'Get to the point.' The man swallowed before explaining that a girl had arrived in the douar two days earlier. 'A lost girl, if you want my opinion.' Nobody knew where she had come from but she was heavily pregnant and she refused to give her name or the name of her village. The farmworker shed his shyness at this point and continued his story in Berber: 'We don't want any trouble. I said we should send her away, that she would only bring us problems. Everyone knows about girls like that. But she cries, she begs, so the women take pity on her. They say we must be merciful and that if we take care of her she will end up telling us who the father is and how she came to be here. Only now, the girl is in my house and tonight she started screaming and shouting. She is twisted up with pain. We brought the midwife over but she says the baby does not want to come out. That it is a child of shame and it will kill its mother. I am telling you, boss, I would rather have a bastard under my roof than a dead kid. That's why I thought you could come, and Madame Mathilde too. We can't leave her like that. To let her die under my roof.'

Mathilde took his hand. 'You did the right thing. We'll take the car and I'll come with you.' She walked over to the large wooden cupboard where she kept the clinic's medical supplies and began tossing them into a bag: a bottle of Betadine, compresses, a large pair of scissors. Amine, who had stood with his arms crossed and head lowered while the labourer was talking, interrupted these preparations: 'No, Aïcha will go. She's the doctor. And I will accompany her. I will not let my daughter go alone into the douar after nightfall.' He went to the terrace and, as he used to back in his days as an army officer, yelled: 'Aïcha, get dressed and come here! Hurry up!'

When they got in the car, Mathilde gave her daughter the small bag filled with medicine. She watched the car move away as the sky turned the colour of ink. They drove to the douar and throughout the journey Aïcha kept repeating that she had never done this before, that she was not, technically speaking, a doctor yet, and that it was crazy to saddle her with such a responsibility. Her legs shook and she felt like she was going to throw up. The landscape began to flicker, she couldn't hear anything any more; her head was empty of knowledge, filled only with a thick fog. 'Would you rather let your mother do it?' Amine asked her, and Aïcha shrugged.

In the headlights' glare the first houses appeared. A crowd had gathered in front of one of them. Women in djellabas, wearing brightly coloured headscarves, were slapping their own faces and wailing. Some of the men were squatting while others paced around, hands behind their backs or smoking cigarettes. The children, taking advantage of the adults' distraction, were throwing rocks at a pack of dogs, all of them so scrawny that they looked like ghosts. The villagers surrounded Amine and Aïcha. They blessed them, kissed their shoulders and hands. Their skin smelled of cumin and charcoal. A woman escorted Aïcha into a dark room with a dirt floor. In a corner an oil lamp emitted a feeble light, casting monstrous shadows on the wall. A young woman, lying on a blanket, moaned quietly. Aïcha went back to the doorway, where Amine was standing, and told him: 'I need more light. How can I help her if I can't see anything?' Amine went to fetch two torches that he always kept in the boot of his car. Aïcha paced about in small circles, wringing her hands, and for a moment she thought about running away, escaping through the dark fields. But Amine turned on the torches and pointed their beams at his daughter's face. 'What else do you need?' She said they should boil some water and that she had to wash her hands. Amine designated two women and warned them: 'Do everything the doctor tells you, understood?' One of the peasant women took care of the water while the other grabbed the torches and aimed them at the pregnant woman. It was then that Aïcha discovered she was no more than sixteen or seventeen. Her face was pale, her skin slippery with perspiration, her mouth distorted by pain. She had slanted eyes and flattened features, as if she came not from anywhere nearby but from the Mongolian steppe. Aïcha crouched down beside her and caressed her temples, her sweat-drenched hair. 'It'll be all right,' she said. 'Everything will be all right.' Delicately she lifted up the girl's blouse, exposing her naked belly. She palpated it, glaring at her assistant now and again to make the woman hold the torch steady. Then she knelt between the girl's legs and spread them. Concentrating as hard as she could, she tried to remember the lectures about childbirth she had attended. In a firm voice she called for silence. The conversations from outside, snippets of which she could hear, were bothering her. She also lost her temper with the two women helping her, whose lamentations sounded like the buzzing of insects. They kept droning 'Ya Latif, oh my God!' and sniffling.

Aïcha slid her hand into the girl's vagina. The cervix was soft, dilated. She had been having contractions for hours, but they did not seem to be working and they were exhausting her. The birth had to be accelerated. It was the only way to relieve her pain. Aïcha rummaged in the bag that Mathilde had given her, but she couldn't find anything useful in there. She looked around. 'I need something small and pointed. Do you understand what I mean?' Struggling to express herself in Arabic, Aïcha grew annoyed. She went out of the house and called her father: 'Tell them to find me something small and pointed enough that I can insert it into that girl's body. I have to break her waters.' In the darkness, Aïcha did not see the proud smile stretch across her father's face. The villagers moved into action. They searched through what little they possessed. At last a woman came over, triumphantly holding a fork. Aïcha took it. She dipped the fork in the boiling water, sprayed Betadine over it and, slowly, with assured, precise gestures, inserted the object into the girl's vagina. A silence fell. A heavy, devout silence. Then the patient gave a cry of surprise and relief. Transparent liquid, mixed with a few clots of blood, flowed between her thighs. 'You'll start to feel better now,' Aïcha told her. She moved her face closer to the girl's and kissed it, watched by the outraged Berber women. The patient's dry lips parted and she muttered: 'Help me.' Aïcha smiled. 'Yes, of course I'm going to help you.' But the girl repeated: 'Help me. Help me never to have any more children.'

In the morning she gave birth to a stillborn boy.

Returning to the farm at dawn, Aïcha took a hot shower and then collapsed onto the bed. She slept through the morning and part of the afternoon. She dreamed she was swimming in a pool whose clear blue water transformed into amniotic fluid; she was struggling, drowning in the lukewarm liquid. Mathilde woke her from her nightmare. She shook her shoulder and said: 'Monette is here. She wants to go to the cinema with you.'

Aïcha dragged herself out of bed. She had no desire to go out or talk to anyone, but she got dressed anyway. She tried to fix her hair, then gave up. She arrived in the living room waxy-faced and puffy-eyed. 'I've heard about your exploits!' her friend said excitedly, and Aïcha gave an embarrassed smile. Mathilde asked Monette for the latest gossip from Meknes. 'This girl knows everything!' Monette told tales of sex and divorce to which Aïcha paid no attention. She slowly drank her coffee, reliving the night's events minute by minute. She saw again the girl's face and the cyanotic, lifeless body of the child she had brought into the world. In the douar, she thought, the men must have dug a hole at dawn to bury the baby's corpse. A tiny little hole, so narrow and shallow. The child's death suited everyone: it erased the sin, the dishonour; it was a blessing. I have to go back, Aïcha told herself. I have to examine the patient, make sure she's not bleeding, that she has regained her

69

strength. But she felt certain that her presence was unwanted and that all the inhabitants of the douar would act as if nothing had happened. As if that night had never existed. Perhaps the girl had already been kicked out, despite her exhaustion, despite the big, flabby belly she would have to hold up with one hand as she walked. No, Aïcha did not feel like going to the cinema. But nor did she feel like staying where she was and enduring her parents' questions, her brother's silent resentment.

Monette looked at the oval face of the slender gold watch she wore on her wrist. 'We should get going if we want to find a parking space near the cinema.' Aïcha heard herself saying 'Okay' and, like an automaton, she followed her friend out the door while listening to Mathilde's advice about alcohol, boys and bad drivers. Monette, who never seemed bothered by anything, kept saying 'Yes, yes' and Aïcha let herself be led to the car.

Behind the wheel, Monette gave a sigh of relief. 'Thank goodness! I thought she was never going to stop nagging us.' Mathilde stood on the front steps and waved, gradually becoming tiny before disappearing from their field of vision. The vehicle turned onto the narrow dirt path that ran across the farm. The branches of olive trees tapped the windows as they passed and this noise reminded Aïcha of the car journey they used to take to her school on cold winter mornings. To the right of the path some farmworkers were crouching inside the vast greenhouses. Beneath plastic sheeting, their slumped bodies and their dark clothes were visible among the bushes. To the left, the stables had been transformed into garages for the machines. A child had fallen asleep, his face resting on the steering wheel of a tractor.

'The danger's over. You can come out now.' Aïcha stared in astonishment at Monette, then turned around to see two men huddled in the back seat.

'What the hell! You said it'd only take a minute. I'm going to have backache for a week now . . .' A man in his forties carefully stretched his limbs. He moved his head from side to side. He looked a bit like Cary Grant, with tanned skin, dark hair cut short and a muscular neck. On his left wrist he wore a gold chain; Aïcha was able to observe it quite closely when the man put his hand on Monette's neck and caressed it. Through the rear-view mirror Aïcha tried to make out the boy sitting behind her, who had said nothing. She could not see his face, only a thick mass of black hair and a bushy beard. Eyes turned to the window, he seemed completely absorbed by the passing landscape.

'All this is yours?'

Aïcha did not realise he was speaking to her.

'Is this your farm?'

'It's my father's.'

'Ah, the father we had to hide from. Is he really that scary?'

'He's just my father.'

'And how big is this farm?'

'I don't know.'

Two men were walking along the roadside. Two farm-workers in rubber boots and woolly jumpers with holes at the elbows. When the car passed they looked up and greeted Aïcha by putting their hands over their hearts. She felt ashamed. Her shame deepened when they passed the huge sign at the entrance announcing, in blue painted lettering: 'Domaine Belhaj'.

'Your father's a colonist?'

'No. He's Moroccan, and this land belongs to him.'

'Moroccan or not, it's the same thing. Your father's not so different from the Russian landowners with their serfs. You live like Europeans. You're rich. You don't have to be a colonist to treat people like natives.'

'You don't know what you're talking about.'

Monette started laughing, then said: 'Aïcha, allow me to introduce Karl Marx. And this,' she added, stroking her lover's fingers, 'is Henri. They paid me a surprise visit today, and I didn't know what to do with them. But I couldn't leave them with my mother. We'll try to find them a hotel.'

During the trip Monette explained that Henri lived in Casablanca, where he was an economics lecturer. Marx was one of his students. She had met them two years earlier, during a Jacques Brel concert at the Rif Cinema in Meknes. Henri interrupted her a few times to add an amusing detail or remind her of something she'd forgotten to mention. Like the fact that she had been wearing a blue dress and crying when Brel sang 'Ces gens-là'. That night, after the show, they had gone to the Hôtel Transatlantique and had seen – yes, seen with their own eyes – Jacques Brel himself, sitting at the bar and staring into space, his long sad hands resting on the countertop. Monette slapped the steering wheel.

'But I haven't told you the news! Aïcha delivered a baby last night, in the middle of the countryside . . . with a fork! Tell them!' Monette urged. Aïcha's lips moved but no sound came out. 'She's being shy. But I always knew she'd be a great doctor. Even back in school she was miles ahead of the rest of us.'

Karl Marx sniggered. Annoyed, Aïcha turned around and stared at the boy's face. His hair was just like hers, only darker, and it looked as though he'd backcombed it to make it even frizzier. His cheeks were covered by a dense beard and he wore a pair of glasses with very thick lenses. His huge, bulging forehead gave him a serious and vaguely disturbing look. She could not have said if he was handsome or not, but she was instantly gripped by his presence, by the aura of sadness and violence that he emitted. He was frighteningly alive, she thought.

'What's so funny?' she asked.

'Only the bourgeoisie can be doctors. Your father must have loads of money if he can afford to pay for all those years of studies.'

'So what? He worked hard for it. Earning money isn't a crime.'

'We'll see about that.'

'Don't take it personally,' Henri reassured her. 'That's why we call him Marx. But he's not a bad person, believe me. So, have you chosen a film?'

They did not go to the cinema. Monette said they should make the most of the mild night air instead, so they sat on the terrace of the Café de France. Monette couldn't stop touching Henri. She put her hand on his thigh, then on his arm, and finally intertwined her fingers with his and did not let go. The look she gave him was filled not only with love but with the desire she felt to get away from this place, the hope of being lifted at last out of her rut. She asked him about his life in Casablanca and did her best to listen to his answers. But her mind kept wandering: she found it hard to think about anything other than Henri's naked skin and the moment when he would kiss her. He had come for her. She kept repeating this to herself. 'He came for me.' Since their first meeting in 1966 they had kept up a regular correspondence. Henri wrote letters of such beauty and intelligence that Monette found them intimidating, and she spent days on end staring at her yellow letter paper without ever managing to say what she felt in her heart. He had phoned her at Christmas and on her birthday, and in January 1968 they had gone walking in Ifrane, amid snow-covered cedar forests where Barbary macaques swung from tree branches. Now he was here and, like those dreams that come true only after we have stopped hoping, his presence left her confused and speechless. They paid little attention to Aïcha that evening, and she sat there, arms crossed, chewing her straw, her tangled hair making her look like a grumpy little kid. She had no intention of making conversation with the pedantic boy who sat across the table from her, tapping his foot. 'The music is really crap here. Hasn't anyone in Meknes heard of jazz? Or rock 'n' roll, maybe?' Aïcha shrugged. Beside her, Henri and Monette whispered to each other. Her friend giggled and twisted in her chair, and Aïcha felt embarrassed. Monette kept touching her hair as if worried that her bun was about to collapse. Unlike Aïcha, Monette had always liked boys and she had given herself to them carelessly, uncalculatingly, perhaps thinking that her sincerity, the gift of her body, would make them love her. People talked about Monette; they said she wasn't shy. She had often used Aïcha as her alibi and as her lookout; Aïcha would sit on the ground or on the boot of a car while her friend let some boy caress her breasts. Aïcha had never felt any jealousy about this. In fact, what she felt was closer to pity. It seemed to her that Monette was giving away pieces of herself to boys who did not love her.

Marx cleared his throat. 'Um, you know, I didn't mean to offend you earlier. I'm sure your father is a good man. And he must be very proud of his little girl becoming a doctor.'

'And you're studying economics?'

'Yes, that's right.'

'So what will you become?'

'Me?' he asked, smiling. 'I want to write.'

Before going to bed, Aïcha locked herself in the bathroom. While she untangled her hair and slowly pinned big blue curlers in it, she thought about what Karl Marx had said. The boy's words obsessed her and cast a shadow over her parents in a way that made her shiver. She could not believe that her father was an exploiter, or even that he could be indifferent to the poverty that surrounded him. She would have liked to prove to Marx that she was not the bourgeois airhead he had described, but the more she thought about it the more it seemed to her that his depiction of her was accurate. She knew nothing about the world, about her own country. She lived only for herself, in a sort of shameful individualism. Never in her life had she rebelled against anything. She asked no questions, disputed no orders. She had never looked at – really looked at – those men and women around her, living in such destitution. Those lines of men who went to war for others, who died for others, who used up their youth and their strength in work. For others. All of this struck her now, but in a confused way: more a feeling than a thought. She felt remorseful but not outraged. Had she dared, she would have asked Karl Marx to explain things to her; she had so many questions. He must have thought her stupid, and that bothered her.

'I want to write,' he had said, and every time she thought about this phrase she was bowled over by it. She did not think anyone had ever described to her such a beautiful dream, such a noble ambition. If she'd been less gauche and ignorant, she would have asked him what kind of books he would write, on what subjects. If he would invent his own stories or tell the truth. He had told her that his name was Mehdi. Mehdi Daoud. And from that day forth, she had only one hope: to see him again.

Selim failed his exams, and in September he had to go back to school. He felt humiliated when the headmaster greeted him at the door with the words: 'So, Belhaj, have you decided to start doing some work?' The other students looked at him with expressions that mingled their admiration for this older boy and his athletic prowess with a dash of contempt because he was now reduced to being friends with people in the year below. But his position had certain advantages too. He knew the syllabus already and persuaded himself that he could wait until springtime to start revising. He would devote the first term to sport and to his few friends who had not gone abroad to university.

In October 1968 he took part in a swimming tournament and won the gold medal for the 100 metres freestyle. 'It's strange that such a clumsy boy can swim so fast,' his coach remarked. Yes, Selim was slow and he had been mocked for it many times. He was slow to learn his lessons, slow in his speech, slow even in the way he got dressed. All his movements were awkward, numb-limbed. You had the impression that his mind was forever elsewhere, busy solving an equation so complex that it prevented him from reacting to anything that happened to him. The words Selma had uttered a few months earlier, on the roof of the house, had slowly wormed their way into his mind, gradually infusing his thoughts, and one autumn evening, after smoking a cigarette on the roof, he decided to find out the truth for himself. When his parents went to bed and the house was plunged into darkness, he went out to the corridor and took the terracotta vase from the shelf. He reached in with his hand and his skin encountered the cold metal edges of the revolver. He cautiously picked it up as if it were a grenade, primed at any moment to blow up in his face. Then, after discovering that the revolver was not loaded, he stuck the barrel in his mouth, closed his eyes and pulled the trigger.

He kept the weapon with him day and night. He hid it at the bottom of his schoolbag, beneath his books and pens, and sometimes he would look inside to admire the revolver's partially obscured gleam. He placed it under his pillow before he went to sleep. He fetishised the gun in a way that bothered him, but he couldn't seem to help himself. He imagined pulling the revolver suddenly from his bag and threatening his teacher. Selim would aim at him and his terrified classmates would finally realise what he was capable of. He wasn't just a man now, he was a man with a gun, and he understood that this transformed him. This simple metal object, its butt fitting perfectly into the palm of his hand, awoke in Selim desires for vengeance, destruction, power.

One day at the end of Ramadan in 1968, Mathilde asked him to give Selma an envelope. 'She deserves to spoil herself a little,' she said. Selim took the envelope, containing a bundle of cash, and after school he went to Selma's apartment and knocked on the door. His aunt lived in Rue d'Oujda in the Boucle neighbourhood. It was a well-maintained building between the train station and the little park where Sabah went to play in the afternoons when school was over. On the ground floor of the building there was a grocer's and a shoemaker's. On the third floor was a Jewish dressmaker's workshop, where Mathilde often went despite her repugnance for its lack of cleanliness, its floor littered with rusty pins and balls of dust. The dressmaker, a chatty, nosy woman, had told Mathilde about an apartment recently vacated by a French family. Mathilde, weary of Selma's stony expression and mood swings, had long dreamed of moving her away from the farm. Seizing this opportunity, she had convinced Amine to rent the apartment.

Selim rang the doorbell early that afternoon. Selma opened the door. She was wearing a turquoise silk kimono and she kept tightening the belt as if afraid that the robe might slip from her shoulders at any moment and reveal her naked body. She welcomed her nephew into the apartment and put Mathilde's crumpled envelope on the table next to an overflowing ashtray. She gave him a cup of coffee so strong that he took only one sip. They smoked in silence. Through a small window they could look down on a courtyard where children played and women in worn clothes beat rugs. In the kitchen sink he saw a dirty saucepan, a plate and a glass. Selim wondered why Selma had not had any other children. They might have brightened her life a little, or at least kept her busy. He had heard rumours, of course, but he knew better than to believe the farmworkers' gossip. They all hated Mourad, so that was why they had claimed to see him, on the Azrou road, picking up boys and leading them in secret to fornicate in the cedar woods. Was it possible that any man could be indifferent to this woman who, even now, in a kimono, her slippers hanging off the ends of her toes, was almost unbearably beautiful? Selma swept her hand across the table, gathering crumbs and ash into her palm. And for the first time in his life Selim acted impulsively. He grabbed his aunt's hand and held it. He could feel the crumbs digging into his skin. Perhaps he wanted this gesture to be simply a sign of tenderness, compassion, proof of the complicity that had connected them for years. But as soon as he looked up at her, he knew it wasn't that. Holding her hand in his, gazing into her eyes, he felt the same excitement as when he pressed the revolver to his temple, alone in his bedroom. His penis grew hard and he felt ashamed of himself and of all men. Were women fortunate or cursed in their ability to keep their desires invisible?

Later he would revisit the memories of that afternoon until they became worn and faded, until they disappeared, until he no longer knew what was true and what wasn't. Did he pull her towards him, or was it perhaps she who stood up and pressed her cheek against his? She moved her lips closer and when he felt her tongue, cool and damp, inside his mouth, he thought he might faint or eat her alive. He wasn't afraid. He abandoned himself to her as he abandoned himself to water and felt the same rightness and lightness as he did when swimming. He slid his hand under her kimono and touched her small breasts, the nipples hard against his palm. He stroked the warm, soft skin of Selma's belly. He stared into her feverish, misty eyes, those eyes that expressed her desire to be impaled, and he thought she had never been as beautiful as she was in that instant. Without letting go of his hand she drew him into the corridor and then into the bedroom, shutting the door behind him. Was she thinking about the possibility of Mourad returning or about Sabah coming home after school? She did not seem worried. She lay down and undid the belt of her kimono. Her skin was the colour of the cannabis resin that the farmworkers would crumble between their fingers. She watched in silence as Selim undressed. His movements were calm, almost childlike, as if this was the first time he had ever taken off his clothes on his own. She could see the bulge of his erect penis under his boxer shorts. From outside came the sound of the call to prayer.

To Selim it seemed that he was the one penetrated that day. She entered him. She unfolded him like the fingers of a hand. Selma's body was fragile, creamy and cloudlike. She enveloped him with an overpowering softness. This woman was his destiny. Her body had been made to melt into his and he wanted to disappear into her hollows, to hide there from all the horrors of the world. There were no words for this, no explanations for the intense happiness that filled him, for the joyful rage that made him gasp and moan. She tamed him and he had no desire to resist. No words were spoken. They loved each other, cradled in a solemn, tranquil silence.

In the weeks that followed he often came to see her in the afternoons and they made love on the wooden bed, undisturbed by the headboard banging against the wall. Selim could think of nothing else, wanted nothing else. All he wanted was to do it again and again, for the world to disappear, for his afternoons to smell of her. He stopped sleeping, stopped eating, wandered around like a lost soul. At the club, his coach was concerned by his poor punctuality and weak performances and he told Selim he would have to pull himself together if he wanted to keep competing. Selim was like those snakes in Place Jemaa el-Fnaa, neck stiff, eyes wide, as if he'd seen a ghost. If someone had looked into Selim's eyes during those weeks, if they had really looked, they would have seen Selma's image engraved in the depths of his pupils.

At school, at home, he stared in a daze at everything around him, incredulous at its normality. Selma was there, so close by, and he was almost sick with desire for her. At every hour of the day or night she would appear to him in flashes, like a succubus taking possession of his thoughts and dreams. She gave him no respite, becoming more painfully unforgettable with each passing day. He saw the dimple in her lower back, he saw her face when she turned to look at him as he penetrated her. An innocent, lustful face that said: 'I want you.' Endlessly he breathed in the memory of her scent: her neck, her silky armpits. He remembered the coolness of her breath and the way she would put her hands on his buttocks and caress him. Stretched out, naked, facing each other, they would kiss for hours on end. They fell asleep together, their bodies pressed close, their legs intertwined, his mouth against the back of her neck, covered by that pale-yellow sheet impregnated with the smell of sex. Sometimes it was just after making love that they desired each other most intensely. As if, for them, it was not enough to feel satisfaction; they had to suck dry, to the very last drop, the vast promise contained in the other's body.

* * *

All week Selma would wait for him, thinking constantly as she sat at the kitchen table about the way he would unfasten her dress, push her onto the bed, spread her legs and slide his tongue inside her. She smoked and thought how differently he kissed her now: less clumsy and rushed than at the beginning. She wanted to talk dirty to him, to tell him she dreamed of being seized by him, being shoved against a wall and fucked until she disappeared, until she no longer existed. He learned how to make her yearn for him, to drive her into a rage. He bit her lip. He scratched her back. When she straddled him he would put his hands on her breasts and say: 'Wait.' When he penetrated her, what she felt was not only pleasure but a sweet, heady relief. Selim's cock did not cleave her. Her lover was an extension of herself, he completed her, filling her emptiness, quenching her thirst. Sometimes she worried that she was taking too long to come. She was afraid he would grow weary of her, abandon her, but eventually she managed to stop thinking about this, to let the pleasure drown out all fears. And when she did finally come, she would burst out laughing.

In that bedroom, she and Selim did not talk about their family. The names of Mathilde and Amine were never spoken and they discovered that they had a life of their own, one that had nothing to do with the others and which they had never discussed before. They did not mention Mourad, and Selim asked none of the questions that welled up within him. He was too afraid of ruining these moments and it seemed to him that no love was more beautiful than that which remains unspoken.

To begin with, they were amused by those Sunday lunches when they had to sit facing each other across Mathilde's dining room table. Of course they feared being caught, feared that someone would notice a glance between them, a change in their behaviour, and that their love would lurch into tragedy. But, at the same time, that fear excited them. Their hands brushed under the table. They made jokes that no one else could understand. They looked at each other, then lowered their eyes. And on Christmas Eve in 1968, when the whole family was gathered in the living room listening to Tino Rossi, they climbed up onto the roof to make love.

They would stroll peacefully through town like a respectable family. They would wait for Sabah outside the school gates and she would throw herself unreservedly into her cousin's arms. She felt sure that her schoolfriends were watching her, wild with jealousy at the idea that she was loved by this tall, blond swimming champion in his moccasins and his white trousers. Together they would go to get ice creams. Selim talked about his own school, about his friend Moshe's moped, about a party they wanted to go to that weekend. He was kind to her. A little distant, but kind. Sometimes they would spend the afternoon at the cinema and in the darkness Sabah would lean her head against Selim's shoulder while he stroked Selma's thighs.

Sabah was simultaneously an obstacle to their love and an indispensable alibi. In a small town like Meknes their walks together did not go unnoticed. Often, while out and about, Selim would see his schoolfriends smoking on café terraces or hanging around a motorbike in the hope of attracting girls. When Mathilde learned that Selim had been seen with his aunt, he told her that he enjoyed spending time with his cousin. They were only five years apart in age, after all, and they were friends. Not once did Sabah contradict him.

But she did ask questions. She wanted to see more of her cousin. Sometimes, entering the apartment, she would say that she could smell chlorine and she felt certain that Selim had been there; her mother's denials were never enough to convince her otherwise. When he came to see them she would

85

cling to him so desperately that in the end he would find it annoying. She begged him to help her with homework or to teach her how to swim one day. Winter ended and anxiety began to gnaw at Selma. This situation struck her as absurd, perilous, unsustainable. She did not open up about this to Selim. How could an eighteen-year-old boy understand her fears? She was afraid of the concierge, a vulgar man with sun-sullied skin who spent his days watching the tenants' comings and goings. One day he asked Selma who the tall blond man was who came to see her every afternoon. 'He's my nephew,' she answered nervously. The concierge raised his eyebrows, sniffed noisily and said: 'And what does your husband have to say about this nephew of yours coming to visit you?' Selma was afraid of the neighbours, the Jewish dressmaker and fat Fanny who worked at the grocer's where Selim would go to buy cigarettes. She was afraid of anyone who might in any way have noticed something off in this dangerous game they were playing. To her, this town, this neighbourhood and its inhabitants, seemed smaller, narrower than ever, and she had the impression that the people here did nothing with their lives except spy on others. She hated the fact that she was never alone, never truly alone, invisible. She wished she could scratch a hole in the wall with her fingernails and slip through it to a place she had never even imagined before. For her too, she thought, there must be a promised land. Like those little girls she had seen in films, she wanted to pass through the looking glass, fly over the rainbow. Escape.

When they made love now, she was no longer able to abandon herself to it completely. Occasionally she would tell him to be quiet or she would pull the sheet over his head. She would think she had heard the sound of a door being unbolted, or someone knocking, or Sabah's heavy footsteps in the entrance hall. More and more often she would fly off the handle at her daughter who stood there moping stupidly, asking her for this or that, wanting to be fed, this girl whose mere presence prevented her from dreaming about her lover. Yes, Selim was only eighteen. By some strange irony, by some sort of time travel, she found herself once again in the arms of an eighteen-year-old boy. As if the years that separated her from her youth and the pilot Alain Crozières had never existed. Past and present intermingled, Selim became Alain, and sometimes she wasn't even sure if what she was experiencing was real or just a memory.

One Sunday in March 1969 she went to the farm with her husband and her daughter. The breeze was still quite cool but Mathilde had moved the table outside, by the edge of the pool. Selim was absent and Selma didn't dare ask why. She waited for him, on edge, pale and half-crazed, jumping at the slightest noise, incapable of following the conversation. Then Sabah asked where her cousin was. 'Oh, who knows,' Mathilde sighed. 'With friends, I suppose. Or a girlfriend. He never tells me anything about his life.' Sabah started crying and Mathilde, surprised into tenderness, kissed her forehead. 'There's no need to get upset. Perhaps he'll drop by this afternoon. I'm sure he'll want to play with you.' But Sabah kept whining and snivelling and Selma, unable to bear it any more, yelled at her to shut up. 'What the hell is wrong with you?' She grabbed her daughter by the arm and dragged her into the house. 'Stay here. You're punished.'

Fear and remorse were not the only emotions that Selma felt. Sometimes the craziest thoughts would run through her head. She wondered if sex with Selim was so good because they were from the same family, because the same blood flowed through their veins. She thought about their names, so similar, the Ss, Ls and Ms swirling before her eyes until she saw the sickening confusion in which they had entangled themselves. In those moments, lying on her bed, she felt nauseated and the image of her own naked body writhing against her nephew's inspired only disgust. Did she love him? Was that kind of love even possible for them? Of course she had tender feelings for this boy who never told her no and who looked at her with such passion that it scared her sometimes. But love? She didn't know what that was.

Nothing could be born from this unnatural coupling, this sin. No future together was possible. And because of that, she started to resent Selim for his youth, his freedom, his life without ties and responsibilities. It killed her, the idea that one day – because one day it would have to end – he would seek solace with other women, on other continents, and that she would have nothing to console her in her grief but this apartment full of memories of her lover and this kitchen that stank of cigarettes.

More and more often they would argue. Sometimes Selim would ring the doorbell and hear it echo emptily inside the apartment. And the only reason she answered the door to him was her fear of scandal. Because if she didn't he would shout her name and hammer his fists against the door. One day he told her about the revolver. He took it out of his schoolbag and placed it on the yellow sheet. Selma stared incredulously at the gun. A thousand pictures flashed through her mind. 'What are you doing with that?' Selim assured her that he knew how to use it if necessary. Nothing would happen to them: he would defend her against Mourad, against Amine, he would find a solution and they would escape. Suddenly Selma thought: He's stupid. There was a big difference between carrying an unloaded weapon around in a schoolbag and aiming it at a man. As for escaping . . . Where could they go? She decided to pretend not to have heard him.

One day, standing naked in front of the full-length mirror on the wardrobe door, she swore to put an end to the whole sad story. She would not give in. She would not open the door to him even if he begged her. She found herself talking to God, even though she never set foot in a mosque. Alone in her bedroom, she asked Him for advice, begged His forgiveness, and in that moment Allah blurred with the image of her elderly mother. If Mouilala found out the truth, she thought, if my mother knew. She bought incense, which she burned in a terracotta brazier, and the scent flooded the apartment. She explained to Sabah that she wanted to get rid of the demons that had invaded their home and were tormenting her.

She often wondered whether Mourad suspected something. She always took a shower after Selim left, and yet she worried that his odour clung to her. Her sin was tattooed on her skin, it was visible in every movement she made, and it seemed only a matter of time before her husband caught her. But Mourad said nothing, saw nothing, felt nothing. Ever since their wedding he had slept on a bench in the living room and he had never had occasion to sniff the yellow sheet on her bed. There were times when she would have preferred him to beat her, imprison her, drag her by the hair along the floor and scream insults at her. Anything seemed better than this cold, heavy, heart-crushing silence.

In early April 1969 Amine decided to have a well dug on one of the plots of land he had bought. He imagined hiring a local well-digger, but Mourad dissuaded him. There was no need to spend his money and allow a stranger onto his land. Mourad could do it himself with the aid of two or three labourers. 'It's not complicated.' The foreman chose two people: a young boy who could go down into the hole and a giant of a man, his eyes too far apart, whom everyone called Zizoun the Mute because he had never spoken a single word. They armed themselves with shovels, pickaxes and two wheelbarrows with squeaking wheels. They used three logs to build a hoist and began to dig. The boy cried because he was scared of going down into the hole, one foot inside the bucket tied to a rope. He kept saying 'I don't want to' and repeating the name of his mother, a peasant woman from the douar who had not had any other children. The giant lifted and dug in silence, frowning with concentration. He pulled on the rope to bring up buckets filled with earth and rocks. To start with, Amine came to the site quite often and was pleased with the progress they were making. Each time, Mourad would say, 'We'll find water soon', and Amine would believe him.

One day Zizoun ran to the farm. He knocked at the door and when Amine opened it the giant began making a series of wild gestures. He banged his head with his huge hands and beckoned the boss to follow him. At first Amine thought something must have happened to the boy, and as he drove the pick-up truck along the dirt path, the mute beside him, he cursed himself for ever having listened to Mourad. He swore it would be the last time, that in future he would stand up to his foreman and reject his hare-brained ideas. But when he got there, the boy was sitting on the dry, cracked earth. He said to Amine: 'I called out but he's not answering. The rocks fell on him. He wanted me to go down there. He got angry with me. And now he's not answering.' Amine leaned over the hole and shouted the foreman's name. He kept shouting even though he knew it would do no good. The walls of the well had collapsed and Mourad was lying at the bottom, his body smashed by rocks.

The police were called. The officer, looking suspicious, asked Amine if he had any reason to believe that it had not been an accident. Arms dangling, mouth tight with nerves, Amine stammered a response. Of course it was an accident! What was the policeman insinuating? That someone might have wanted to kill Mourad? The policeman paced around the hole. He did things by the book. He asked to see their papers. Did they have authorisation to dig in this location? Who exactly was this dead foreman? He made it clear that he would have to carry out an investigation, to interrogate the farmworkers; it would be a long, unpleasant process, but it was his job and there was nothing they could do about it. Amine led the policeman to his office. He served tea, which the policeman drank slowly, eyes fixed on the portrait of Hassan II which hung on the wall. Amine asked if they could come to an arrangement and the policeman smiled. It was just a simple accident. This kind of thing happened all the time. It was the downside to employing illiterate peasants: those imbeciles always thought they knew more than they actually did. Amine was a gentleman, that was obvious, and the policeman had no intention of stopping him doing his work. How well did he know this foreman? Did he have any family? Because that was the problem with people like that. The family would come knocking, they would weep and complain, they would claim compensation from the boss. Those ingrates would drag their kids along and tell them to whine just to make you ill at ease, and then for months – no, for years – they would harass you with their poverty and their grief. 'The only problem,' the policeman repeated, 'is the family.' Amine nodded. He opened an envelope, put some cash in it, and handed it to the policeman. 'Don't worry about the family. I'll deal with that.'

'You're a generous man, that's obvious. I'm sure you can make them see reason. What's the point of nosing around, of wasting all our time? It is what God wanted, after all. And nobody can defy the will of God.'

Did God answer evil prayers? Had Allah done this for her? These were the thoughts that ran through Selma's head when Amine told her that Mourad was dead. And even though he didn't look her in the eyes, she knew that her brother was thinking exactly the same thing. Amine promised to continue taking care of her and Sabah. 'I owe him that.'

The night after the accident, Amine wandered alone on the quince tree hill. He could not believe that Mourad was dead, his corpse rotting under rocks a few miles from the house, in the middle of nowhere. He was sure that his aide-de-camp would reappear one day, just as he had reappeared years earlier one rainy night in his baggy, ragged clothes. Mourad would come towards him and call him 'my commander' with that mixture of tenderness and submission that Amine had never under-stood. Amine saw once again his imploring, disturbed eyes, behind which flickered occasionally the shadow of a nightmare. How strange it was, Amine thought, to know beyond any pos-sible doubt that someone was ready to die for you. Until the end, Mourad had remained a soldier. Submissive and brave. Obedient and violent. He had never returned to civilian life. He had never left the world of war, orders, massacres. He had continued to live in a reality that no longer existed, a soldier without a country, without a uniform, without medals. His hands dripped blood. His guts still bore traces of the amoebic dysentery he had caught in Indochina, and Amine remembered the way he used to eat, very slowly, chewing with difficulty. He had been raised to destroy and now he had been destroyed.

They decided not to try removing his body from the well. Mathilde was offended by this; after all, Mourad had been her brother-in-law. 'We can't just leave him there. What will people think?' But Amine preferred it this way: in that deep grave, nobody could disturb Mourad's rest. As a child he had heard the story of a military governor, hated by the population because he had collaborated with the French, whose body had been exhumed by the villagers and chopped into pieces. They had exposed his profaned corpse to the sun and sworn that they would do the same thing to the man who took his place.

A funeral was organised, a funeral without a body. That day Selma, Sabah and Mathilde, all dressed in white, sat together on the living room sofa. Every time someone entered the room they would stand up, almost at the same time. Mathilde kept adjusting her headscarf and Sabah wept. Tears rolled over her acne-ridden face. On the verge of a nervous breakdown, she demanded to be taken to the well. 'I want to see where my father is.' But Amine dissuaded her. 'I am your father now. You will always be able to depend on me.' What? How did he dare say that? She didn't want him to be her father. She would never have a father again, because hers had died. Selim, standing there in front of her, could not be her brother. She didn't love him like a brother. She stood up, pressed her face against his chest and, using her grief as an excuse, held him tight.

Selma could not have explained the feelings she experienced in the days after Mourad's death. Strangely, her husband had never been as present in her life as he was during that time.

Since he was dead and had gone to heaven, she imagined that he knew everything about her. From his new location he could see down into the depths of her heart and she no longer had any secrets from him. He knew about Selim, and Selma – even when she was alone – would blush at the idea of her private life being exposed to his eyes. As a dead man, Mourad became a confidant, almost a friend, who no longer judged her. And she understood then what it had been impossible for her to see while they had lived together: this man's loneliness. His suffering. His absence of desire for her, which she had for a long time simply been happy about instead of wondering at its cause.

One day, as she was making Sabah's dinner, a memory came to her. They had just moved into the apartment that Amine had rented for them and one night Selma was woken by screams. At first she thought something must have happened to Sabah. Mourad adored that child and worried ceaselessly about her. Selma stood up and went into her daughter's bedroom. Sabah was sleeping peacefully. She went into the living room and saw Mourad's body, stretched out on the bench. His face was pouring with sweat. He screamed again and she was so frightened that she almost ran back to her bed. But she forced herself to move closer. Her husband was like a stray dog dreaming that it is running, paws twitching frantically as it lies there in the street. She touched his shoulder and whispered: 'Wake up.' Mourad's eyes opened wide, like a drowned man coming back to life. She warmed up some milk and sat beside him, and that night, for the first time, he talked to her. He told her that he had a recurring nightmare. He was lost in a dense, suffocating jungle, his skin bitten by swarms of parasites, and in the distance he could hear men yelling, the whistling of bullets. He ran desperately, knowing that he had left behind him his dying comrades and his own sense of honour. In his dreams he could smell the thick odour of blood and mud, he could feel the tree branches scratching his face. He saw the boat where the corpses were piled high and the abandoned villages where their enemies lay in wait. He heard harrowing screams and the word 'Mama', which he understood even though he didn't speak that foreign language. The men, their guts spilling through their hands, the naked and abandoned children, were all calling out for their mothers the way you might pray to Jesus or Allah to come and save you. He told her that these nightmares did not come to him only at night when he was sleeping on the bench in the living room. Sometimes he would have visions in the middle of the day, in the middle of a field, on a country road. He would hear a tractor engine and see a tank. The peasant farmers appeared to him as enemy soldiers. Once, seeing a flock of birds attack the orchard and eviscerate peaches with their beaks, he had started sobbing loudly. 'I deserted. Me and my men, we killed the captain and we fled. We left his body in the camp and we all went our separate ways. That's the truth. I wanted to save my own skin, so I ran away. Sometimes there is nothing else you can do.'

In the days after remembering this, Selma was haunted by Mourad's words. It wasn't merely a memory, she felt sure, but a message from her dead husband. He was trying to tell her something and she fretted over what it might mean. 'Run away – there is nothing else you can do.'

Aïcha was like her father. Touchy, violent. '*Soupe au lait*,' Mathilde would say, and what annoyed Aïcha was not the accusation itself but the idiocy of that expression. Why did 'milk soup' mean short-tempered? The phrase always made her think of those soups that Mathilde used to make, with pieces of boiled vegetables floating around in them, stringy bits from turnips that had so disgusted Aïcha when she was a child. In Strasbourg she had fought against her own nature, following her parents' advice, and she had forced herself to be discreet. 'We don't want them saying that Arabs don't know how to behave themselves.' Aïcha had behaved herself.

Aïcha felt a mix of excitement and fear when she began working at the hospital in Strasbourg and was put in charge of her first patients. She knew all the theory, of course, and was practically infallible when it came to reporting a pathology, but she feared the questions of her patients who wanted to know exactly what was wrong with them but who did not listen when she tried to explain it to them. The patients did not take her seriously and often, when she left a room after her morning visit, one of them would say: 'But I haven't seen the doctor yet. Could you call for him?' She had to get used to being mistaken for a nurse, while male nurses were often presumed to be doctors.

One day she saw a female patient complaining of stomach aches who told Aïcha that she had thrown up copious amounts of blood-red vomit. Aïcha immediately thought it might be a perforated ulcer. She ordered blood tests, put the woman on a drip and asked about the possibility of a transfusion if the woman lost too much blood. When her department head was informed of this by the laughing nurses, he took her aside. 'You may be a brilliant student, mademoiselle, but maybe you should get your nose out of your books for a while and take a look at the world around you. It's strawberry season, didn't you know? And here people like to mash up strawberries with pots of cream. So don't be surprised if you have quite a few patients coming in over the next few days with acute indigestion.' She had to learn to recognise the effects of unsanitary lifestyles, and of alcoholism too. In the end she got used to the lies told by young women who came in with their trousers covered in blood, followed by a parent shaking their head and repeating: 'The shame . . .'

But what most struck Aïcha, and what raised a torrent of questions in her mind, was her superiors' advice that she not tell her terminal patients that they were soon going to die. They recommended ignoring the facts and giving these doomed patients hope, and Aïcha could not accept this. She could not see the benefit in what she regarded as a lie, an act of dissimulation and, worst of all, the denial of a precious piece of information that the patient might have used for good in his life. During a department meeting she raised this subject with regard to one of her patients, a woman called Doris of whom she had become very fond. Doris had lung cancer and the marks that had recently appeared on her skin showed that the disease had spread. Doris kept asking if she would be cured by Christmas, wanting to know when she would be allowed to leave the hospital and live with her husband and their three-year-old son again. Doris died one night when Aïcha was absent, and in the morning she met Doris's husband in the corridor. He was forty years old and he was wearing a sky-blue jumper over a check shirt. He hadn't shaved for at least two days and his hair was lank. All her life she would remember, almost word for word, what this man said to her and the lost look in his eyes as he stared at her and at the salmon-coloured corridor walls. 'Excuse me, Doctor. I'm sorry to bother you. I know you must be very busy, but I just wanted to ask you a question. Could you tell me what Doris died of? Could you explain it to me?' Aïcha kept her head lowered and tried to hold back the tears that were welling behind her eyes. They were tears not only of compassion but of rage, because she knew she had been guilty of lying. And the husband went on: 'I'm sorry, but I don't understand. I tried to remember what you told me and what the other doctor told me, the tall gentleman with the white hair. I know you did your best and I won't forget your kindness towards me. But I'm finding it hard to understand. Just yesterday you promised me that she would be well again soon, that you were going to try that new medicine, I can't remember what it was called. You said everything was under control and that I could go home to take care of our son. You told me that but when I came back this morning, with a clean jumper for Doris in my bag, she wasn't in the room any more. I know you've already explained it to me and I know what she had was serious. And I know these things happen, but I need you to tell me again, Doctor. I need you to tell me why my wife is dead.'

Was it this contact with her patients? Or was it Karl Marx's words, which continued to obsess her? In any case, something in Aïcha had changed. During the winter and then the spring of 1969 she felt an anger, a rebellion, rising inside her, along with a desire to open herself up to the world, to understand it. It seemed to her that she could not do her job properly unless she knew what life was like for other people, unless she understood what they were going through. Once, when she and David were smoking a cigarette in the hospital lobby, he raised his eyebrows and smiled when he noticed a copy of *The Second Sex* in the pocket of Aïcha's white coat. 'You're reading that?' he asked, incredulous. Aïcha replied coldly: 'Yes, why? Did you think I couldn't read?'

Just as she used to do when she was at school in Morocco, Aïcha would sometimes fly off the handle. One day a girl approached her at the hospital cafeteria. The girl had a very small face and her blonde hair was tied in a sophisticated bun. When she spoke, the movements of her chin and the way she kept sniffing made her look like a shrew. She sat across the table from Aïcha and told her that she was Moroccan too. Well, she was born in Morocco anyway, although her parents had eventually returned to France. She didn't remember anything about it because she had been very young when they left. Then she leaned over her plate of sliced ham and whispered: 'My father often tells me about his memories. He says there were lepers in the cities, begging for money.' Aïcha stared at her, then laughed contemptuously. The shrew looked taken aback. 'You're not Moroccan,' said Aïcha, 'and those weren't lepers that your father saw. They were poor people.'

But the person who irritated her more than anyone, the person who drove her mad with rage, was Madame Muller. Aïcha knew that her landlady went into her room when she wasn't there. She could only imagine what that almost bald Alsatian woman did there behind her back. Perhaps she lay in Aïcha's bed to inhale the smell of the African on the sheets. No doubt she rummaged through the fridge, curious what this skinny girl ate, and she must have grimaced with disgust when she saw those open sardine tins and the mouldy carrots at the back of the vegetable drawer. Maybe she even inspected the toilet bowl to see if the rumours were true and Africans really did leave black stains on the shiny white enamel. One day Aïcha went home and found Madame Muller sitting on a chair in her kitchen. She was startled by the sight of that solid body in the half-dark. The woman was holding a white tissue in her hands and she unfolded it in front of Aïcha, who leaned down and saw what looked like a wet, grey strand of hair, covered with a phlegm-like residue. In an outraged voice Madame Muller said: 'This is why the pipes are blocked! Although, with hair like that, it's hardly a surprise. Didn't they ever teach you that in Africa, to clean up after yourself?' She placed the damp tissue on the table and left, slamming the door behind her.

Aïcha nursed her anger for weeks, imagining scenarios in which she would knock at the landlady's door and tell her exactly what she thought of her and her nosiness. But she knew she would never find the courage to do it, and when she passed the old woman in the corridor or the street she just pretended not to have seen her. One day in June 1969, about six in the afternoon, Madame Muller came to Aïcha's door and handed her an envelope. 'You have a letter.' Aïcha knew that the land-lady opened her post. It was easy to picture Madame Muller in her office, holding envelopes over a saucepan of boiling water. She resealed them afterwards but in such a careless way that

Aïcha could have no doubt that her privacy had been violated. She grabbed the letter without a word and shut the door in the Alsatian woman's face.

Then she sat down and, smiling, read Monette's letter. Monette had moved to Casablanca a few months earlier and was now working as a secretary at the Moulay-Abdallah secondary school. Throughout the winter Monette had been sending her friend beautiful postcards, which Aïcha had stuck to the kitchen wall, just above her desk. The Corniche beach, vivid with sunlight, with men in white trousers strolling along its promenade. Young people diving, undaunted, from the high board into the biggest swimming pool in the world. Women in bikinis lying on orange deckchairs. This time she had sent not a card but a long letter; Aïcha had instantly recognised the jerky, messy handwriting that had so upset the nuns at their boarding school years earlier. Monette was writing to announce her decision to move in with Henri. They had rented a beach hut at Sable d'Or, between Rabat and Casablanca. They had no intention of getting married. They were just living together, without any concerns for the future, with no other aim than to enjoy their love. Monette's mother was furious. 'But she'll come round.' Monette had included a photograph on whose glossy surface Madame Muller's fat fingerprints were clearly visible. In the picture Monette was lying on the sand and reaching out, palm upwards, as if she didn't want to be photographed. Three other people were sitting around her: two young suntanned women and Henri, who had a football between his feet. Empty beer bottles were lying on a tablecloth and in the distance you could see the front of a cheap hotel and a few tents under which some holidaymakers were lying in the shade. At the end of her letter Monette wrote: 'Come and spend the summer with us. I think this is the most beautiful place in the world and there's nowhere you could be happier.'

A week later Aïcha moved out of her apartment. Madame Muller watched as she loaded her belongings into a car driven by a young Jewish man with curly hair. She did not say goodbye to her tenant or wish her good luck. As far as she was concerned it was good riddance: the African had packed her bags and was returning to her own cursed continent. Madame Muller was relieved. She knew she would have no trouble finding someone else to rent the room. The city was full of students and it would take less than a week to find a decent candidate, preferably an Alsatian whose parents would be prepared to pay six months of rent in advance. Of course, it would need a big clean-up. She would have to air the room, tidy the cupboards. The day after Aïcha's departure Madame Muller entered the apartment, bucket in hand. As soon as she opened the door, a foul stench assailed her nostrils. A smell she would remember to the end of her days as the smell of humiliation. She pinched her nose, walked through the living room, and when she came to the bedroom she saw, above the stripped bed, written on the wall in faecal matter: 'The African shits on you.'

Karl Marx saw the world as a succession of scenes in which extras repeated gestures they had learned by heart. He was convinced that a destiny would be accomplished through him and that he had no choice but to yield to it. Sometimes he felt annoyed with himself for his failure to mask this sense of certainty, with the consequence that he came across as arrogant and pretentious. His life, he believed, would have the density, the logic, the grandeur of a novel. He would be a character and watch himself live, eager to find out the next scene in which he would play. In his mind a series of heroic stars jostled for the lead role and when he thought about himself it was not his own face he saw but that of John Wayne or Marlon Brando.

He would haul himself far above his friends and family. So high that they would not be able to follow him. Of course he would send them money and let them know that he had become someone. He thought about this constantly: what were you if you weren't *someone*? His family understood nothing about the future. They lived in Fes, in the bowels of the imperial city, petrified – like the city itself – in a nostalgia for past glories. All they cared about was satisfying their immediate desires. They were the exact opposite of the characters in the films he watched, who were always working towards a goal. Who knew that, sooner or later, something important was going to happen to them.

Mehdi had grown up in Fes, in a cramped apartment above the Rex Cinema. His mother, Farida, would never let him buy a ticket, take a seat among the other cinemagoers and watch a film. She said the dark theatre was a den of iniquity populated by criminals and fallen women. He would learn things there that were not suitable for a boy of his age, and it was not good for children to believe in what did not exist. She would spit on the pavement whenever she saw those big black-and-white posters of velvet-lipped, long-haired actresses insolently staring at her.

In their apartment, Mehdi could hear laughter from the cinema below. He could hear gunfire during the action scenes. In the living room, when they ate dinner in silence, they would hear the spectators impatiently yelling: 'Turn off the lights! Start the film!' They whistled at the pretty girls on the screen, applauded the cowboys and booed the Indians. Mehdi soon discovered that the bathroom was the best place to hear the lines of dialogue written thousands of miles away, in the Hollywood Hills. The *oh mon amour*s that Mehdi would repeat uncomprehendingly under his breath, his ear glued to the cold zellige tiles. One day, when he was about twelve years old and had been staring at the mirror, inspecting the first hairs to sprout from his chin, Mehdi decided to remove one of the tiles. Then another. Then, using a screwdriver, he scratched at the damp-rotted wall until there was a hole through which, miraculously, he could see the cinema screen. To start with, he did not tell anyone about this. Certainly not his two brothers, who would have fought to steal his place from him, who would have pulled at his shirt and, despite the respect they owed him as their older brother, would have showered him with prayers and pleas. For a few months this pleasure, this source of delight, remained his alone. He would lock himself for hours on end in that bathroom, freezing in winter and stifling in summer, gazing one-eyed at the Warner and Paramount classics. The women's hair, always uncovered, looked diaphanous in the black-and-white flicker of the projectors' light. In the streets of those great American cities, the women would run to their cars in high heels. They would kiss men in packed restaurants or at the top of the Empire State Building. They would drink cocktails, holding the martini glass in a silk-gloved hand. He loved all of this so much that he never even noticed the pain in his bent back, the pins and needles in his calves.

In the end his brothers realised what was happening and they threatened, in voices rusty from constant colds, to tell their parents if he didn't let them take a turn. At first Mehdi hated the idea of sharing his secret and he would shake with rage when his brothers giggled or made vulgar remarks about actresses he revered. But it wasn't long before his brothers had learned the films' dialogue by heart and the three boys would have fun reciting lines together. In the living room where Farida gave them their dinner they would sometimes suddenly start acting out one of those scenes. Mehdi would be Humphrey Bogart or Fred Astaire; he always took the lead role. Whenever their mother caught them, laughing and squawking in French, she would blow her top, screaming at them: 'Stop speaking French in my home!' They would burst out laughing, despite their fear of her. 'Aren't you ashamed, mocking your own mother?' And she would slap them. If he really wanted to enrage her, Mehdi would recite poems by Pierre de Ronsard. In a quivering voice he would declaim

'Sweetheart, come let us see if the rose . . .', and Farida would run after him down the stairs. The sounds of that language disgusted her. Those incomprehensible syllables spoke of her misfortune, her powerlessness. They betrayed the oppression of her people, her lack of education as a woman.

Once, when Mehdi had spent almost an hour inside the bathroom, Farida lost her temper and hammered her hands against the wooden door. In French, Mehdi shouted: 'Leave me alone', then started to laugh. Farida punched and kicked that damp-rotted door as hard as she could, until finally it gave way. She grabbed Mehdi by the collar, threw him to the floor, and slowly bent down to peer through the hole. Startled, she jumped back from it, intoning 'May God protect us from Satan', 'Ya Latif, ya Latif.' Through the spyhole she had seen a blonde woman with a painted mouth. A woman sitting on a chair in a very dark house, crossing her naked legs. She was aiming a revolver at a man in a raincoat and hat. Farida would never have admitted this to anyone, but had it not been for the presence of her son, her idiot son lying on the floor right next to her, she would have kept her eye to the hole a little longer, just to find out what was about to happen to that woman. Instead, she turned around and began hitting Mehdi, who shielded his face with his arms. There was the sound of laughter, then a gunshot.

* * *

Even now, at twenty-four, Mehdi would still sometimes wake with a start, his forehead covered in sweat, after dreaming of his mother. He remembered her as a woman with dazed-looking eyes sunk deep in her tobacco-coloured face. Black rages would engulf her at the slightest provocation and she would lash out, so as not to hear, not to feel pain. She beat her children. Since breaking several bones in an accident, Farida had been addicted to morphine, a fact that everyone pretended not to know. At night she would slip away over the roof terraces. Often she would be seen up there, walking in her brightly coloured djellabas, her hair loose. In those streets, lit by the big candles each family kept outside its front door, she would pass men coming back from the hammam, white towels wrapped around their heads, their skin still steaming. Farida didn't notice them. She walked faster and faster, frantically wiping her hands over her djellaba, desperate to reach the pharmacist who dreaded her arrival. He had even started closing his shop earlier than usual in the hope that she would find another pharmacist outside the old town. 'Let her find some charlatan to supply her,' the old man wished. 'Let her forget me.' But Farida kept coming back, sweaty and determined. She knocked at his window and she knew the pharmacist could hear her because he lived above the dispensary. She also knew the old man would open the door for her because he feared a scandal and felt some pity for her. In the end he would always come downstairs, grumbling to himself, and he would open the shutters even while swearing this was the last time. Invoking Allah, he begged Farida to pull herself together in the name of decency, for her own salvation, for her children. Farida didn't hear him. The shutters were raised now, she was close to her goal. Soon the pharmacist would head towards the back room. She heard the sound of little metal tubes and felt a wave of relief sweep through her. He spoke and all she was aware of was her slimy mouth, her mouth which felt as if it were full of sweat.

Mehdi was a lively, curious child, adored by his father. Old Mohamed, who worked as a butler for a rich Frenchman, decided he wanted to send his son to the European school. He asked his employer for help and the Frenchman, after meeting the young prodigy, agreed. Farida never forgave her husband for pushing their son into the arms of the French. 'You'll make him a stranger in his own home.' Years later Mehdi had to admit that she had been right.

Mehdi was eleven when Morocco achieved independence. Like the other students, he had watched the crowds gather, had witnessed the explosion of joy that followed the return of the king, and he had felt proud of his country, its regained sovereignty. He had ambivalent feelings towards the French. In front of his classmates he would pretend to hate white people, Christians, those horrible imperialists. He insulted them and said that the only reason he was learning their language, their laws and their history was to help free himself from them. To play them at their own game, as the nationalists said at the time. In reality what he felt for them was admiration mixed with jealousy, and he believed he had only one ambition in life: to become like them.

When he started secondary school in the late 1950s he would sometimes earn a bit of pocket money by acting as a guide for tourists in search of exoticism. They thought he was funny, this little Arab with his bulging forehead, his thick-lensed glasses, who knew the alleys of the old town like the back of his hand. In a knowledgeable tone he would warn them:

'Without a guide, you will soon get lost. The city was designed that way: to close like a trap around foreigners, invaders.' The tourists followed his every footstep. They were startled by the sight of the artisans' ravaged faces, were frightened by the yells of the men pulling donkeys or rickety carts who would shove them roughly against a wall. They were horrified by all the legless cripples, the dwarves, the blind men in their grey woollen djellabas, holding a knotty stick and a little metal cup in which a coin would occasionally rattle. Few of them knew how to be silent in the face of the beauty of this swarming crowd, knew how to let pass the mules carrying piles of pink or indigo-dyed wool. Mehdi ran. He leaped over puddles and cowpats, slipped out of the tourists' sight and took delight in the scent of terror that reached him in his hiding place. He wanted to give them the impression that the town belonged to him, that he was known and loved by all its inhabitants. He feigned friendliness with the men selling vegetables and olives. He told tall tales, recounted legends, never caring about the truth. They got their money's worth, those tourists sweating in their woollen coats who walked around staring at their shoes, afraid of stepping in shit.

Mehdi knew more about French history and geography than any of those French people from Limoges or Orléans. And for them he invented extraordinary myths. To start with, the old Fes shopkeepers had snarled at this ugly child with his skinny calves who made them unroll their rugs or show their leather pouffes. They didn't like being interrupted in the middle of a sales patter they had spent their whole lives perfecting, a patter that had worked for them again and again. But little Mehdi turned out to be an extraordinary salesman. He demonstrated to them something that they had not understood before: that it was not enough to boast about the quality of their wool, the softness of their leather, the subtlety of their embroideries. They had to tell a story. 'This is no simple rug,' Mehdi would tell the open-mouthed tourists. 'It is all that remains of the home of an old pasha who died in a tribal war.' And soon, in their living rooms in Limoges or Orléans, those delighted travellers would invite friends round to share a glass of wine and tell them the tale of that rug and the defeated pasha.

The tourists asked him questions. They wanted to know more about him, to understand why he had no accent ('If I closed my eyes, I would swear you were French'), how he knew all these extraordinary stories. Mehdi answered them with more stories, stories in which he was the hero, the kinds of stories that these tourists, the women especially, were expecting to hear. The story of a little savage who becomes civilised in the warming presence of enlightened foreigners. The story of a gifted child lost in a limbo of mediocrity and barbarism. The women, after a tearful glance at their husbands, would lean towards him. They would make him promises. That they would write to him, send him books and money, take care of him when he was old enough to escape this place and – why not? – go to university in France. They told him there were other Arabs, young people of exceptional intelligence, who were studying at the best institutions in the country. That he must be a good boy, well behaved and studious, if he wanted this dream to come true. He said 'Thank you' without ever feeling that he owed them anything. From beneath his disguise of poverty and childhood – which were, to him, one and the same – he observed them through the eyes of the man he would later become, never fooled into thinking them anything more than mediocre.

Sometimes, however, he did not manage to smile, to play along. The tourists' condescension would irritate him and he would answer their questions coldly. Biting his tongue, he would listen to their idiotic commentaries, their remarks about the filth and poverty, about the stupidity of his people. When that happened, he would nurture a desire to disappoint them, or rather to confirm – with his hate, his violence, his rudeness – that he was exactly what they thought he would be. He wanted their nightmares to come true. To a little girl with braided hair, in a bottle-green woollen coat, who was wrinkling her nose at the tanners' stinking vats, he whispered: 'You'd better watch out, or an Arab might come and eat you!' The girl cried out and hid in her mother's skirts, the mother concluding: 'This isn't for children. She's far too impressionable.' The mother did not seem to have noticed that Mehdi wasn't much older than her daughter, and that he was sitting and laughing on the guardrail of a balcony just above those vats full of pigeon shit.

There, along the fifty miles of coastline between Casablanca and Rabat, Marshal Lyautey had dreamed of building a French California. He believed it was the ocean that would give this country its strength, its fortune, and he was bewildered that its inhabitants had lived for so long with their backs turned to its potential. He made Rabat his capital, relegating the once-great city of Fes to the past. And in the small port town of Casablanca he intended to construct a symbol of modern Morocco. A land whose inhabitants would work hard to earn money and enjoy the pleasures of life. A land very different from those imperial cities, those stifling medinas, those riads with their windowless walls behind which whole families were preserved in the old traditions. No, it was here, by the sea, that he would build a city for the conquerors, the pioneers, the businessmen, the party girls and the tourists in search of exoticism. A city of labourers and billionaires, its broad avenues shaded by palm trees, lined with restaurants and cinemas, with immaculately white art deco buildings. Here, the city's best architects would raise concrete towers fitted with lifts, central heating and underground parking. A city like a film set, bathed in golden sunlight, where passers-by would play the roles assigned to them. No more plump pashas, no more yawning sultans, no more veiled women imprisoned in humid palaces. No more tribal wars, no more peasant famines, no more of that prudishness and backwardness that had flourished in the shadow of the mountains. The coastline was the new frontier, and all men with ambition would dream of conquering the West.

* * *

In July 1969 Aïcha went to stay with Henri and Monette in the beach hut they were renting at Sable d'Or. The house was surrounded by a small sun-yellowed lawn. At the back, a wide terrace led down to the sand. The incredibly messy living room adjoined a narrow kitchen. Near the always-open front door there were piles of sandy shoes, raffia baskets, wet towels that smelled of mould. Between the two sofas stood a coffee table littered with newspapers, books and seashells. A cat slept on an armchair. Another, which Monette had found at the local shop, was sitting on a windowsill. 'I wouldn't get too close if I were you,' she warned Aïcha on her first day. 'They're both wild. They'll scratch you if you try to stroke them.' Despite, or perhaps because of, the hut's chaotic appearance, there was something pleasant and welcoming about it, and everyone who entered it immediately shed the suffocating corset of social etiquette. This was a place of pleasure and relaxation, where you could let it all hang out. Behind the kitchen a concrete staircase led up to the first floor, which contained Henri and Monette's large bedroom and a smaller guest room where Aïcha would sleep. It was a cramped little room with only a simple bench for a bed. 'But don't worry,' Monette told her. 'We basically live outside here.'

When she awoke on the first morning, Aïcha sat up in bed

and looked out the window. A white sun was shining through thick mist. The beach looked as though it was caught in a vast spiderweb, where vague, frightening figures would sometimes move, dragging behind them boats with peeling paintwork. Monette knocked softly at the door. 'Are you awake? I heard a noise.' She was wearing only a flimsy nightshirt and she got in bed with Aïcha, pressing her frozen feet against her friend's calves. 'We can't both fit in here!' Aïcha protested. 'It's much too small.' But they stayed there, huddled together, whispering as they had once done at the back of the class when they used to share secrets and fear the teacher's cane. Monette talked about Henri in such glowing terms that Aïcha felt moved. She also described her job at the secondary school. The girls who hid so they could smoke and who learned the French dictionary by heart. 'The police tell us to keep them under surveillance, to take their photographs. But they're only kids. Who are they going to hurt?'

That morning they hung around the living room, drinking coffee and tossing their dirty cups into the overflowing sink. Then the fog dispersed and the impossibly blue sky appeared, like the first sky ever seen. It seemed to have absorbed all the blue in the world, leaving the ocean nothing but green and grey. Aïcha went out onto the terrace and the light hurt her eyes. The sand appeared to consist of tiny copper sparkles which reflected the sun in a never-ending dazzle. Around noon a fisherman knocked at their door and showed them his day's catch: sardines, mullet, a handsome sea bream that Monette grilled on the terrace barbecue. They ate lunch at three in the afternoon, on the terrace, looking out over the deserted beach. Henri watched them as they ate the fish with their fingers and giggled like schoolgirls. 'This must make a nice change from boarding school.'

In the first few days they saw nobody. The nearby houses were empty during the week and their wooden walls creaked in the wind. A few streets away there was a local shop that stocked vegetables and canned food, and several vendors selling kebabs and koftas. In the afternoons, while Henri worked on the terrace, the two women would go swimming in the freezing sea. They would lie on the sand, smoking salty cigarettes, then fall asleep like children, heads buried in their arms. In the neighbourhood the rumour spread that there was a doctor holidaying at the hut, and the day after Aïcha's arrival people began coming to her with their medical problems. The grocer brought his daughter, who had earache. The man who ran the car park asked for medicine for his asthma. But it was Aïcha herself who insisted on examining the wound that the fisherman had on his foot, which wasn't healing. She disinfected and bandaged it and told him that he must not get it wet for at least a week. The fisherman clapped his hands and laughed. 'And how am I supposed to work if I can't get my feet wet?'

At the end of the day the sky turned orange and mauve. The sea grew calm, ready to swallow the sun. The waves no longer crashed onto the beach but died softly, in near silence, stroking the sand like the hem of a silk dress. Dusk was a magic spell, enchanting the elements and the population alike. Children began to yawn. Some fell asleep on their mothers' bare thighs. Young women nestled in their lovers' arms and together they contemplated the horizon, their faces bathed in the reddening light, as if watching a fire. At that time of day the wind blew more strongly, drowning out laughter and voices and making swimmers shiver. The sand took on the colour of melted gold and blonde strands appeared in the hair of the languid girls. The light made everything more beautiful. It erased fatigue and worry from people's features and even the most sinister faces seemed sweet in its embrace. It was during this hour, the most splendid of all, that some friends arrived from Rabat and Casablanca. All weekend the house was full of people, abuzz with laughter and music and passionate discussions. On the coast the traffic was bumper to bumper and the local peasants gaped in astonishment at this ballet of cars heading for the beaches, parasols poking from open windows.

Along that fifty-mile stretch of coastline were concentrated all the people of the Court and the capitalist bourgeoisie. That strip of land was home to the comings and goings of an elite who had, a few years earlier, developed a taste for the seaside, spending their afternoons in the sun at private clubs with swimming pools. They went from Rabat to Skhirat, from the Sable d'Or beach to the Bouznika beach, from the Fedala casino to the Corniche in Casablanca. Restaurants, run by Spaniards and Frenchmen, served grilled fish which the customers ate with their fingers while drinking low glasses of tannic wine that made them fall asleep in the afternoon. On those terraces the air was scented with grilled garlic, fried fish and orange zest. Jazz songs and French *chansons* played in back rooms and the laughing customers, knowing every word, sang along.

If a stranger had entered Monette and Henri's beach hut one summer evening in 1969, he might well have been surprised to see such a motley bunch assembled under the same roof.

Some of the guests had come from the palace while others came from nowhere and had no tribe, no support, no money. A student union leader, married to a bookseller from Lille, rubbed shoulders with a rich industrialist from Casablanca, a pro-Palestinian Jewish student or a young mathematics prodigy from Sidi Kacem. Men who orbited circles of power drank with men who wanted to overthrow them. Lower-middle-class students, the sons of artisans or shopkeepers, imagined that they would one day become ministers and have a house with a swimming pool in a chic part of Rabat. They all had one thing in common, however, something that was still unusual in that new country. They had been to university, and that gave them the right to dream of a radiant future.

One night Aïcha met Ahmed, a close friend of Monette and Henri, who kissed her hand and introduced himself. A man in his early forties, Ahmed had graduated from a prestigious engineering school in Paris. After returning to Morocco he had been recruited by the Ministry of Economic Affairs. Originally from Fes, the son of an illiterate shopkeeper, Ahmed told her how he had received a grant from the nationalists. 'When I left home I still had a guern – a braid of hair that some boys wear at the back of their shaved head. I had some old sirwal pants and a linen shirt. When I arrived in Rabat to take the train and then the boat, I used my savings to pay for a haircut. Then I bought some new clothes. In not much more than a quarter of an hour, I had entered the modern world.'

There were not many women among Henri's students. When Aïcha saw Ronit, she immediately recognised her as one of the girls in the photograph Monette had sent her. Ronit was small and slim but as soon as she appeared in a room she seemed to magnetise all the male attention. She was beautiful, of course, with her tanned complexion, her grey eyes shaded by false eyelashes and her long hair which she kept tied in a ponytail that hung halfway down her back. But what drew men to her was her self-assurance, her sense of humour, the way she would snap her fingers, wink, flash a lopsided smile. Ronit was Jewish, from an extremely strict Orthodox family who lived in the mellah of Fes. She had run away from home at sixteen, leaving her parents shattered by the scandal, and had begun by taking refuge with some cousins in Essaouira before settling in Casablanca. She lived above a garage with her brother, and even though everyone knew she was so short of money that she had to work a number of crappy jobs, she never complained and always bought a round of drinks. Aïcha was impressed by the way she dressed. Ronit would take old kaftans and shorten them, using thick leather straps to tighten them at the waist. She wore raffia sandals, like the Rif peasants, and Aïcha thought her the most elegant woman she had ever seen. Ronit hated Marxists, whom she accused of blindness and complicity with the crimes of Stalin and Mao. She was particularly vituperative about Abdellah and his group of long-haired boys. Abdellah was a green-eyed Slaoui who claimed that one of his distant corsair ancestors had abducted then married an Icelandic woman. He wore flared jeans that were too tight around the thighs and garnet-coloured ankle boots of which he was as fond as he was of the portrait of Che Guevara that hung above his bed. Ronit spent her time mocking him. 'You think we'll still be able to live like this when your communist friends are in power? Go on, piss off somewhere else to have your revolution!' Everyone thought Ronit and Abdellah were sleeping together. At night, when the air was less humid and people gathered under blankets in little groups, Ronit and Abdellah would always be in a corner of the garden together, and everyone could hear the boy laughing at Ronit's taunts. He adored her.

Ronit placed three bowls on the kitchen countertop. In one she put olives, in the second pieces of cucumber, and in the third some still-warm grilled peanuts, so salty that they gave you stomach ache. On the terrace the boys grabbed cans of beer from an icebox and sucked up the foam that poured out when they were opened, running down over their chins. 'Look at those hypocrites,' Ronit said to Aïcha. 'They say they're in favour of women's liberation, that they're not like their fathers. I bet you as soon as they're married they'll all expect their wives to forget their diplomas and become good little housewives again.'

'We'll need some help around the house!' Ronit yelled at the men, who ignored her. 'You're a doctor, aren't you?' she asked Aïcha, who was busy slicing the *saucisson* she had brought with her from Alsace. 'Is it true what they say about the pill?'

'What do they say?'

'You know! That it makes your hair fall out, gives you cancer, and that it can sometimes make you infertile.'

'I don't think *they* know much about science if they're saying that.'

'Do you take it, then?'

'What? The pill?'

'If it's not harmful, why don't you take it yourself?'

Ronit did not wait for Aïcha to reply. Abdellah had come over to nibble some *saucisson* and pick a fight with Henri.

'Did you know that Roland Barthes is going to teach in Rabat?'

'Everyone knows that,' said Henri. 'It's all they talk about at the university.'

'It's unbelievable. The country's on the verge of revolution, the people are living in poverty, and Monsieur Roland Barthes is going to pay us the honour of teaching us Proust and Racine! What the hell do Moroccans care about Proust? We wear your clothes, we listen to your music, we watch your films. In the cafés of Casablanca, young people read *Le Monde* and bet on horses racing in Paris. When are we going to understand that we need to develop our own personality, understand our own culture, take control of our own destiny?'

'What would you prefer?' asked Ahmed. 'Don't tell me you're like those people in the Istiqlal Party who want Quranic schooling, total Arabisation and a return to traditions that are basically nothing more than folklore for tourists?'

'Don't put words into my mouth! The truth is that the government has no interest in educating the masses. As long as Moroccan students are taught by young Frenchmen on military service, the education they'll get is colonial and bourgeois and they'll keep on defending their class interests. I'm not saying this about you, Henri. You're different. But you must agree that your French colleagues only come here for the money.'

'I think that's a little unfair,' their host replied. 'We're here to pass on our knowledge, and to help Morocco train its future elite – the people who will take control of the country.'

'The elite? Oh, give me a break! Every year this country breeds millions of illiterates to work in the fields, clean the streets, shoot rifles. The elite, as you call it, has a responsibility. We need to go to the factories, organise evening classes, raise awareness among the masses!'

Ronit stood up on top of the counter. 'Ugh, you're ruining the party with your boring speeches! Why don't we go to a club? I want to dance!'

They went dancing every night in the clubs along the coast. Sometimes they would drive as far as the Corniche in Casablanca and strut their stuff in one of those establishments that, fifteen years earlier, would have had signs on the door announcing: 'No Moroccans'. By the edge of the world's biggest swimming pool, girls in bikinis took part in beauty contests and were named Miss Tahiti or Miss Acapulco. They went to concerts by groups who modelled their style on French pop or American rock. The Moroccan singers would slick back their frizzy hair with brilliantine and rent sequinned jackets from a boutique in Maârif. All night long, at Le Balcon, Le Tube or La Notte, Henri and his friends would wiggle their hips to songs by Elvis Presley or The Platters and slow-dance to Gilbert Bécaud. At dawn they would walk to a stall where an old man fried sfenj, Moroccan doughnuts, which he rolled in sugar and hung from strings. The young people devoured these sweet treats and licked their fingers afterwards, their lips gleaming with grease.

Aïcha did not dance. Nor did she take a drag on the joints that were passed from hand to hand, leaving all the others red-eyed.

She often stood apart from the rest of the group and thought about Karl Marx. There was still no sign of him. Every day she hoped he would knock at the door of the hut or appear suddenly on the beach. Her heart raced whenever she thought she had spotted him, but there were lots of men with thick beards and long hair and her disappointment would bring tears to her eyes. She wondered if he and Henri had argued or if he had gone off somewhere to write and she would never see him again. At night, when her bedroom window banged in the wind and she shivered with cold, she imagined that he had been arrested or had disappeared. Ever since she had been here she had heard so many tales of kidnappings, conspiracies and arrests, and she wondered if Mehdi could be involved in that sort of thing.

One afternoon, as the three of them were finishing lunch, Henri stood up and announced that he was going to Rabat to do some shopping and make a few telephone calls. They had tried to have a phone line installed at the beach hut, but without success. 'And maybe I'll drop in on Mehdi. You remember Karl Marx?' he asked Aïcha. 'I was the one who gave him that nickname.'

Aïcha looked up at him, wide-eyed. There were a thousand questions she wanted to ask him. Where was Mehdi? Why didn't he come to see them? Was he okay? But in the end she just replied: 'Yes, I vaguely remember him.'

'He accepted a job as an assistant lecturer at the university in Rabat. I warned him against it. Since all the strikes began, it's become almost impossible to work there. And with his qualifications he could easily get a good position in the government. But he's obsessed with writing a magnum opus about the psychological consequences of underdevelopment. If he thinks he's going to win the Nobel Prize for Economics, he's kidding himself.'

That afternoon, as he drove towards the capital, Henri remembered how he had almost left Morocco in 1964, only a few months after his arrival. He had packed his suitcase and called the dean of the university to inform him that this was not the life he had come looking for. He had left his ex-wife, his family, his dull friends. His life in France had been so grey and insipid, it had made him feel as if he had already entered the corridor of his own decline. But he hadn't fled all of that only to find himself in a land of fire and blood, a country where his own students could be killed in front of his eyes. Today he had no regrets about his decision to stay. Had he given up and taken the plane back to France, he would never have met Monette, never have lived in the beach hut, never have enjoyed this life which was, he believed, the happiest and most beautiful imaginable. And it was precisely this happiness, the simple pleasures of his existence, that sometimes struck him as obscene, indecent. Because behind this floating bubble of bliss, behind the cheerful blue sky and the big yellow sun, he could feel the fear, the narrowing of souls.

He was haunted by his memory of those days in March 1965 when hundreds of young students had invaded the streets of Casablanca to protest against a rule forbidding anyone over the age of sixteen from attending secondary school. Back then Henri still lived in the city, in the Gauthier neighbourhood. He had seen them marching through the sunlit avenues to the working-class neighbourhood of Derb Sultan. The boys had carried girls on their shoulders and they had yelled: 'We want to learn!', 'Down with Hassan II – Morocco doesn't belong to you!', 'Bread, work and schools!' Joined by their parents, by the unemployed, by the poor people from the shanty towns, they had built barricades and set fire to buildings. The next day, Henri had passed the central police station and seen the crowd of parents, their faces pale with anguish, begging for news of their vanished children. Against the city walls of the new medina, hands tied behind their backs, schoolchildren had stood in line to be shot. Henri could still hear the sound of gunfire, the explosions of mortars, the screaming ambulance sirens. And, loudest of all, the blades of a helicopter from which, it was said, General Oufkir had fired bullets at the crowd below. In the days that followed, Henri had seen bloodstains on the cobbled streets of Casablanca and believed that the government had sent a warning to the masses. Here, we shoot at children. Law and order are non-negotiable. On 29 March, Hassan II had declared: 'There is no greater danger to the state than the so-called intellectual. It would be better for you to be illiterate.' The tone had been set.

Zippo was a tall Berber man with grey eyes and a bull neck who ran l'Océan, the best beach restaurant for miles around. He owed his nickname to the lighter he was constantly playing with: thumbing it open, snapping it shut, his hands smelling strongly of naphtha. That lighter had been a gift from some American soldiers who had been quartered at the Kenitra Air Base in the 1950s. 'Fantastic guys with teeth so white they looked fake. I'd never seen such handsome, strong men before. Ah, America, what a place . . .' The soldiers had been crazy about him too. They played him the records they received one week after their release. Records by Elvis and Bill Haley, to which the young Zippo would dance, making the Americans laugh.

Often Zippo would say: 'I thank God I never went to university.' He was convinced that too much knowledge muddled the brain and he attributed his enormous financial success to his instincts. No need to study for hours every night to understand how to run his little restaurant and the nightclub next door. The key was simple: music. At l'Océan the jukebox blasted out hits all night long, at top volume. The music made the young people dance, dancing made them thirsty, and they ordered beers at the bar. The easiest equation ever. Zippo spent his nights trying to rouse his customers from their lethargy. He would walk over to tables where groups of shy, spotty boys stared silently at the dancefloor, each of them slowly sipping from a bottle of Coke. He encouraged them to be bold, to make the most of their youth, to ask those giggling girls to dance with them. He monitored the entrance and was wary of the fist-fights that would often break out around midnight. The Moroccans, he claimed, could not take their alcohol and would throw themselves at the pretty Spanish girls, only to be punched in the face for their insolence by the Spanish girls' brothers. 'You want independence? Go hunt on your own land, then, and leave our women to us.'

On 21 July 1969 Henri, Monette, Aïcha and the others were sitting on the terrace of l'Océan. Monette had convinced Aïcha to wear a figure-hugging white muslin dress. She had told her that she ought to make the most of her slim body, and she'd lent her some bracelets and a ring too big for her finger that Aïcha was afraid she would lose. She had tied her hair back to show off her suntanned face. During dinner Monette had encouraged her to drink some rum and Coke and promised her that there was nothing to fear from the drunkenness that started to loosen her gestures and turn her cheeks pink. They ate sizzling shrimp, grilled fish, tomato salad and cumin-dusted sweet peppers. It was hard to have a conversation because the music was so loud and they soon left the table and headed for the dancefloor. It was then that Aïcha saw him.

In the middle of the crowd, Mehdi was dancing.

To understand Mehdi, you had to see him dance. There was, in his gestures, in his movements, a sort of casual mastery. He appeared to abandon himself to the rhythm of the music, letting it guide and control him as if he were a puppet coming to life under an invisible hand. He closed his eyes, held his arms against his chest, fists balled, and became completely indifferent to the world around him. Then he opened his eyes again and stared defiantly at the other dancers. 'Look what I can do,' his eyes seemed to say. He raised his right leg and began to do the twist. Now he was no longer in a nightclub on the coast but starring in one of those musical comedies he used to watch as a child, through the hole in the bathroom wall. He was Gene Kelly, he was Fred Astaire, dreaming that Cyd Charisse was making her way through the crowd to give him her hand. Aïcha watched him, fascinated. The jukebox played 'The Great Pretender' and Mehdi danced alone, snapping his fingers in time with the beat, eyes lowered to the tips of his leather shoes. He was slim and graceful. Aïcha noticed that he had changed his glasses; the pair he was wearing now were more fashionable, with a thick tortoiseshell frame.

Then the dancefloor emptied. A crowd of customers were gathered around a television set. Zippo had agreed to put the television on the copper bar as long as people kept drinking and dancing. But the customers were staring at the screen, where the image began to flicker and then died. There were shouts of impatience. Someone said they should go up to the roof to check the aerial. When the first images appeared, a man turned the music down so they could hear what the commentator was saying. Everything had come to a standstill by now, and even the barmen, cloths hanging over their forearms, were watching open-mouthed as the American astronauts moved on the screen. The nightclub owner could no longer hear the music, he was no longer beating time with the tip of his shoe. He was just standing there, arms by his side, staring at these images that he could not help regarding as diabolical. What was this witchcraft? Boxes that talked and showed pictures? Men flying to the moon? He shuddered and shook his head.

Mehdi takes Aïcha by the hand and they walk down to the beach. They can hear the muffled sound of applause and the beat of a French pop song. Aïcha is tipsy. She looks like a little girl about to fall asleep in the back seat of a car. She is not really listening to what Mehdi is saying. 'I'd like to sit down,' she says, and lowers herself onto the sand before she has even finished her sentence. He sits beside her. He wants to touch her but doesn't dare. He is waiting for a sign, an invitation. He picks up a handful of sand and lets it run through the gaps between his fingers. She turns towards him and he kisses her. Now, even more than before, she looks like a child, an innocent, and he is surprised by the way she kisses him back. Mouth open, her hand on his neck. There is nothing vulgar in her attitude or her movements and he does not think, as he has sometimes thought about other women, that her kisses show traces of other kisses given to other men. Her mouth opens wider and she lets Mehdi's tongue inside. She leans forward, her long swanlike neck illuminated by moonlight. Her lips touch every inch of Mehdi's face. Her eyes are squeezed tightly shut, as if she has withdrawn deep within herself and has, by some miracle of the night and alcohol and this starry sky, succeeded in conquering her own shyness. This drives him wild and he kisses her with the same hunger, the same passion. He senses, he feels certain, that he is the first man to awaken this passion in her. He discovers her like Columbus drawing close to the shores of the New World. This woman is a distant island, an unknown continent, a planet that nobody has ever seen before. Or at least not the way that he sees her.

She opens her eyes. They sparkle like frost, like ice, in the morning sunlight. He was afraid that her eyes would be hazy, bleary, the eyes of a drunk woman who does not realise what is happening, who might look at him as if he were a thief, a looter, just another guy. But she is not like that at all. In fact he is troubled by the lucidity of her gaze, by her determination. There is neither defiance nor submission in the way she looks at him. She kisses him, fully aware of what she is doing, with all her strength and all her will, and this makes Mehdi's heart overflow and he holds her in his arms as tightly as he can. He sinks his fingers into the muscles of her back and is astonished by her birdlike delicacy. He can feel every one of her ribs. Aïcha's back is like an ancient musical instrument, a Persian zither, an Indian lyre. Now he imagines her trembling, the luminous nudity hidden beneath this thin dress, this dress so beautiful that he noticed it as soon as the music ended and, alone on the dancefloor, he looked up.

In the distance they can hear shouting, applause, a quiet roar coming from the bar where they got drunk. Mehdi and Aïcha don't care. What is happening behind them, back there, strikes them as pointless and ridiculous; nothing can matter more than what is taking place here, on this freezing sand, a few feet away from the whisper of the waves. They belong to another geography now, to a timeline distinct from that of their friends, whose absence does not worry them.

Young customers, faces reddened by alcohol, shirt collars soaked with sweat, keep rushing back and forth between the terrace and the bar. They look up at the sky and stare laughing at the moon. They say things like 'Unbelievable' or 'It's crazy.' Some of them are lying on the damp deckchairs, and the boys, rendered pompous by the circumstances, proclaim that this night is going to change the world. From now on, nothing will be impossible for mankind. Having conquered the moon, we will bring an end to poverty and oppression, we will cure all diseases, stop all wars. The young women giggle and feel proud, even though they haven't done anything. After all, they think, it's true: this is not just another night. Progress has brought them this far and now it will open up a new era of freedom, and to celebrate this it is surely not asking too much that they agree to sit in the lap of the boy they love. On this night of all nights they could surely dispose of their scruples, dispose of their clothes and go forth naked into this new world that is beginning, this nascent world full of promise. The alcohol, the dancing, the languorous movements and that boot leaving its imprint in the dust of the moon, all of this goes to the heads of these young people who bellow in French and in Arabic on the terrace. They howl like wolves in deep, dark forests. Twenty years from now, thirty, even a hundred, people will still talk about this day when man set foot on the moon. They will say: 'I remember exactly where I was.' They will tell their children about that television set on the gold-coloured countertop and the music playing in the background. And each time that someone mentions this night, Aïcha will think of their first kisses and she will repeat to herself: 'One small step for man, one giant leap for mankind.'

'Dinner's ready!' Mathilde shouted. No response. 'It'll go cold!' she shouted. Selim appeared, looking absent-minded, and shuffled into the dining room. Amine finally arrived too, and sat facing his son. Amine unfolded his napkin and began complaining about the farmworkers. He railed against the man who had sold him some poor-quality seed and told Mathilde: 'I'm going to sue him.'

'Sit up straight,' he said to Selim, who replied that he wasn't a child any more. 'Act like that, then.' While her husband and son insulted each other, Mathilde watched the lentils going cold. The sauce would not taste the same, she thought, and the meal would be ruined. Losing patience, she grabbed their plates herself and served them. She wanted them to shut up and eat but they kept arguing, ignoring the pleasant smell of the dish she had prepared. 'You didn't even manage to get your baccalauréat at the second attempt!' Amine grumbled. 'If you keep lazing around like this, I have the solution, believe me. I'll send you off to do your military service. Then you'll understand what being a man is all about. I was at war when I was your age!' Selim rolled his eyes and Mathilde stopped listening. She wanted them to eat, that was all she wanted.

'Why didn't you let Sabah live here instead of sending her to that horrible boarding school?' Selim demanded.

'Your mother and I raised our children. We worked for years so you would never lack anything. We deserve some peace. Selma just needs to look after her daughter instead of strutting around Rabat. All she's ever brought to this family is shame and disappointment.'

Selim threw his napkin onto the table. 'I've lost my appetite. I'm going out.'

That day, leaning over a saucepan, Mathilde wondered: How many times have I watched water boil? How much time have I spent shopping for this family? She looked up at the fridge as if it were her worst enemy. She swore that cold, white beast swallowed up the food she put in it. Like those pierced barrels in Greek mythology that Danaus's daughters were doomed to constantly refill. Mathilde was the same: always having to start again and again. Always repeating the same actions, with nothing to show for it. She felt so ashamed. She thought about all the years that had passed, about her life with her family and the tons of food they had guzzled. She imagined a room filled from floor to ceiling with pieces of meat, loaves of bread, boiled vegetables. She felt sickened, by them and by herself. And to think she had believed all those idiotic tales about the girl in rags who becomes a princess. Poor Cinderella, who had spent her youth cleaning up after her sisters, who had not been allowed an education, and who, having married her prince, must have brooded over her shattered dreams for the rest of her miserable life.

Mathilde could look at a man now and instantly know how many women he depended upon in his life. One for placing a bowl of steaming food in front of him, another to make his bed, to clean the mirror he used every morning to check his hair. Behind every ironed shirt, every polished shoe, behind every fat belly hanging over a tightened belt, she saw the hands of women. Hands plunged in icy water, rubbing soap against sauce-stained sleeves. Hands covered with little burn marks or wounds that never healed. She could spot a man with no women in his life too. They were the easiest of all to recognise. She sought them out, desired them. Single men, forever betrayed by a frayed collar, scuffed shoes, a missing button.

Mathilde had just turned forty-three. She felt old, useless. Like damaged goods. She felt certain that the best years of her life were already over and that nothing remained to her but the long wait for death, demanding from her even more patience and self-sacrifice than she had shown up to now. Single men did not look at her and the idea of love had become humiliating. Love? Who could love her now? Who could desire this body, grown fat from years of stuffing herself? Amine criticised her for not doing anything, for spending money on junk and wasting her time having tea with stupid women. He imagined her gulping down cakes, taking long naps, reading books about people who had never existed and events that had never happened. In the evenings he often found her sitting at the kitchen table, one hand resting on the plastic tablecloth, staring into space. Dinner was ready, the house was clean. She had put away the invoices and account books. In the clinic, the bin was full of Betadine-soaked compresses, bandages stained with dried blood.

While her daughter was at university, while Selma was living her life in Rabat, she was here, in this kitchen, breathing in the smell of the damp tablecloth. What can anyone learn in a kitchen? Century after century, women have worked in kitchens to cure the sick and raise children, to console the sad and to spread happiness. They have made decoctions to soothe the agonies of old people approaching death and to solve the problems of young pregnant women. They have warmed up oil to be rubbed into the belly of a child with colic and, with nothing but flour, water and a bit of fat, have kept whole families alive and kicking. And all of that was nothing? Hadn't women learned anything?

In such moments, she wanted to explain it all to Amine. Tell him that it might look like she was resting, but that he was mistaken. He thinks she does all of this out of love and she wants to yell at him: 'What you call love is actually work!' Were women really so filled with affection and kindness that they could spend an entire lifetime – yes, an entire lifetime – taking care of others? When Mathilde thought about this, it made her almost enraged. There was something wrong here, a trap into which she had fallen but whose name she could not remember. She didn't talk about this to her friends at the Rotary Club with whom she had tea. No, she smiled, she licked the cream from her lips with the tip of her tongue, she put a hand to her belly to check whether she had put on weight. She ate like someone punishing herself.

Sometimes, in the house, she no longer felt at home. And in those moments she never imagined another house that would feel more attuned to her, less hostile. She understood that every house was a trap that would close around her. Chaos was not a sad or even frightening idea; it was the only thing Mathilde wished for, the only thing that might give her back some semblance of exaltation.

Selim got on his moped and rode into town. He hung around the empty, baking streets of Meknes. It was the end of July, the shops on the avenue had closed for the summer and his friends had all left for the seaside. As he came out of a garage in the medina, Selim heard a woman yelling in a language that sounded like German. She was arguing with a group of boys who had surrounded her and were shouting insults at her. Selim walked towards them. The young woman was wearing a pair of skintight trousers, low-waisted trousers held up by a drawstring. Her white, muscular stomach was exposed to the eyes of the world and her cotton tunic covered only her shoulders and her breasts. She was tall, as tall and blonde as Mathilde, but so thin that Selim could see her ribs. He heard one of the boys calling her a whore and without thinking he grabbed the boy by his hair. 'What did you say? You should be ashamed of yourself!' The kid fought back, kicking Selim, and his friends joined in. They encircled Selim and swore at him, eyes bulging, all of them in a fury. They beat their chests and one of them spat on the ground and swore that this would not end here.

Selim went up to the oldest and calmest of the boys and asked him who this woman was. 'She walks around like that in the medina, looking for hash. What does she expect, the stupid hippie? You can't do that here.' Selim explained that she was just a foreigner, a girl on her own, probably lost, with no understanding of the country's morals. The boys stared at him incredulously, apparently shocked that this huge, blond boy could speak Arabic so fluently. Selim seemed to know their codes, their insults; twice he mentioned God, and eventually the swarm of boys dispersed. One of them shouted 'Go home!' in English and spat on the ground. Throughout this conversation the young woman had not moved. She did not appear frightened and she had even smiled when Selim lifted the boy up by his hair. She thanked him in French, her accent obviously Germanic. She asked him if he was from here and said she had never imagined Moroccans could look like he did. He told her his mother was from Alsace but that he had grown up here, on a farm.

He felt bad just abandoning her there, in her ludicrous, dangerous garb, but he wasn't in the mood for a long conversation and he sensed something clingy about this girl. A propensity to impose herself on people, to insinuate herself into others' lives. She followed him as he walked away and told him she was from Denmark and her name was Nilsa. One month ago, some friends from university had written to her: they were staying in Tangier, and they invited her to join them. So she had packed her suitcase and left Europe for the Third World. She stopped for a moment and leaned over a stall selling dried roses and black soap. She asked the price and the vendor put a few pieces of rhassoul clay in her hand.

'So,' asked Selim, 'have you found them?'

'No, when I got to Tangier they'd already left. I took the bus here, with the chickens and peasants, you know? Tomorrow I leave again and I go south. You know the south?'

No, Selim did not know the south. And he did not think it was possible for such a young, pretty woman to travel through a foreign country by bus. He wondered if Nilsa was mad or if he was the one who had no understanding of life, of all the possibilities open to a human being. Nilsa took hold of his arm and moved her lips very close to his ear. 'Could you find me some hashish?' He asked her where she was staying and she gave him the name of a seedy hotel in the medina where, Selim imagined, she had been sleeping in a filthy, cockroach-infested bed. 'I'll see what I can do. I'll drop by your hotel tomorrow, okay?'

He accompanied her to the central market, where she was planning to find something to eat. She seemed to think everything here was wonderful. She kept repeating: 'It's so different from Denmark. Back there, everything is grey. Here, wherever you go, there are so many colours.' Selim had never thought about this before, about the greyness of the other world and the colours of this one. While Nilsa bought some olives and some candied carrots, he looked at the people around them. The pink djellaba worn by a woman with a child in her arms. The saffron-coloured slippers worn by an old man sitting in the entrance to the patisserie, where pyramids of pistachio-green cakes were on display. Nilsa talked a lot and she couldn't stop touching Selim: squeezing his arm, hugging him whenever she saw something surprising. She shouted: 'Fantastic!', her arms thrown wide open, and passers-by stared in horror at her naked belly.

Selim left her there. Night was falling and as he rode the moped back to the farm he felt slightly guilty. What would become of her in that dark, hostile medina, in that hotel where someone might try to rape her or beat her? He thought about this all night, seeking reassurance in the idea that she was crazy and not even a very nice person, and besides he wasn't responsible for her or her senseless urge to discover Africa.

The next day, after his chemistry class, he approached a group of boys he very rarely spoke to, because he felt certain they would be able to provide him with what he needed. Selim saw one of them, a skinny kid called Roger with an acne-scarred face, walking through the school courtyard, so he drew him aside. He was momentarily lost for words. How to phrase his request? He was afraid that Roger would make fun of him or sell him some adulterated crap for twice the normal amount. 'Do you know where I could get hold of some hashish?'

Roger frowned at him. 'You smoke hash?'

'It's not for me, it's for a friend.'

'Piss off. I don't know you and I don't want any trouble.'

Selim decided not to go to any more classes that day, and when the bell rang he took advantage of the general chaos to slip out through the back door of the school. Without even thinking about it, without having made a decision, he headed towards Nilsa's hotel. Outside the front door sat a small dog with grey fur so tangled that it looked painful. There was no lobby or reception desk inside the hotel, but there was a man sitting in a chair at the far end of a dark room, and Selim asked him if the Danish girl was still there. The man leaped to his feet and began shouting. There was no Danish girl here and he wasn't the type of man to let women stay in his hotel; these accusations were baseless and he would make this blond bastard regret ever saying such a thing to him. Selim apologised and left. He had no idea what was going on. Had he misunderstood what Nilsa had told him the night before about where she was staying? Had she set off earlier than expected with her friends, headed for adventure in the south? Selim was alone in the street now, the grey dog following at his heels. An immense sadness weighed down on him. A sadness he could not explain but which made it hard to breathe. He started crying and his tears burned the freckles that covered his cheeks. He didn't want to go back to school or the farm and he abandoned himself completely to his sorrow. He thought about Selma, who had lit some fire inside him, a desire to live and to love, only to leave him with no outlet for that desire. He felt even more regretful that he had not managed to find the drugs for Nilsa, because at that moment it was the only thing he felt like doing. Drinking, smoking, drifting aimlessly through a fog of forgetfulness . . .

It was noon when he found himself close to the Jardin des Sultanes, where his mother used to take him when he was a child to see the monkeys in their cages. Just then he heard a voice calling him – 'Hey, you!' – and when he turned around he saw Nilsa's naked belly. She was lying in the grass, surrounded by three boys sitting cross-legged and smoking cigarettes. One of them was languidly playing a guitar. Nilsa stood up and jumped into Selim's arms so excitedly that he felt embarrassed. 'It's my Moroccan friend!' she told her companions. The three boys were Germans who had decided to flee their families and capitalist society and who had spent the last two years living in a commune. 'They're all Nazis,' explained Simon, the boy with the guitar. Selim sat facing him and noticed his red eyes, the dilated pupils. He realised they had not needed him to find hashish. They all had long hair which fell down to their waists. Nilsa handed him a cigarette and Selim took it. 'Why don't you come with us? There's nothing keeping you here, is there?'

All Selim would remember afterwards of those three days spent travelling were a few hallucinatory images, like fragments from an endless dream. He smoked hashish and drank huge gulps of a bitter eau de vie that Nilsa had brought with her. In her suitcase she also had some tabs of LSD, a transistor radio and records by Pink Floyd and Janis Joplin. Several times Selim had to ask Simon to stop by the roadside near some field or village so he could throw up. Through the car's windows he saw landscapes he could not believe, landscapes that must, he thought, be the product of his imagination. He barely spoke a word. The others talked in German or English and the sounds of those foreign languages added to his sense of unreality. He kept thinking: I'm not really here, nobody can see me. To soothe his nausea he would close his eyes, and occasionally he would fall asleep with his head on Nilsa's shoulder. Then he no longer knew if he was in a car, in the carriage of a train or in the hold of a ship, sailing towards some unknown destination. His organs felt as if they had been swapped around. He ached all over his body: his lower back, his heart, his stomach. When the pain in his belly grew unbearable, he would sink his fist into it. This was the only thing that brought him any relief. His body was rotting from within, he thought. Inside him there was one of those massive piles of black manure that were always left by the edges of fields at the farm, their fetid odour spreading for miles around.

One day Selim woke up in the middle of nowhere. Some tiny village, a stop-off point for lorry drivers, with a high street lined by a series of butchers' stalls. A crowd gathered to stare at these hippies, who seemed unperturbed by all the attention. Animal carcasses were hung from hooks and on a white enamel counter there sat a sheep's head, its eyes closed, its fleece greyish, tongue hanging from the side of its mouth. On the ground was a pink bowl full of tripe. Selim closed his eyes again. He turned his face to the other side. Droplets of cold sweat ran down the back of his neck. He pretended to be asleep because he didn't want anyone to call him over, to ask him to act as an interpreter. He wanted to be forgotten, to no longer be part of this world, this country which, the further south they went, seemed to him ever more implacably foreign. They had been sleeping on beaches under ominous starry skies. Nilsa and the others would go swimming naked and wash their hair in the sea while he lay on the sand, his knees pressed tight to his chest. All night he would be attacked by mosquitoes and when he woke in the mornings his eyelids and hands were swollen from all the bites. The hippies wanted to shove him in the water. They said that he stank, that they couldn't stand the smell of his sweat, his vomit breath. But Selim would not give in. In reality he was afraid of being abandoned and in his rare moments of lucidity, when the effects of the drug waned a little, he held on tight to his bag, in which he kept his clothes, his revolver and some cash stolen from his mother.

Several times they got lost and Simon could not understand why Selim refused to help them question a passer-by. Then, after a while, there were no more passers-by. There was nobody at all. Nothing but a road in the middle of a rocky desert where all that grew were some thorny trees deformed by the wind, with goats perched on their branches. Selim burst out laughing. A maniacal laugh that sounded like a hyena or a lunatic and which made the others feel uncomfortable. His laughter grew louder, and even more chilling, when a white horse, skinny and filthy, appeared in the beam of the car's headlights before vanishing into the darkness. Selim was the prisoner of a sticky, slimy dream, deep as a swamp, and he could not pull himself out of it. He was like those characters in fairy tales who dream that they are dreaming that they are dreaming.

By the roadside tall thistle bushes grew, covered with greyish dust. Inside the car, nobody talked any more. The wind carried an odour of iodine and walnut, which made them think that they weren't far from their destination. Hundreds of seagulls shrieked and wailed. They filled the sky like a battalion of scavengers and it was impossible to tell if they were mourning their dead or plotting against the humans. Ahead of them they saw Essaouira.

The city itself was part of a dream. At its entrance, near the Porte du Lion, stood a large sign: 'Town For Sale'. Nilsa was afraid that Selim would start laughing again, sending Simon into a rage. But Selim did not laugh. He was slumped on the back seat. His face was the colour of earth, his shirt drenched with sweat. He was shivering with cold. 'He looks ill,' the girl said. They parked the car at the port. Night had fallen and there was no one around. Not a single living soul, just the howling of the wind and the creaking wooden hulls of the trawlers in dry dock. The city looked like one of those medieval cities depopulated by plague, its streets deserted except for a few skinny cats and half-crazed survivors. Some disaster must have driven the entire population into exile; perhaps a tidal wave had carried them away or a corsair raid had left them all bleeding to death or abducted. The hippies wondered if they had come to the wrong place. This gloomy, torpid town could not be the famous hippie hotbed that they had heard so much about. Later they would find out the reasons for this desertion. Because there had been no plague in Essaouira, no witch's curse; its silent and empty streets had a more prosaic cause. The factories had closed and the high rate of unemployment had driven the city's youth to other, more prosperous and welcoming places. But, most importantly, the news of Israel's victory over Nasser's Egypt in June 1967 had finally reached this outpost at the edge of the world. Most of the Jewish families had fled, taking with them part of the city's soul.

* * *

'When the Jews leave a town, it brings misfortune, and ruin is not far off.' This was what Lalla Amina would tell Selim during one of their long conversations on the terrace of her house in the medina. Two days after his arrival in Essaouira, Selim woke up in a room he had never seen before. He had no memory of how he had got there, no idea how much time had passed. Only his body remembered: the violent stomach cramps that had prevented him from sleeping and the endless vomiting that had drained him of all strength. He threw up everything he swallowed, even the water that some gentle, maternal hand brought to his lips. Several times he had called

148

for his mother and Lalla Amina had held him between her flaccid breasts and reflected on how all men were like this, tied to their mothers like dogs tied to their kennels.

His benefactress was a tall, bony woman with black skin and white curly hair which she sometimes covered with a square of coloured cloth. There was a large wart on her chin, with a few thick grey hairs sprouting from it. With her dry thin lips, her small myopic eyes and her high cheekbones, there was a hardness, an air of authority in her appearance. Lalla Amina, however, turned out to be a good-humoured and touchingly hospitable woman. When this handsome blond boy, lost in the delirium of a fever, was handed over to her care, she first thought he must be one of those hippies who came here from the other end of the world in search of God knows what. She communicated with him through mime, joining her hands together and placing them under her cheek to invite him to sleep. She buttered slices of bread and brought her fingers to her mouth when she wanted him to eat. For two nights he was delirious and in his dreams he saw the white horse again, the trees deformed by the wind, and that woman whose face became mixed up with that of Aïcha Kandicha, the sorceress with goat's hooves who picked her teeth with the bones of children. He dreamed of Selma. He buried his head between her breasts, breathed in the smell of her skin, and he felt himself dying.

* * *

Selim woke with a start. It was not yet daytime. A violet glow came through the little window in his bedroom. Instantly he thought about his bag, about the money it contained and the revolver. He looked for it in that tiny room and tears rose to his eyes. He banged his forehead against the wall. How stupid he was, what a stupid idiot – his father had been right when he called him all those names. He had been robbed, he had been betrayed, and somewhere someone must be bragging about that stolen treasure. He stayed where he was for a long time, his forehead pressed against the wall, incapable of thinking straight or making a decision. There was nothing he could do, no way out of this mess. He wanted to shout 'Maman!' Then Lalla Amina appeared. She cautiously approached him, as if he were a wild animal. She stroked his back, his hair. 'It's a beautiful day,' she said, 'and since you're feeling better you'll be able to explore the town. But first, you should go to the hammam.' The old woman stood on tiptoe then and from the top of the wardrobe she pulled down Selim's leather bag. 'Here are your things. Pick out a change of clothes and then I'll take you.'

Selim followed Lalla Amina through the streets of the medina. He told her it was nothing like the town he was from. In Meknes the alleys were narrow and winding, shaded from the sun, whereas here, between those high ramparts, everything seemed open to the sea and the sky. The old woman started to laugh. 'You're as white as I am black. And yet we're the same, you and me.' Selim did not understand what she meant. She spoke strangely, in an Arabic that was unfamiliar to him and in an accent that confused him. But he enjoyed listening to her and he thought she was funny with her vulgar expressions, the way she told everyone to go fuck themselves, and her hands, wide and dark and thin, which she waved about in the air whenever she told stories. She said there had been signs that the world was ending, signs that were never wrong, and of which those odd birds, the hippies, were the heralds. She had grown up here, in this city whose glorious past she liked to remember, the city at the height of its elegance, and she was sorry to see it now in such a state. 'But you'll see, my boy. Essaouira is not so easily invaded. With its grey skies and this wind, it ends up spitting out those without a soul solid enough to put down roots here.'

One evening, during dinner, they heard a knock at the door. A young boy came into the living room and kissed Lalla Amina's shoulder.

'I won't stay long,' he promised. 'Just a night or two and then I'll find another solution.'

Karim was Lalla Amina's nephew and he lived in Marrakech, where he was still in school. He stayed with his aunt whenever he had an argument with his father and ran away from home.

'What happened this time?' she asked while Karim sat down at the table, next to Selim.

'He tried to cut my hair while I was asleep!' he shouted. 'I opened my eyes and there he was, above me, holding his razor. He can go screw himself if he wants me to have short hair.'

Selim watched as Karim dipped a piece of bread into the fish tajine. The boy's brown curly hair hung down to his shoulders, and he was so slim that from behind it would have been easy to mistake him for a girl. He was wearing a blue linen shirt and a big orange scarf around his neck.

'Say what you want,' mumbled Karim, his mouth full of bread, 'but your brother is a fascist. He's an animal. I'm not going back this time, believe me.'

Karim knew the hippies. And he couldn't stop wondering what strange miracle had brought them here. By that summer of 1969 Essaouira had become a gathering place for their kind. The port was full of parked Volkswagen vans decorated with flowers and peace symbols. On the walls of houses, and on horse-drawn carriages for tourists, the locals saw garish murals appear. They got used to the sight of girls in long dresses selling flower necklaces or knitted clothing in the alleys of the medina. With pearls from Guelmim they made shimmering necklaces that were all the rage. Thickly bearded young men strummed guitars in the city's squares, begging for money.

The day after his arrival, Karim took Selim to the Hippie Café, a former judge's house converted into a café. The patio was littered with benches, cushions and rugs on which boys and girls lay. On wooden tables there were stacks of books stained with mint tea. The café did not serve alcohol but everyone there appeared drunk. At the back of the room the clouds of smoke were so thick that you could hardly see the outlines of the smokers. The hippies passed around long sebsi pipes or animal-shaped chillum pipes. One young man was playing the guitar while another tapped softly on a drum that he held between his thighs.

The owner was a quietly efficient Moroccan man in his early forties who always wore a pair of sirwal pants which he pulled up over his knees, exposing his sinewy calf muscles. He wore a grey shirt and an elegant, foreign-made waistcoat. He spent his days wandering around the patio and the upstairs floor, serving glasses of tea and fresh orange juice, bowls of home-made yoghurt drizzled with honey and sprinkled with crushed walnuts and pistachios. He seemed to pay no attention to his customers' strange behaviour. He cleaned the tables and stepped over the intertwined bodies, his face betraying no hint of shock at their moans of pleasure. Sometimes, and this was something Selim had seen with his own eyes, the owner would even unfurl his prayer mat in a corridor and prostrate himself, facing Mecca, while the hippies toasted the sexual revolution and universal copulation. Selim observed the praying man. He watched him kneel down, press his forehead to the floor, turn his head to one side and then the other. The owner's lips moved. He seemed completely indifferent to the huge fresco that the hippies had painted on the wall facing him. It showed a naked woman, a siren or an ancient goddess, holding a drum in one hand and a reptile in the other.

Selim returned to the café several times but never saw Nilsa. She had vanished into thin air. The hippies assumed Selim was one of them. They asked him about his story, but Selim began to stammer so badly that he couldn't get the words out. There were lots of Americans there, from Montana, New York, Michigan. Two enormous young men with long red beards told him that they had left their country to avoid being drafted. They swore they would never cut their hair and said they preferred exile to killing innocent Vietnamese people, as poor and oppressed as the poor of this country. For some of them, Essaouira was just a stepping stone. After this they would go to Ibiza, Syria, Nepal. There they would buy cloths and embroidered shirts, brightly coloured saris and wool-lined coats which they could sell for a fortune in the fashion boutiques of Manhattan or Amsterdam.

Selim was greatly impressed by the intellectuals: the way they spoke, the books they kept in the pockets of their long woollen cardigans, the speeches they gave about the atomic bomb, Buddhism or bourgeois morality. Among them was a French sociologist with old-fashioned manners who never looked you in the eye when he talked to you. He appeared to be scanning the horizon, as if you were merely ectoplasm pierced by his gaze. He was often accompanied by an American theatre director, whose gaunt cheeks and white-blond hair made him look like a vampire. His troupe of actors, thirty-strong, rehearsed near the port in an abandoned warehouse that still smelled of sardines and brine. The gossip around town was that they had been involved in a scandal in Europe and had fled shame and opprobrium, ending up here. They were rumoured to appear naked on stage, insult the spectators, even urinate on them. The governor had warned them: 'Stay here if you like, but I don't want any trouble. Don't forget this is a Muslim country.'

One day, however, trouble erupted. It was a Saturday and the café owner grabbed Karim by the collar and, surrounded by apathetic hippies, started slapping him. The sociologist stood up and defended the boy. He was horrified by violence, he said, and this was no way to treat someone so young. The owner, in pidgin French, called Karim a thief. He had seen him stealing a camera from another customer's table. 'I don't want problems. No police,' he kept saying. Karim struggled free. The sociologist held him by the shoulder.

'You wanted to sell it, did you? You need money?'

Karim looked up at him with dark, insolent eyes.

'No. I didn't want to sell it. I want to take pictures of the girls on the beach.'

The sociologist laughed with relief. The kid wasn't a poor beggar, just a typical horny teenager.

'Oh, take it, then. I'm sure whoever it belongs to wouldn't blame you. You see, that's why we need to free ourselves from all of this and choose a simple life, with no complications, in touch with nature. Ownership is war, you understand? Go on, go home. Just don't let us catch you stealing again.'

Selim and Karim met in the street. As they walked together, Karim looked through the camera lens.

'Why did you steal that?' Selim asked.

'You're not going to lecture me too, are you? I know what hippies are like. They might be dirty and look like beggars, but the truth is that they're all hypocritical mama's boys. What do you think they do when they run out of money? They go to the post office and call their parents. Reversing the charges, of course. Then they queue to pick up their packages. Peanut butter – they can't live without it. They start crying when they dip their finger into it.'

Selim talked to Karim about Nilsa. He still hadn't found any trace of her.

'Is she your girlfriend? You sleep with her?' the boy asked him.

'No, not at all. I came here with her, that's all.'

'So why do you care, then?' Selim shrugged. And Karim, apparently repenting his rudeness, added: 'Have you checked the noticeboard, near the post office? Maybe she left you a note.'

On a wall opposite the post office the hippies stuck up pieces of paper. They arranged meetings, rented out rooms or searched for friends. Sometimes parents would put up posters of their missing children. Selim looked at the photographs of smiling teenagers, so normal and happy-looking, beneath which their bereft mothers and fathers had written a name and the offer of a reward. Would Mathilde come here to add the portrait of her son to this legion of the disappeared? One name kept cropping up on all these scraps of paper: Diabet.

Selim asked: 'What's Diabet?'

'Diabet?' laughed Karim. 'That's hippie paradise, man.'

Three days later Selim was given the opportunity to go to paradise. Karim turned up late in the afternoon, out of breath and so excited that what he said made no sense at first.

'Man, this morning, I swear on my father's life, this luxury car stopped in front of the Hôtel des Îles. And this guy got out of it, this tall Black guy with frizzy hair, leather trousers and cowboy boots. You'll never guess who it was, man!'

Selim shrugged. 'Who was it?'

'Jimi Hendrix, man.'

'I've never heard of him.'

'What? You've got to be kidding me! You don't know who Jimi Hendrix is? He's a star, man. A star! And tonight, believe me, we're going to a party like nothing you've ever seen before.'

They walked for almost an hour: along the coast then through a forest of tamarisk, eucalyptus and thuja trees. Buffeted by the wind, these trees had taken on strange shapes, like tortured bodies or frail peasants bent double under the weight of a stack of firewood. Around here it was said that there were wolves and wild boar in that forest. Nobody went in there, especially not after dark. Selim and Karim crossed a small stone bridge over the Oued Ksob. A herdsman in a white djellaba was sitting on a rock, watching his goats. On a hillside to the left Selim saw the village of Diabet. It was a tiny place, just a heap of small whitewashed houses, most of them containing no more than one or two living spaces. He spotted a group of young people lying on the sand and a naked child, barely old enough to walk, who was crying. A girl, presumably the baby's mother, was calling to it in Italian.

The hippies lived there, alongside the villagers. Or, rather, *with* the villagers. They would rent a room from them for a few dirhams and share their uncomfortable lives. They would do their business in the forest and wash in the public fountain or in the sea. They lived by candlelight and when they were sick the villagers would treat them using traditional remedies. The people here liked them. They said: 'They're just poor people like us. Poor people help one another.' Like them, the hippies put up with fleas, stink bugs and those huge oily cockroaches that crawl into your bed at night and lay eggs inside your ears. To pay for their rooms, the hippies would barter. A jar of peanut butter or jam would provide them with a roof for a week or more.

The villagers saw them as poor foreigners, Europeans who owned nothing. The hippies were always in a good mood. They liked to sing and dance. They took care of animals and children, showing a tenderness towards them that the inhabitants of Diabet found touchingly naive. 'They're like children themselves,' they told each other when the hippies weren't around. The older villagers were sometimes more suspicious. They didn't understand. A long time ago the white people had come; they had promised them trains, roads, schools; they had said there would be electricity and aeroplanes and brand-new hospitals where they would be healed for free. But there was no road, no school, no train. And now here were the white people again. But this time they wanted to share the villagers' simple, rough life. It was all so strange. The children of Diabet fled the village as soon as they could. They went to Marrakech or even further away, to Agadir or Casablanca. And other people's children came here and said there was nothing more beautiful, nothing more real than this primitive life among the goats and the cockroaches.

From the other side of the road you could see the ruins of a chateau devoured by sand. Dar Soltane, built in the eighteenth century by a rich merchant and then given to the governor of the town who would meet there, in those rooms with their European furnishings, with ambassadors and other dignitaries. Stripped of its luxury by looters and sandstorms, the chateau was now nothing more than a pile of ruins, like those abandoned maharajas' palaces in the middle of the Indian jungle. The bases of the adobe walls were indistinguishable from the sand dunes beneath, and nothing remained of the richly decorated ceilings, the courtyards made from zellige tiles, the marble fireplaces or Italian chandeliers. Selim and Karim walked, guided by the sound of tom-toms and guitars. There, amid the ruins, the party was in full swing. Most of the guests were hippies from the village. They were drinking and smoking near the fire. To shelter from the cold night wind some of them had covered themselves with hessian sacks normally used to transport flour or sugar. In a corner, dealers with glistening lips and hazy eyes warmed mahjoun in their hands. In the middle of the crowd, Selim spotted Nilsa. She was sitting in the sand, her long hair hanging over her bare shoulders, and when she saw him she jumped up and flung her arms around his neck.

'My Moroccan friend!' she said. 'What happened to you? I was worried about you!' She held Selim's face in her hands and kissed him, sliding her tongue inside his mouth. Her thick, furred tongue caressed his teeth, the insides of his cheeks. And Selim felt something soft and viscous melting on his palate.

A man and a woman were kissing on the ground and Selim stared at the man's hands. Big white hands covered with red hairs. The fingers ran along bare thighs like an enormous spider. Then they disappeared inside the woman and she threw her head back, gazing up at the sky, and began to moan. What was Selim doing here? Amine's face appeared suddenly before his eyes and he felt ashamed, terribly ashamed, as if his father could see what was happening here through his eyes. A girl took his hand. A bushy-haired girl who smiled at him, revealing gaps between her teeth.

A group of musicians came up from the beach. They had long frizzy hair and were wearing dark djellabas. On their heads they wore woven hats with little seashells hanging from them which clinked together as they walked to make a bell-like sound. They sat around the fire. Some of them held darbukas between their thighs and began tapping them with their palms. Others had huge metal castanets which they clapped together by moving their fingers. Around them the hippies whooped with joy. 'They're Gnawas,' Karim explained. But Selim wasn't listening. He was thirsty. Terribly thirsty. He thought about the water, down there below, and about the sound of the waves that had now been drowned out by the clatter of percussion. He staggered to his feet and held on to a girl who was dancing in front of him, turning around and around to the rhythm of the darbukas. One of the musicians started to sing, or more accurately to growl and howl as if trying to wake the ghosts hidden in the abandoned chateau.

To Selim, the ground seemed soft. It gave way beneath his feet, and around him the world had lost its contours: all shapes had melted and he could only walk forward by raising his knees high in the air and reaching out with his hands, as if in search of some invisible wall. His thoughts were so frantic, so fast and confused, that he could never follow them to their end or draw any meaning from them. Then one of them grew bigger than all the rest. It was not really a thought. Selim was filled with a desperate urge, an overpowering desire to have sex. He wanted to tear off his clothes and lie naked on the ground with a woman, to fuck like wild animals. The others, sitting around a fire, called out to him. But no matter how far Selim walked, their figures always looked small and distant. He had the impression that he was sinking into the sand as he heard his companions' laughter. They saw him, they shouted his name, and Selim was filled with love for these strangers. He would hold them in his arms and tell them a thousand things about himself. Yes, he just had to keep walking, a few more steps and he would rest his head in the lap of the boy with the guitar and tell him who he was and where he came from and how happy he was to be with them all. No, not happy, he thought, it was something different from happiness, it was release, the end of the struggle, and Selma's words overlapped his own. He had stopped resisting and the dog that was gripping his calf with its teeth had lost interest and trotted away. Someone was pulling at his shirt. 'You okay, man?' Selim smiled. He wanted to reply but when he opened his mouth all that came out was a gurgling sound. He fell to the ground. His hands reached out to the face of the man next to him. The man let Selim caress his cheeks, his nose. Selim parted the man's lips with his fingers and the man bit him softly, like a playful puppy.

Around them people were laughing. Moonlight illuminated the abandoned chateau. Selim stared at the walls. He could make out sculpted stones and the remains of what had once been an engraving. The walls started to move. The chateau itself seemed to detach from the ground and the adobe walls came closer to Selim. As clearly as he could see the ocean, he saw the figures of those who had lived here long, long ago, when the chateau had still had a roof, when rotting wooden boards had been windows. Ghosts from books he had forgotten ever reading appeared out of nowhere and mingled vaguely with the young people sitting on the sand.

He didn't see them arrive. He just heard the applause, the screams of girls close to fainting. The Black man was here. The man Karim had told him about and whose name Selim had now forgotten. His face was lit up by the embers flying in the wind. He looked like a character from a film. An Indian chief or a voodoo priest. An imaginary entity of some kind. When he picked up his guitar and his long fingers began moving over the strings, Selim burst out laughing. The same laughter that had so scared Nilsa now echoed within the ruins of Dar Soltane.

Selim was on his feet. He didn't know where to go. He could no longer move forward through the crowd of half-naked bodies, feet stamping the ground rhythmically, eyes closed. They span around so fast that Selim felt dizzy. Some of them beat their chests, reached up towards the sky and threw their heads from side to side until they were in a trance. And the musicians' hands slapped ever faster against the taut skins of their darbukas. Selim could hear each person's heartbeat. Their hearts were huge, about to explode, to burst out of the chests that held them prisoner. The dancers swung their arms, their hips, as if possessed by spirits. A man jumped up and down behind the musicians and repeated ecstatically: 'That's it, man, yeah, that's it!' The dancers' feet kicked up sand which flew through the air and stuck to wet skin. It filled mouths, the grains cracking under teeth.

Selim moved forward, drifting beside himself, watching himself live then forgetting himself. His body had been set free; it had its own life now. His eyes saw, without understanding. He had lost all notion of time and events came to him in flashes. His body was caught between a strange weariness, a feeling of faintness and a hazy serenity, a dilution of consciousness that allowed it to be everything, say everything, live everything. He unbuttoned his shirt and caressed his stomach, his chest. Oddly, there was something reassuring about the feel of his hand on his own skin. He would have liked to make love to himself, to eat himself whole. To feel every pore of his skin, to excite every nerve end. He wanted a hand, a superhuman hand, to possess him, from his fingertips to the back of his neck, from his lips to his inner thighs. He flapped his arms as if trying to embrace the landscape, surprised that the world around him could not be hugged tight. Then the sand grew cold. His bare feet were wet. He drank something warm and bitter that made him feel better. He nodded while a boy spoke and he didn't understand a word. It needs to slow down, he thought. He lay on the ground, bare-chested, and fell asleep.

'Selim has disappeared.' On the other end of the line Mathilde was crying and Aïcha could not understand what her mother was saying. She had gone to the post office in Rabat to call her parents and let them know that she was planning to stay with Monette for a while longer. But as soon as she answered the phone Mathilde said: 'Selim has disappeared' and Aïcha didn't dare talk about herself. She asked questions. When had her brother last been home? Had they contacted his friends? Did they have any idea where he might have gone? Mathilde could only answer her daughter with sobs and sniffles. 'He stole money from me. Can you believe it? He stole my money.' Aïcha said: 'Have you called the police?' And Mathilde, her voice suddenly cold, replied: 'The police? Of course not. We don't wash our dirty laundry in public. Whatever you do, don't mention this to anyone. If someone asks you, Selim is in Alsace and he's fine.'

Mehdi was waiting for her outside, on a café terrace, under the arches on Avenue Allal Ben Abdellah. When she got back from the post office he suggested they go to his apartment on Rue de Bagdad, a few yards from the Bab er-Rouah. He had been thinking about this for days, imagining Aïcha sitting on his living room sofa, legs crossed, her long hands resting demurely on her knees. Or perhaps she would stand to take a closer look at the books in the bookcase he had built himself out of bricks and wooden planks. He would put on some music, a record by Sarah Vaughan or Billie Holiday. He would make her some tea and they would stay there, sitting side by side, in the white-hot sun-soaked living room. He would open the window that overlooked an old palace and he would hold her close to him, hugging her so tight that her ribs would crack like a walnut shell. He would try to find the words but would not say them. But no matter what he did, he felt sure she would understand. They had spent every day together for the past three weeks. They had kissed, hidden in the car, awaiting nightfall so that they could find some remote place, a beach or a corner of Henri's garden. Not once had they had a living room to themselves, and of course Mehdi thought about it. About Aïcha's naked skin. About the desire she aroused in him, about what it would be like. He didn't want her to feel trapped or frightened. But the truth was he had no idea what she thought of sex. They had never talked about it and neither of them had ever dared ask the other about their past experiences. He drank his coffee, closing his eyes at each sip. He was taking so much pleasure from this anticipation that he hoped her telephone call would last forever. She had told him that her mother's name was Mathilde and he didn't know why but he had been impressed by that.

She came back from the post office with red eyes. Mehdi knew instantly it was all over. 'I have to go home,' Aïcha told him. 'My parents need me.' She would take the train that evening. Mehdi insisted on going with her. 'I don't mind. We'll travel there together and then I'll come home. No one will see me.' And that is what they did. Aïcha packed her suitcase, she hugged Monette and Henri. Then her friends, standing outside the door in their wet bathing suits, waved their arms until Mehdi's car disappeared.

They drove in silence in the old beige Simca, the warm, heavy air pouring through the open windows. Mehdi drove without leaning back against the burning seat. Sometimes he would let go of the steering wheel and put his hand gently on Aïcha's shoulder or thigh. She wished his fingers could stay on her skin for all eternity, become embedded in her flesh. While they were driving through the Maâmora Forest they were overtaken by police cars. The policemen signalled to all the drivers they passed to park by the roadside. A royal cortège was about to come through. Mehdi stopped under a cork oak and they waited. He hated August with its cloud-choked skies. August was the month of massacres, abductions, riots. Like all Moroccans, Mehdi was wary of summer, the heat that rose from the ground and drove people so mad that they would commit murder. Aïcha turned to face him. She wanted to speak, to say some sweet nothing, but she remained silent. Mehdi looked at her and bit his lip. He stared deep into her eyes as if they were coffee cups whose grounds might reveal the future. In the depths of her pupils he saw his own sorrows, glories, shames and betrayals in the years to come. In her irises he saw the entirety of his existence unfold. Aïcha contained his future the way the lamp found at the back of the cave contains the genie's evanescent body. If he took her hand, if he turned Aïcha's palm up to the sky, he was sure to read his own destiny in those lines.

They waited for a long time in the shade of the trees. At last those Mercedes, gleaming brown and black, appeared on the road. They sped past. The police signalled to the parked drivers:

they could now go on. Mehdi wished the journey would never end. If only they could keep driving into infinity, towards an ever-receding destination. If only the world could shrink to the inside of this car, the two of them alone, untouchable. Ahead of them the heat-pounded hills appeared to be floating, and on the tarmac the refracted sunlight created the illusion of vast puddles of water. In the distance tall cypresses loomed into view, followed by fields of olive trees. They passed the acres of vineyards belonging to the Belhajes' neighbours. The trip was over, they had arrived. Already Aïcha was showing signs of nerves. She kept glancing at the rear-view mirror as if afraid they were being followed, as if her parents might appear within its frame at any moment. She kept her face lowered, like a fugitive. Then suddenly she told him: 'Stop here.' A few yards away they could see the big sign with the Belhaj name upon it.

'Here? Are you sure? There's still a long way to go. I could take you a bit closer. No one will see us.'

'No, no, it's better if I get out here.'

'But isn't it dangerous? I don't want to leave you alone in the middle of all these fields.'

'Dangerous?' Aïcha smiled. 'This is my farm, remember. Nothing can happen to me here. I know this place like the back of my hand. Even in total darkness, I'd be able to find my way home.'

There was no cinematic kiss, no tearful farewell. Mehdi hugged Aïcha then watched her walk away as he stood next to the car. She jumped over a fence and her graceful figure eventually vanished into a line of trees. Mehdi remained motionless. He couldn't bring himself to get back in the car and drive away. He looked at the rows of olive trees and started imagining the little girl Aïcha had once been. He saw her, a child, running through fields and he could picture her face as it had been, her grazed knees, her headstrong expression, her small round-nailed hands covered in nettle stings. He even thought he could hear her laughter ring out, her little-girl laughter, and spot her thin, agile body swaying on a tree branch. He felt then as if he had always known her. That little girl was no stranger to him, and nor was the teenager she had been afterwards. A serious, austere teenager, fully focused on the tough business of growing up. She had been his soulmate forever and all the years he had lived without her seemed to him like lost years, pointless and wasted. Not only was he in love with *her*, this woman he knew now, but also all the Aïchas she had been before and all the Aïchas she would later become. He smoked cigarette after cigarette, sitting in his car with the door open. Some peasants walked past and greeted him suspiciously. Mehdi didn't care. This woman, and the intensity of the love he felt for her, proved that he had been right to believe in the greatness of his destiny. Yes, an extraordinary destiny awaited him, a destiny in which Aïcha would take centre stage, and not for a second, sitting there in his Simca, did Mehdi consider that he was trespassing. That he was on the property of another, richer, more powerful man who could have him removed if he wished. No, he didn't think any of that. He was filled with happiness, with an unshakeable serenity. At last he stubbed out his cigarette, closed the car door and set off.

He drove slowly along the dirt path. The estate struck him now as even bigger and more impressive than it had the first time. He kept driving and found himself at a dead end, facing an immense hangar sheltering a row of agricultural machines. He put his car into reverse and almost ran over a man who was jogging towards him. The farmworker came up to the car and put his callused hand on the door.

'Where are you going, kid? Are you lost?'

'I'm looking for the house. I want to see the owner.'

'Sidi Belhaj is in his office. Come on, I'll show you.'

The farmworker began jogging forward again and Mehdi followed him, feeling slightly intimidated. Soon the house appeared. The high palm tree, the storehouse and, behind a hedge, the swimming pool edged by red bricks. Mehdi stopped for a moment and observed the tall blonde woman standing next to the water. She was wearing a mauve swimsuit and beneath her very white skin she was as muscular as a young man. She raised her arms, brought her hands together and dived in. Mathilde.

'Aren't you coming?' asked the farmworker impatiently. 'It's just here.' The man half-opened the glass door, holding his woollen hat in one hand. 'Boss. There's someone to see you.'

The first thing Mehdi saw when he entered the office was the portrait of Hassan II hanging on the wall. It felt as if the king was watching him, mocking him. A second later his attention switched to Amine, sitting in a leather chair. He was a handsome man, Mehdi thought, nothing like the vulgar, pot-bellied peasant he had imagined. On the contrary, with his finely sculpted moustache, he looked more like a film star. Mehdi held out his hand and introduced himself.

'Hello, monsieur. My name is Mehdi Daoud.'

'And what can I do for you, Monsieur Daoud?'

'Well, I've come to ask for the hand of your daughter, Aïcha.'

'I beg your pardon?'

Amine was stunned. He put his hands on his desk and stood up, ready to attack this insolent young man.

'Is this a joke?'

'No, not at all. I have come to ask for Aïcha's hand in marriage,' Mehdi said, his voice embarrassingly high-pitched.

'What are you talking about? Who even are you? Mehdi Daoud, you said? My daughter has never even mentioned you.'

'I am an economics lecturer at the Mohammed V University in Rabat. I intend to apply to become the dean of the law faculty and I am currently working on a book about—'

'Are you out of your mind? Did my daughter put you up to this?'

'Oh no, not at all. Your daughter had nothing to do with it. She doesn't even know I'm here. My intentions are extremely serious, Monsieur Belhaj.'

Amine turned to the corridor that led to the house and yelled 'Aïcha!' so loud that Mehdi recoiled. She was there. And in a moment or two she would appear at the door and she would see what Mehdi was capable of. She would be swept away by his courage and the romantic nature of his actions. She would persuade her father and they would be married here, in this farm, under the high palm tree.

Aïcha appeared. She walked barefoot towards her father, like a guilty child ready to be punished. When she saw Mehdi, her eyes widened. She looked very angry.

'Do you know this young man?' Amine demanded.

Aïcha lowered her eyes.

'He says he knows you. So have you met him before or not?'

'Yes, I know him. Monette introduced me to him.'

'All right. Well, guess what? This boy came here to ask for your hand in marriage. What do you say to that?'

'What?' Aïcha said, almost shouting. Her cheeks were bright red and she could feel the blood beating at her temples.

'Are you behind this little scheme?'

'No, not at all!'

'You mean you didn't know about it or you mean you don't want to marry him?'

'I mean . . . I don't know!'

'How can you not know? You think I'm an idiot?' Amine looked at the two of them, suppressing a smile. 'I don't have time for all this. Work out what you both want and we can talk about it later. Now get out of here. Go on, out of my sight!'

Aïcha,

The storks have returned. They fly around in the permanently blue sky over Rabat, they fly in circles above the river, above the roofs of the medina, they build enormous nests in dead trees and those piles of rocks in the ruins of the Chellah, and I have the feeling that they are signalling to me. I often go to the necropolis to watch them soar around, with their red beaks and their white bodies and their huge black wings, the flight feathers spaced out like combs. I observe their reflections on the muddy waters of the Bou Regreg. Sometimes they swoop so low that I feel I could reach out and touch them. I am captivated above all by the sound they make. I listen to them endlessly calling, as if they have a message to deliver to me. They came from you in a straight line, from your green and cold Alsace, gliding without a single beat of wings, perched on clouds. I try frantically to decipher the message that you have given them to deliver to me. Because surely you have something to say to me even if you don't reply to my letters. You preferred to send me these ambassadors to announce your return. I'm right, aren't I? The storks are your scouts. If they have come all this way, then you will too. Aïcha, it's not over between us.

172

I know from Monette that you are still in Strasbourg, that you are renting an apartment above someone called David. I called your number and I think it was him who answered, but how can I know if he even told you about my call? Does he know who I am? Have you told him about me? And then I wonder: who is he for you?

My heart is weary, my stomach is in knots. My thoughts are no longer anything more than a letter I am writing. My head is filled with a mountain of words all for you. It is a blundering, endless process, an obsession that pursues me even into sleep. I am haunted, Aïcha, haunted by the mistake I made, by the thought of what we had begun to experience, our love which was cut short by my ridiculous approach to your father. I want to believe that you are, like me, in a state of painful confusion. I wish I could hold you in my arms, forget the thunderclap of your departure, and tell you that nothing can ever separate us, not even you. Because I can't stop myself hoping. Nothing and nobody can fill the void you have left in my life. I should build a nest in that void where I can sleep through my grief, where I can hibernate like a bear, bathed in the eternal summer of my soul. I can still feel your eyes on me, as real and invisible as the wind on my skin.

Surely you can't be *this* angry with me. I was wrong, I admit it. Perhaps you thought I wanted to buy you from your father as if you were a horse or a cow? I surrendered to a mad impulse, without asking you, because I was so sure of the love that filled me like hot air and carried me far above all ordinary considerations. Everything seemed so simple from up there; I felt as if nothing could stop this force. Your father would smile and give me his consent, and you and I would take off together towards the brilliant future that was promised to us. I had not even the shadow of a doubt, believe me. It was just a question of momentum and the sky would open up, revealing our dazzling destiny. Everyone calls me Karl Marx, after all: glorious futures are my specialty.

I was vain enough to believe that you shared this faith in my powers, Aïcha. I thought I was being admirably courageous and determined, but instead of those qualities you saw in my attitude arrogance, brutality, the desire for possession. You were right on that last point: I wanted you to belong to me. I wanted to make sure that no one other than me would ever hold your hand or embrace you or breathe in your smell. When you were there, when I touched you, when I talked to you, when I listened to you, when I dreamed of you, I had the feeling that my love made you even more beautiful, carried you towards yourself, towards the pure beauty that is within you. How glorious you were, caressed by my hands, by my eyes! That pretension oppresses me now. The memory of the taste of your lips, the smell of your skin, our kisses, is a poison that burns me.

I walk endlessly, aimlessly. I go to the end of the kasbah to look out at the sea that separates us, as if I might be able to spot you: isn't that you, that little dot on the horizon, and aren't you waving to me? The rest of the time, I watch my life take place as if I were a spectator, or rather as if it had not yet begun.

Let me give you some news from your homeland. In three months I have taught only three or four classes. The students are in such a fervour that they keep going on strike, which at least gives me time to read, go for walks and think. I applied for the position of assistant dean. Unfortunately the dean does not like me as much as he likes all the fawners that surround him. When I told him about my plan to write a thesis on the psychological consequences of underdevelopment, he laughed in my face. There is no intellectual life in this country any more. Everything is stunted, restricted, disappointing. They have replaced philosophy with Islamic studies; the Institute of Sociology has been closed. If I had been born in France or America, I could have been interested in something other than politics, I could have written my poems without having to justify myself to anyone, without having to endure the sermonising of these so-called revolutionaries. Last night I went to Jour et Nuit with Abdellah and the gang. Abdellah was more fanatical than ever. He spends his time in the Chinese and Cuban embassies. The other night he dragged me to hear a speech by Alejo Carpentier, which I found so much more subtle, appealing and rousing than all our tinpot Che Guevaras. Ronit isn't wrong when she says it would not be good to live in a country run by men like Abdellah. I know what you're going to say. Not so long ago I was stuffed full of theories too, convinced that I could write a book that would change the world. What madness! Becoming a starving artist, going out into the desert to preach . . . None of this is going to help me. I have thought about it a lot and I have other plans now. Please listen to me, Aïcha: I feel certain that an extraordinary destiny awaits me. You are the first person I have dared say this to, and it doesn't matter if you are rolling your eyes now, wondering if I am arrogant or just naive. I could not explain why, but I can tell I am fundamentally different from most people of my generation. I sense a unique strength within me, and I am telling you now that this strength will carry me far and that you will be with me, I know it. So there you go, now you can have a good laugh. And I will laugh with you, even though I am perfectly serious.

I have a story about Roland Barthes for you. As you know, I often eat dinner at La Pagode, the Chinese restaurant below my apartment. Well, the other night a man came in, an elegant-looking European with white hair and a slightly sad face that struck me as familiar. He was with a tiny elderly woman – his mother, I presume. The next day I saw the old lady in the stairwell of my apartment building. I realised that she lives on the floor above mine. I checked the letterbox in the lobby and saw the tenant's name: 'Roland Barthes'. Can you believe it? Everyone here talks about him. At the university the other lecturers are proud that such a famous man should be giving classes here in Rabat. The students couldn't care less, of course: all they think about is strikes and general assemblies. You will think me ridiculous, but I went through all my articles, carefully rereading and revising them, then put them in his letterbox. He might be reading them now, as I write this! My present existence consists solely in waiting. For a letter from you. For a response from Barthes. I am a man who waits. Imagine if he likes my writings. Imagine he offers them to a Parisian publishing house. Imagine that I go to France, maybe even Strasbourg, to publicise my book and give you a copy! Then you could tell your father that I am more than just some economics lecturer, and you'd have to admit that you have no choice but to live the rest of your life with me.

Aïcha, our life began one night on the terrace of the Café de France. I have not forgotten a single moment of that evening.

I remember the spark in your eye every time you looked at me. Not that you let yourself meet my eyes for long. Perhaps you knew that if you looked deep into them you would never come back to the surface. But I felt your gaze on my hands, my lips, and especially my forehead. You stared at my forehead so avidly, trying to guess what strange thoughts might be bubbling away inside it. You wanted to know! Even though we were careful not to say too much, I realised that we would soon be together. In that moment my entire being wanted to enter you. It all began there. Before that we were embryos, unhatched larvae. Nothing remains to me of the years that preceded your appearance. I can't remember a life in which you did not exist.

One day, later, during one of our walks, you told me, laughing, that I was an atheist of life. But that isn't true. Life possesses me, Aïcha. I believe in it fiercely. Life illuminates me, it tears me apart at every moment, I love it in its every aspect: pleasure, happiness, pain, silence. And, thanks to you, I have never felt so close to it. I recognised you. I had been waiting for you since the limbo of childhood, and you arrived. I look up at the sky now, the light in the palm trees, the circling storks, and I am in awe. Believe me, this beauty is made from us. It is made for us.

MEHDI

Mehdi posted his letter and walked back up Avenue Mohammed V towards his apartment building. He passed the train station and in the distance he saw the white towers of St Peter's Cathedral. When he first moved to the capital he had felt a profound antipathy towards it. The white, torpid city made him suspicious. It was too quiet, he thought, too bourgeois. The kind of place where nothing happens. Nothing visible, anyway, and all the vices, all the lies, were hidden behind the high walls of the bourgeois houses which, in spring, were ablaze with flame vines. Mehdi hated the pretty avenues neatly planted with palm trees. He hated the eucalyptus forest at the entrance to the Agdal neighbourhood; those greyish trunks made him anxious. In this city of diplomats and civil servants, courtiers and lackeys, he felt as if he were being constantly spied upon. He was suspicious of waiters in cafés. Behind every caretaker, every taxi driver, he saw an informant.

Then Mehdi got to know it better. After leaving work, he got into the habit of walking through town, as far as his legs would carry him. He went to the central market, at the bottom of Avenue Mohammed V. He wandered through the indoor vegetable market and admired the fruit stalls. The mandarins and pomegranates that the vendors split open to expose their glittering freshness, and the skinny, dirty cats that ran through the peelings on the ground. He never bought anything but he enjoyed observing the busy stallholders, especially the fish-mongers who sat on plastic chairs behind wide marble counters where scarlet-gilled sea bass and John Dory lay dying. He went to the Kasbah of the Udayas and explored that bohemian district with its walls painted white and blue. Sometimes he would go down into the valley and walk along the marshy banks of the Bou Regreg river. Clouds of dense pale-blue mist floated muddy and motionless above the water's surface. Dozens of white birds perched on grey leafless branches. The locals avoided the river because they said it was full of corpses. Mehdi went up to the Chellah necropolis, where the majestic ramparts turned orange at dusk. And in front of the white-walled, round-roofed marabouts, those buildings where the holy men were buried, women came to leave hard-boiled eggs and bottles of milk as offerings.

Since it had become the theatre of his heartbreak, he had begun to like this city. He walked his melancholy through it, like a dog on a leash, roaming the streets in search of a woman who he knew was far away. And strangely, it was because Aïcha wasn't here that the streets seemed to him so horribly alive. His quest opened his eyes to the smallest details: the beauty of a building, the golden light on the palace walls, a blacksmith's gaunt face in Rue des Consuls. He sank deeper into the sands of regret, he brooded over his grief, and the city was his accomplice, his protector.

The day was ending and the shopkeepers on the avenue were closing their shutters. Mehdi walked past a bakery and watched the flies hovering over pyramids of Ramadan patisseries covered with honey and sesame seeds. As he walked, the streets grew more and more empty. The government employees had already gone home and were probably taking naps on their living room benches while their wives stirred the soup and took care of the kids. The schoolchildren had gone home too and now only a few stragglers were out on the streets, with their pale faces, dark-ringed eyes and fetid breath. The whole city was hungry.

For the first time in a long time, Mehdi thought about his family. He had burned his bridges with them, but now the memory came to him of those long Ramadan evenings in Fes, when he would watch his father play cards with some friends from the neighbourhood. He remembered the way old Mohamed would sit at the table and pray before taking small sips from his glass of cold milk. 'Hamdoullah,' he would say before opening a fleshy date for each of his children and handing it to them. Sometimes there would be a worm inside the date, a fat, white, shiny worm that Mohamed would flick away with the tip of his fingernail. On Fridays the patriarch would take his sons to the mosque. On the way he would stop at the grocer's and buy round loaves of bread, bars of chocolate and tins of sardines, which he would hand out to the poor people sitting in the square outside the temple.

Mehdi jumped. He had been so lost in thought that he had not seen the man coming towards him. The man was about forty years old, tall and unhealthily thin. He wore sunglasses and a permanent smile. Mehdi noticed something moving under his beige raincoat. The man was carrying a small dog with white curly fur. He bent his neck and kissed the animal on its muzzle. During the conversation that followed, he never stopped stroking it.

'Are you Karl Marx?' Before Mehdi could answer, the man started laughing. 'You're so clever! I went to your lecture this morning and I didn't understand a thing.' He did not introduce himself or offer to shake hands. He just stared at Mehdi, smiling inanely. Mehdi started walking again and the man followed him, matching the rhythm of his footsteps. 'I never even finished school. But I admire educated people. Your parents must be proud of you.'

Mehdi threw a few threatening looks at the man, but he didn't dare tell him to go away. He upped his pace a little, clutching his satchel to his chest. On the pavement a boy was selling a meat cleaver. An old, worn meat cleaver that was clearly worth nothing but which the boy had placed on top of an incongruously clean piece of cloth. Next to him was an elderly woman, her face wrinkled as a fig. She was selling home-made pastries out of a little wicker basket. The man stopped and leaned slowly towards the old woman. Mehdi, who felt absolutely sure that the man was a cop, expected him to get angry, to kick the basket and the cleaver out of the way. Instead he smiled.

'My compliments, el hajja,' he said to the woman. 'You're a good cook.'

He staggered sideways and to stop himself falling grabbed hold of Mehdi's arm.

'So, tell me, why do you write all those articles?'

Mehdi could not stop staring at the man's enormous Adam's apple. It was so big he could imagine it slicing apart the thin red skin of the man's neck.

'It's my job. I'm a professor and I publish my research.'

'Ah, okay, I'm sorry. You publish your research. Of course.' The little dog was increasingly fidgety under the raincoat. It looked as if it wanted to escape its master's arms and leap down onto the pavement.

'And does it make much money, this research?'

'That's not really the point,' Mehdi replied coldly.

'Hang on, I don't understand. All that work you do, all those books you read, you don't get paid?'

'I told you, money doesn't interest me.'

'Did you hear that?' he asked the trembling poodle. 'Money doesn't interest him. But you must have a family, right? Everyone has a family. And they'd probably be happy if you sent them some money. You don't look like one of those bourgeois types who can afford to work for free.'

Outside an empty restaurant two men were setting out trestles and planks. Every evening, when the fasting ended, they gave out soup and hard-boiled eggs to the city's poorest people. Mehdi came to a stop in front of a blown-up photograph of the king dressed for a round of golf.

'It's nearly time to break the fast. I have to go.'

'Ah yes, that's true,' the stranger said. He lowered his glasses, brought his watch very close to his eyes and nodded. 'It's a shame. We could have gone to the café and continued our conversation. Before, people used to eat at cafés during Ramadan, remember? Apparently there were arrests. What do you think of that?' And he fixed Mehdi with his dark, impenetrable eyes.

'I have to go.'

'Okay, of course, I'm not stopping you. You must have a lot of work to do. I can see you're a serious man. This country is lucky to have young people like you.'

II

The carnival was over. Workaday humiliation had begun.

Milan Kundera

Omar undressed, as he did every evening before going on duty. He laid his trousers out on the bed and tossed his shirt, the collar of which was stained with a few drops of blood, onto the floor. In the shower Omar used an exfoliating glove to rub at the blotches that covered his arms and legs. The doctor had told him not to do this. And he knew it would be even more painful in the next few hours, when the fabric of his shirt rubbed against his skin, when his trousers irritated the sores on his thighs. But in that moment, under the jet of hot water, he felt powerless to stop himself. He scratched and scratched. His shoulders, his armpits, his skinny swollen neck. It was as if he were trying to erase himself. Or at least erase some trace that he bore on his skin. He put the glove to his face, rubbed his cheeks, pulled at his eyelids, mouth tensed. For a short while he stood there, naked, in the middle of the steamed-up bathroom. Then he wrapped himself in a big white towel and sat on the edge of his bed. He picked up the clippers from his bedside table and cut his fingernails and toenails, one little bit at a time, his gestures nervous but precise. He collected the nail clippings in his bath towel and dropped them into the bin.

He left his apartment building and got into his car. He sat in the passenger seat, beside his chauffeur, Brahim. His men were waiting near Place de France; he saw them leaning against the back wall of a grocer's. He had to let them into the car himself. They smelled of diesel and cheap beer and they kept noisily sniffing. They were dirty. And yet Omar had told them so many times that their appearance was a fundamental part of their work. How could they hope to be respected if they went around acting like boors? Was this how they expected to impress those little intellectual pricks who had been to Paris or Brussels and who would try to humiliate them with their knowledge, their theories about the future of capitalism?

Omar took good care of himself. His trousers were always perfectly ironed and his shoes so clean and shiny they might have just come out of the box. He fastened his shirt buttons all the way to the top even when the heat was stifling, even if the collar rubbed against his eczema rashes and made them bleed. He saw in this refinement a form of intelligence. An element of surprise that left his prisoners in awe. No, the police chief was no savage; he knew how to behave.

'No smoking in the car.' In the back seat, the two men put the cigarettes behind their ears. No one argued with Omar's orders. It started to rain and they drove through the city streets, the light fragmented into shards by the raindrops. 'We can't see a thing,' one of the policemen complained. Omar wondered if the man was trying to provoke him. Behind his back, his colleagues called him The Mole. Speccy Four-Eyes. They threatened the prisoners: 'You'd better watch out or we'll send for The Bat.' And the prisoners, their eyes blindfolded so tightly that the fabric tore at their infected skin, would start to shake. Omar's reputation preceded him.

'Open the window, then, you idiot.' The policeman lowered his window and stuck his head outside. He looked as if he were searching the pavement for a wallet or a bunch of keys that he'd dropped.

'There!'

The chauffeur braked suddenly. The two men in the back seat leaped out of the vehicle. It was true that Omar was, if not blind, then extremely short-sighted. All he saw now were figures running and others pursuing them. He heard men shouting insults. The sound of a leather boot against a body. A yell of pain. Something banging against the iron shutter of a shop doorway and the rain hammering on the car roof. He sat there, immobile, staring at the windscreen streaming with raindrops that reflected the light from a street lamp and a few passing automobiles.

Then the two men got back into the car. In their filthy, sodden suits and their mud-spattered shoes.

'So?' Omar said.

'The van's here. They're going to take them away.'

'How many were there?'

'Two tramps.'

'You made a lot of noise. The neighbours saw you.'

'Those fuckers were drunk. That's why they put up a fight.'

'I don't want any noise. I don't want any scenes. Understood?'

The next day the king was due to welcome a delegation of foreign leaders and, as was always the case for such events, Omar and his men had been ordered to clean up the streets. To rid the city of its population of homeless people, lunatics, troublemakers. That evening they were making one last round and in the morning the streets would be clean. There would be nothing to see.

'What cannot be seen does not exist.'

If someone had asked him what his work consisted of, Omar would simply have told them that. To make the things that should not be seen disappear. To swallow them up, erase them, suffocate them, bury them. To veil them. Build walls around them. Dig holes for them. Omar was a master in the art of burial. A secrecy artist. Nobody could respond to questions as well as he could with a calm, opaque silence. Nothing could make him weaken, not even the tearful faces of mothers searching for their children or the pleas of a young wife whose husband had simply vanished one morning. In 1965, during the student riots, he had played his part in erasing all traces of the massacre. He and his men had taken control of the Ain Chock morgue and for days no one had been allowed to enter or leave without Omar's approval. Families had gathered outside the building, demanding to see their children's bodies. He had had them removed. Then, one night, he and his men loaded the corpses into the back of a pick-up truck. The corpses were small and thin; they weighed almost nothing in the arms of the policemen who had to carry them. They drove without headlights to the deserted cemetery and Omar would never forget the reflection of the moon on the gravestones or inside those holes that had been dug in various spaced-out parts of the cemetery, in a pattern intended to look random. Someone had wanted to pray, but Omar had stopped him. God had no business there.

In this poverty-stricken country all it took was a few small bribes. For the doctor who would testify that he had not seen any wounded people. For the gravedigger who, for a handful of dirhams, would forget the graves he had dug for the murdered children. Omar had been offered bribes hundreds of times, but he had always refused them. Often he would see his colleagues take brown envelopes stuffed full of cash. He saw them get rich and climb the ladder. They married rich girls from good families whose fathers were thrilled to have a son-in-law in the police. But Omar took nothing. He had only a modest apartment in town and a car, a beautiful Chevrolet that he had bought with his share of the inheritance Amine had passed on to him. Strangely, his integrity caused him only harm. His superiors considered him arrogant and puritanical; they resented the cold, proud way he displayed his austere life. They grew increasingly suspicious of this man who had never married or had children, this man who did not even appear to have affairs. He had no life beyond the police station. Who could trust such a man, a man with no vices? Omar knew they talked about him behind his back. His job was surveillance and he wondered who had been ordered to keep an eye on him.

'We going to the station, boss?' Brahim asked, startling Omar from his thoughts. The chauffeur had stopped at a cross-roads and was awaiting orders.

Omar turned to the two men in the back seat and told them to get out. They concealed their rage at being made to walk through the rain and hail a taxi. When they had gone, Omar turned to the chauffeur: 'Take me to her place, Brahim.'

* * *

As a young man Omar had been capable of going several nights without sleep. He would work in the basement of the police station, interrogating prisoners who were half-mad from the lack of sleep and the physical violence. The questions he asked them were always the same, in Arabic and in French. He spoke in a calm voice, almost gentle and reassuring, which the prisoners found disturbing. But tonight he lacked the courage. He felt overwhelmed by fatigue, sickened by his colleagues' stupidity. He felt as if he would never accomplish his mission, that he was forever doomed to keep silencing mouths, eliminating those who talked too much. He was tired of punishing, tired of violence. He was growing soft. For some time now he had been letting the prisoners speak and listening a little more attentively to what they said. One man in particular had made an impression on him. A man in his mid-twenties who printed a communist newspaper in his bathroom. Omar's men had abducted him one day and taken him, blindfolded, to a secret detention centre. There were dozens of such places all over the country. Labour camps and abandoned palaces. Townhouses and grimy basements. Places that nobody knew about, with walls so thick that the screams of the tortured would never be heard. Omar, though, heard everything. As his sight had deteriorated, he had become a giant ear, an immense ear capable of perceiving the faintest creak, the softest whisper. Even at a distance he could hear what people were saying on café terraces or in the back seats of public taxis. He had informers everywhere. Guards who feigned sleep in their wooden sentry boxes. Maids who rummaged through drawers when their employers were absent. Peanut vendors, shoe shiners, newsagents: they all had to report to Omar.

But this boy, this young communist, was different. With remarkable courage he had come through the endless torture sessions. His face swollen, his hands and feet bloody from being whipped, he had told Omar that this country was heading to its ruin. 'Can't you see that they're just using you to do their dirty work? They live in their grand palaces, drinking their whisky, swimming in their pools, playing on the bright-green fairways of their private golf courses while our children die of hunger and thirst. Tell me, where does that water come from? Is that why your generation fought the French? Today's bourgeoisie deserve nothing. They are corrupt neo-colonists who treat our people the exact same way the Europeans did. Open your eyes!'

The rain kept falling and Brahim, who drove quickly, left the city and took the coastal road towards Rabat. Less than an hour later they had reached the outskirts of the capital. By the roadside, a wall was visible. 'The wall of shame', as it was called by the left-wing militants, the trade unionists, all those opposed to the government. In clandestine meetings and in articles for illegally sold newspapers, this wall was held up as an example of the country's decadence. One month earlier Omar had learned that a documentary had been secretly filmed outside the shanty town of Yacoub El Mansour. 'To start with, I didn't understand,' explained the informer, a slum-dweller who made a little extra by talking to the police. 'The car was parked outside the neighbourhood, just in front of the wall. Inside there were three men. Two Moroccans and a European. The European was sitting in the back seat. He was the one with the camera.' The informer had done a good job: he had described the vehicle, noted down its number plate, and given detailed information about the physical appearance of the driver and his partner. It had taken Omar less than a day to discover that the Renault belonged to a communist activist who was being interviewed by a French journalist. They had tried to get into the shanty town to question the inhabitants, but the people there had been too afraid to talk. So they had had to make do with filming the wall. The journalist had been expelled, his films destroyed, and the communist had disappeared. Nobody would ever see that film.

The wall extended along part of the coastal road between Rabat and Casablanca, and it was high enough to hide the shanty town from passing motorists. Omar had supervised its construction. He had made the slum-dwellers build it themselves, explaining that it was to protect their children, who might wander out onto the road and be crushed to death under the wheels of some rich man's car. The wall was for their own good, and for the good of their wives, who, like all women, could not help flirting with the pretty boys who drove past. This wall, he told them, is to protect you from the shame you feel at the ugliness of your existence, your corrugated-iron shacks, your muddy streets, your worn old clothes hanging from washing lines. Do you really want the whole world to see your wives' knickers flapping in the wind, to see the holes in your children's jumpers?

His forehead pressed to the window, Omar thought about the young communist's clear voice. One night the prisoner had told him the story of that queen of Russia whom her ministers had wished to spare the sight of poverty and desolation in the countryside. And while she travelled around her lands, among her subjects, within her vast empire, she had no idea that the beautiful villages she was contemplating were merely painted cardboard sets. Brahim parked the car on Avenue de Temara, a few yards from the Orthodox church. The first glimmers of dawn were illuminating the dome-shaped belltower and the golden cross atop it. The pavements were full of puddles and men were walking, heads lowered, rugs under arms, towards the local mosque. The caretaker was sitting on the front steps of the apartment building. He was a thin man of indeterminate age, his chin covered in stubble, whose cigarettes smelled of bleach. He wore a grubby woolly hat and a brown woolly jumper given to him by some bourgeois woman. He and his wife had six children and they all lived cooped up together in a single ground-floor room. So he often stayed here, on the steps, smoking cigarettes that left a greyish residue on his tongue. Occasionally he would sweep the steps or rub the guardrail with a dirty rag. When he spotted Omar's car he rushed over to him.

'Hello, boss.'

'Hello, Hocine. Any news?'

'All quiet, boss. Nothing to report.'

'Is she here?'

'Yes, boss. She came home two hours ago. She came back on foot, boss, and she was carrying her shoes. I told her it wasn't a good idea to walk like that, in the middle of the night. I told her there are thugs around, but she said she didn't care. She says nothing can happen to her.'

Omar took a coin from his pocket and dropped it into Hocine's callused palm.

'Go buy yourself a coffee, my friend. And stop smoking. You're not looking too good.'

She opened the door and Omar looked at her ankles. Her slender, tanned ankles. He noticed she was bleeding.

'Did you get hurt?'

'Oh, it's nothing. New shoes. Are you hungry? Do you want a coffee?'

'Later. Let's sleep a bit first.'

He went through the little corridor and into the bedroom. He took off his jacket and his shirt and lay on the bed barefoot in his vest and trousers. A small dog with curly white fur was lying on a rug.

'Don't close the shutters.'

Omar claimed he loved this room because of the sunlight that poured into it early in the morning to warm his bones, even in the middle of winter. He said it was good to sleep enveloped in those golden beams, like an old cat or a lizard on the wall of a house. The truth was he was afraid of the dark. He was frightened, like a little kid. Afraid of closing his eyes. Omar's job was dangerous. Every day he risked his life and yet nothing, nothing at all, scared him as much as those moments when his eyelids grew heavy, so heavy that he couldn't hold them open a second longer and he fell asleep. In his dreams he fought with the night, and in the deep darkness he felt something move, he sensed the furtive movement of a predator, the threat of a hidden attack. The doctor had warned him. He was going blind. It was inexorable, incurable. Soon the world would be nothing more than a dark, opaque expanse, his life an interminable journey through damp subterranean tunnels in the company of moles, snakes and rats. Deprived of all light.

'What cannot be seen does not exist.'

'What did you say?'

'Nothing. Lie down next to me, Selma. Let's get some sleep.'

Selma couldn't sleep. She had stomach cramps and a sour taste in her mouth. She would have liked to get up, take a long shower, eat something, but instead she stayed where she was, lying next to her brother's body. She watched him, her big brother: he was so thin and his face, even in sleep, appeared nervous. She was holding his hand. This was the only way he could sleep, with his hand in hers, and she could feel Omar's rough, scaly skin against her palm. Her brother had come back into her life and she couldn't help believing that it was Mouilala who had driven Omar towards her. He often talked about their mother. He brought up childhood memories with a tenderness, a gentleness, that Selma had never sensed in him before. When he had knocked at her door a few weeks after she moved to Rabat, she had been afraid. She had thought he was here to punish her, dissuade her, drag her by the hair back to the bosom of the family. But he had visited her apartment in silence, his little dog tucked under his arm. The tiny kitchen with a view of the courtyard. The living room with its blue benches, its black varnished wooden table on top of which stood a large glass bowl filled with matchboxes. And then the bedroom bathed in sunlight.

'So this is where you live?'

Mouilala had warned her. Women had to be patient. Men softened over time. As they got older they became sentimental and sought consolation in the arms of their sisters or their mistresses. Mouilala had been right: Omar came to visit Selma several times a week. He asked her to cook him the meals he'd eaten as a child: split pea soup and carrot tajine. He gave her a record player and together they would listen to songs by Fairuz and Asmahan. He asked her to wear the same make-up as the Syrian diva, with thick black lines under her eyes, and he liked to watch her as she stood in front of the mirror, concentrated on her reflection, a kohl stick in her hand.

First and foremost he taught her to speak. Subject, verb, complement, as the teachers at the colonial school had drilled into them. He taught her a new grammar – of things unsaid, insinuations, the grammar of fear and universal surveillance. He taught her to beware the telephone, confidants, metaphors. He repeated constantly: 'Listen carefully and hold your tongue. What you don't say belongs to you. What you say belongs to your enemies.' He bought her a small leather-bound diary in which, until the end of her life, Selma would record a brief summary of each day in a code known only to herself. She told him once about an air hostess she was friends with. People called her 'the countess of the skies' because she put on airs and wore perfume bought in Paris. She smuggled forbidden magazines and books back to Morocco in her luggage and invited people to her home for clandestine reading sessions. That day, Omar softly stroked Selma's head, like a master rewarding his dog for fetching a stick.

Finally, her brother played the role expected of him. He protected her. Selma's life was not without risks and a few months before this she'd had to deal with a lover's fierce jealousy. The man, from a noble family, spent his days smoking hash pipes, which made him violent and paranoid. He harassed Selma. Interrogated her while they had sex. Forced her to tell him who she had seen, what she had done, and if she had, even in the secret depths of her heart, desired any man other than him. One night, in a fit of rage, he sliced up all Selma's clothes with a razor blade. And Omar found her like that, sobbing on her bed, surrounded by the shredded muslin of her dresses and blouses. 'Think yourself lucky he didn't test the blade on you. He must know you're my sister so he didn't dare.' Yes, she knew she was protected, but this feeling of security was mixed with a bitterness, a regret. Omar was no longer the severe, disapproving brother he had been before. He didn't beat her any more but he still gave her orders, still criticised her. Sit up straight. You smell of cigarettes. Don't laugh so loud. And what are you going to do at this party? Remove that lipstick, the other one was better. You're talking rubbish.

Staring at the ceiling, she thought: I hate them, I hate them all. I wish I never had to see them again. The previous night she had held people in her arms, she had laughed and danced, lifting up the hem of her skirt. She had thrown out *I love you*s and *I adore you*s, phrases she only spoke, in truth, because she wanted to hear something kind in response. The evening had begun at the bar of the Hassan Hotel and had continued at a cabaret run by a former prostitute from Corsica. At midnight the happy little gang had gone to a bachelor flat belonging to a government minister whose own wife was unaware of its existence. 'I should tell Omar that, but maybe he already knows.'

197

The minister liked to have his friends over, and to entertain them he would invite a group of cheerful, docile women. Air hostesses, hairdressers, beauticians and dancers. One of them in particular he was addicted to. A fortune-teller, her right eye blackened by a fist, who read cards all night and spoke in a low voice. He never made a decision without consulting her. Just then, he was nervous. The whole city was talking about the Pan Am affair and the arrest of a businessman accused of attempted corruption in a catering project. Ministers and senior civil servants had been fired. There were rumours of imminent arrests. On television the king had declared: 'Moral integrity is the secret of all success.' And the entire country had burst out laughing.

To see them at those parties, smiling and smartly dressed, you might have thought that these women were powerful. That they had the world at their feet. But, without husbands, they were nothing. Their lives were held together only by the grace of their lovers. Colonels and generals, businessmen and politicians' sons, playboys who would fly to London or Rome on a whim. Selma was one of them. She had left Meknes two years earlier. A former schoolfriend, Hind Benslimane, had told her about a training course for hairdressers in the capital. And Selma went there the day after her arrival. The woman in charge welcomed her enthusiastically. She held her hands and brought her face so close that Selma thought she was going to kiss her. 'You have the most beautiful skin I've ever seen,' the woman breathed ecstatically. Every evening the women who worked in the salon would throw handfuls of hair into bin liners. They cut them from the heads of old plastic dolls or sometimes from one another. 'It's for the police. They go through our rubbish.'

Selma quickly realised that she wasn't there to brush hair or give manicures and that most of their customers were in fact employed by the woman in charge. During the day the women would gather in the salon, where they would spend hours gossiping and filing their nails. They waxed each other's pubes, swapping secrets with their legs spread. In the evenings they would go out in a group to the capital's restaurants and night-clubs. The people who ran the disco paid them a commission.

Selma danced on the tables of the city's clubs. She danced until dawn at Jour et Nuit, Le Sphinx and La Cage, and men whirled her around. Selma spent her holidays in villas at Cabo Negro and went swimming in the Mediterranean. She had gone skiing on the slopes of Oukaïmeden and had even slept in a room at the Mamounia in Marrakech. The following spring, Selma would go to Club Med and eat enormous juicy king prawns with her fingers. Selma shopped for clothes in the most expensive boutiques in the city centre. Her lovers got their chauffeurs to drop her there and returned later to pay in cash for the silk dresses, the blouses and the lingerie made in Paris. Selma wore shoes that matched her dresses and real leather handbags in which she kept her packs of Marquise cigarettes and a lipstick.

Selma dreamed of having a passport and a plane ticket. She prayed that one day one of her lovers would take her to Paris or Madrid. But for now she had to be reasonable. Not ask for too much, not talk too much at all, show herself to be both discreet and amusing, superficial without being vulgar, not deny that she was a whore, and let the socialites take the spot-light. She had to pretend not to know, to play the innocent, the frightened virgin. At first, when she had sex, she didn't close her eyes. Some of the men took offence at this. They thought it indecent. So she lay on her side, placed the man's hand on her breast and, as he entered her, stared at the window or the wall. They weren't happy when she spoke either, when she told them what she liked. Some of them got angry: 'Don't try to teach me what to do.' She pretended to submit. She learned to behave like those dogs that lie on their backs, stick out their tongues and beg to be tickled. She feigned not only submission but docility too. She did not feign desire because the men didn't like that, but she hammed up her surprise, giving little moans. However, she knew what to do to give herself pleasure. She knew how to make her own body feel as light as a feather. From the soles of her feet to the roots of her hair she was a breath of air, a cloud of foam, a drop of liqueur slowly trickling down a throat and warming it. Alone, she came.

The women often argued. About who would receive the most beautiful jewellery. Who would have the thickest wad of cash hidden in her bra. Who would be given an apartment or a car by her lover. They pulled each other's hair, cursed each other with insults. Once, one of them even threw hot sauce from a potato tajine into a rival's face. They hated each other, then made up. Deep down, they had no one else they could depend on. They would slip each other the contact details for a back-street abortionist or warn each other about a man who liked to hit them during sex. 'And he doesn't even pay well. I'd steer well clear if I were you.' And all of them drank. Because there were so many parties, all of them the same, and the joy was always faked, they drank. And, the previous night, Selma had had one too many. She had wanted to please the minister, who boasted about his imported champagne and whisky and who snapped his fingers to summon a young maid to bring them ice cubes.

She had drunk too much even though she knew it made her unpleasant, made her say harsh things, ramble on. Alcohol protected her from the shame but it always drove her to excess. At two in the morning the maid had left the kitchen and one of the female guests had whispered to Selma: 'She looks like a little bitch, don't you think?' Selma had wondered if the girl was an informer too. If she listened at doors and called the police to deliver her report as soon as the house was empty. Selma would not say anything about the alcohol. She would not admit to Omar that she had been sick. She had taken refuge in a room at the back of the apartment, lying on the floor, her legs up against the wall. Her skirt had fallen around her hips, exposing her turquoise lace knickers. Now and again her stomach would spasm and she would hiccup as if she were about to throw up, but nothing came out. She made the same sound that dogs make when they are choking on a bone. First she had hoped that someone would come, and then she had prayed to be left alone, to be forgotten, for the party to end and for nobody to enter this room which, to judge from the clutter within it, was used as a sort of storeroom. She had fallen asleep, legs against her chest, head on the tiles. Someone had shaken her – 'Come on, get up' – and she had opened her eyes. She had got on all fours. 'Time to go home.' 'I'm going, I'm going.' And she had made it to the door of this stranger's apartment and gone outside, the door banging shut behind her.

She no longer felt nauseated, but something was bubbling up inside her. It was anger. Hate, even. Yes, she hated them.

She cursed them. She wished she would never see them again. She wished they would die and she could forget forever what they had turned her into. A pathetic, screeching actress in a bad film. She heard herself repeating the same phrases, the same jokes, and now she was no longer drunk she remembered that one of them, the cruellest of them all, had said wearily: 'Yes, we know, you already said that.' And it had been as if he had spat in her face, his words a veiled threat that she had become too boring to be invited any more.

Selma hated them and yet, as soon as she wasn't with them, as soon as a day passed without hearing from them, she was seized by anxiety. She made resolutions. She believed herself capable of self-sacrifice and imagined becoming a real grown-up, wise and reasonable. She imagined finding a decent job, in a city-centre office or shop. She would not owe anyone anything then; she would live without surveillance. Tidying the house, spending her nights watching television or smoking in the bath. She also swore that she would visit her daughter more often and that one day she would bring her back to this apartment where they would share the same bed. The thought of Sabah made her feel sick. Her daughter, whom she found impossible to love, whom she could not help considering an accident, a misfortune visited upon her. Sabah had always been a hindrance. Even when her daughter was just an embryo, growing inside her belly, Selma had thought of her as a curse preventing her from ever being alone. Men could not understand that. This propensity they had to colonise you from the inside. This desire they had to push themselves into you, to invade you. The foetus crowding your guts. The penises penetrating you, wanting you to be as deep as possible, as wet as a tropical jungle. Women, thought Selma, are like those countries devastated by foreign armies, the earth scorched, the inhabitants forced to forget their own language, their own gods.

Then her telephone rang. She was invited to a party and the weight was lifted from her chest. She jumped for joy, opened her wardrobe and began tossing dresses and silk slips onto the bed.

In January 1971 Mehdi took the national exam for financial inspection and finished top of the year. Only five Moroccan students were given jobs. Three from Fes, one from Casablanca, one from Rabat. Mehdi was put in charge of the tax office. He moved into a large office on the fourth floor of a building in the city centre. Janine, his secretary, was French; she had married a Moroccan man whom she had met at university in Lyon. She was a good secretary, rigorous and organised, but Mehdi avoided her. When she was in a room with him he tried not to meet her eye. She made him ill at ease. He hated her long red fingernails, which made a fast, sinister tapping sound whenever she used her typewriter. Her voice irritated him, as did the way she would take a deep breath before beginning an endless conversation. If you could even call it a conversation . . . The truth was that she generally just talked to herself, answering her own questions without giving Mehdi time to get a word in. He spoke to her through the half-open door of his office, where he recorded a list of instructions on a little Dictaphone. Janine called him *'Monsieur le directeur'* and so did Simo, the caretaker. Mehdi had imagined that this kind of deference, these submissive gestures, the way Simo had of holding the door open for him, bowing his head, agreeing with everything he said, would make him uncomfortable. When he parked his car outside the office building Simo would rush over to meet him. He would wait outside his car then follow him to the building, sometimes even daring to brush some dust off Mehdi's suit with his fingertips. The first few times, Mehdi had slipped the old man a banknote and had responded affectionately to the blessings with which Simo, who smelled of squalor and tinned sardines, had showered him. But then this ritual, repeated a thousand times, had wearied him to the point of contempt. Nowadays he could not bring himself to smile at this servile, devoted man who tried every day to earn from Mehdi enough cash to buy himself a few beers at a bar near the central market.

Mehdi took no pleasure from the exercise of power, from observing the fear or respect he inspired in those around him. All he thought about was work, from dawn until night. He was still that studious schoolboy, obsessed with the idea of pleasing his teacher, and he set out to reform the bureaucracy he had inherited, to turn it into an exemplar of efficiency and modernity. He upbraided the civil servants in an attempt to rouse them from their torpor. Almost every day he would send a letter to his supervisory department suggesting innovations, fiscal reforms, training seminars for civil servants. His old friends from university saw him as a sell-out and a traitor. He had given up his dream of writing a book, he had given up his ambition of becoming an important university lecturer, and now he had to prove he had been right. He wanted to convince them, and convince himself, that it was possible to change the system from within, without losing his way, without being corrupted.

This job at the tax office had not given him the satisfaction he'd been expecting. Mehdi had to put up with the indifference of his superiors, but most of all with the complaints, the tears and sometimes even the fury of taxpayers. Everyone considered themselves wronged, misunderstood. They reacted angrily to Mehdi's coldness, his intransigence, which they regarded as a Western attitude. This chief taxman might be an Arab but he acted like a white man. Refusing their offers of compromise, their envelopes, their explanations. Asking in a severe voice, whenever he spotted a stack of cash hidden between two sheets of paper: 'What is that? You'd better take it back. I'll pretend I didn't see anything.' The taxpayers took offence. They threatened to go over his head and boasted about having friends in high places who would punish him, this little shit, this nobody, who had dared treat them this way.

Sometimes prominent figures from the provinces would come to his office to see him. Older men in woollen djellabas and saffron-yellow turbans who stared in astonishment at this young Moroccan in his ironed shirts and cufflinks. They appeared to understand nothing Mehdi said to them and they remembered that this was how the French had got what they wanted from them. Paperwork. That damned paperwork and all those big words they couldn't read, humiliating them. Paperwork frightened them more than a whole gang of armed men. Nothing was more guaranteed to make them lose their composure. Mehdi felt ashamed. Ashamed of feeling so different from these men who looked like his father Mohamed, his father whom he never saw any more. He played with his cufflinks, he smiled at them. He said: 'Janine will explain the process to you, okay?'

One day he requested an audit on a man who, considering the scale of his assets and revenue, was paying very little in tax. He expedited the investigation, went through the man's case file, and had no difficulty proving that he had been defrauding the government for years. The man's name was Karim Boulhas but he was nationally famous as 'the sardine king'. Boulhas came from a wealthy family that had made its fortune in commerce and he ran the biggest canning factory in Morocco, at the port city of Safi. In recent years he had invested in property, bought up land, and he was planning to build a hotel, convinced as he was that tourism represented the country's future. Mehdi sent him letters and took pleasure in imagining the fraudster's reaction when he saw how much money he owed. Millions of dirhams. Karim Boulhas turned up at the headquarters of the tax office one afternoon. The summer heat had still not abated: Janine's chignons kept collapsing and when she uncrossed her thighs they made a sound like suction pads. Boulhas entered Mehdi's office accompanied by a plump, shy girl. Her black oily hair was tied in a long braid that hung all the way down her back. Drops of sweat beaded on her upper lip and she slowly moved her tongue under her nose to lick them.

The conversation began politely. Karim Boulhas asked Mehdi where he was from. He said he knew some people called Daoud, from El Jadida. Were they relatives of his? Mehdi said no. With his face blank and his eyes fixed on this wealthy man, he rejected all the unspoken rules of cronyism. Boulhas was sweating; he patted his shiny forehead with a handkerchief. Mehdi handed him a sheet of paper covered in figures. Boulhas glanced at the document before pushing it away. 'Oh, but I don't understand those numbers at all! You're the educated man. You have the knowledge and I have the money, as they say. I'm sure we could come to an arrangement.' Nodding at the girl, he added: 'This is my daughter. She's eighteen.' Mehdi did not understand at first. He thought Boulhas was seeking his pity or simply trying to change the subject. Moving the discussion to a more emotional plane, as taxpayers so often did. 'She's a nice girl,' Boulhas said. That was when Mehdi noticed that the girl was smiling at him. Her features were rather coarse, her teeth crooked, but there was something sad and vulnerable about her that touched Mehdi.

'This is between us, right?' Boulhas asked. 'You are still young, full of life, and you must be exhausted from all your work. It's obvious that you're not the type of man to waste his time having fun. I'm thinking about you, you understand?'

Mehdi sat back in his seat. The teenager's hands were placed demurely in her lap. Docile as a mule, submissive to the desires that others formulated for her, used to nodding and obeying. She looked up at him with her lovely aubergine-coloured eyes.

'Maria,' her father ordered, 'say hello to the gentleman.'

A few days later Mehdi received a note from his superiors. Karim Boulhas was an important man and it was out of the question to create a scandal while the country was going through difficult times. 'I'm relying on you, Monsieur Daoud, to find a solution that can satisfy all parties.' Boulhas returned to Rabat on several occasions. He gave Simo and Janine boxes of tinned anchovies and sardines. Mehdi could hear his secretary's giggles through the door. He had to acknowledge that Boulhas was a pleasant, cheerful man whose charm was difficult to resist. When Mehdi told him the sum he had to pay, Boulhas slapped himself on the forehead. 'Are you trying to ruin me, my son? No, no, you have to recalculate. I am happy to pay, as I told you, but I can't let you take bread from my children's mouths. You have to be reasonable, ya ouldi.'

Boulhas proved himself a formidable businessman. After spending so long in his company, Mehdi began to take an interest in his plans. Boulhas was ambitious and clever and he had no intention of devoting his whole life to fishmeal and tinned foods. Of course, he was proud that he was able to sell his products in France, Spain, Thailand, and soon he would be exporting to the USSR and Poland too. But what he wanted above all was to build hotels with swimming pools and holiday clubs for sun-starved Europeans. In June 1971 they signed an agreement and Boulhas was so satisfied that he invited Mehdi to visit his offices in Safi. 'There's no need to discuss it. I'll send my chauffeur to pick you up tomorrow. And don't wear one of your bourgeois suits. You don't need shiny shoes on a sardine boat.'

The next day, at six in the evening, Boulhas's chauffeur parked outside the tax office building. Mehdi got in the car, dressed as usual in his dark suit and his shirt with cufflinks. They drove for hours along a poor road and on several occasions Mehdi was afraid they were going to cause an accident. The chauffeur paid no attention to traffic laws or speed limits, overtaking trucks on narrow two-lane roads even when it was impossible to see what was coming in the other direction. He constantly honked his horn and insulted other drivers, and by the time they arrived on the outskirts of Safi, Mehdi was in a state of nervous exhaustion. It was the first time he had visited the former Portuguese trading post and he was disappointed to arrive after dark, not to be able to admire the impressive fortress overlooking the sea. As soon as they entered the Djorf El Youdi neighbourhood, the smell of fish filled the car.

Outside a café Mehdi spotted Boulhas's imposing figure. The businessman was wearing khaki canvas trousers, a thick woollen cardigan and plastic boots. He got into the car beside Mehdi and started laughing. 'Oh, my son, didn't I tell you to wear comfortable clothes? We're going fishing, you know, not swaggering around a cocktail bar in the capital!' Boulhas's company owned its own sardine boats and Mehdi boarded one of them, wearing a pair of borrowed boots. 'We'll be barefoot anyway.' While the men prepared the cerco, the red net three hundred yards long that was used to catch fish, Boulhas drew the taxman into his cabin. He poured him a cup of tea then opened a tin of sardines swimming in oil. 'For a long time, people from here were afraid of the sea. My grandfather, God rest his soul, told all sorts of legends about that. He said that Moroccan peasants were suspicious of the coasts. Those poor buggers believed water was the territory of genies and evil monsters. These people are not bad at their job,' he added, gesturing to the fishermen on the boat, 'but they're nothing compared to the Spanish or the Portuguese, believe me.' He explained to Mehdi that he planned to buy a bigger boat soon, one on which they would be able to freeze the fish they caught, permitting them to go further out to sea. He was also going to order one of those ultrasound machines, a depth sounder, to locate shoals of fish and to read the profile of the sea bed on an echosounder. The boat left the port. The fishermen walked along the wooden boards and Mehdi observed their feet, which were enormous and covered with wounds, their black toenails eroded by salt. Behind them the city disappeared and the fishermen began searching for shoals of sardines. To spot them, they followed the groups of dolphins and seabirds that were in turn seeking out the phosphorescent reflections of fish scales on the water's surface. They started to sing. It was a song that Mehdi had never heard before, and which surprised him with its cheerfulness and harmony. The men's voices, as they leaned over the rail, were clear and powerful.

'They've found some!' Boulhas announced. They tied the end of the cerco to a small boat commandeered by the chief fisherman and one of his crew and towed it towards the spot where the sardines had been detected. Then the ship began spinning slowly. Boulhas took Mehdi to the hold, at the front of the boat, and they watched as a vast number of sardines

211

poured into it. The captain, back on board, patted Mehdi's back. 'Beautiful, isn't it?' Mehdi had to admit to himself that the captain was right: it really was beautiful, more beautiful than many of the things he had seen in his life. Day broke and the water took on a yellow tint that reminded him of wheatfields in the light of August, the year he had last seen Aïcha. His heart contracted. He had to write to her. He had to tell her about all this.

They headed back towards Safi. The captain sent a radio message and when they arrived an alarm blared loudly in the port. This was the industrialists' version of the call to arms. Vans were driven out to the fields of caper bushes and wheat to collect farmworkers who would come to the port to earn a few dirhams. Mehdi was sleepy and cold. He wished he could lie down in a bed, under a thick blanket, and dream of dolphins, their bodies shining in the moonlight. But Boulhas had no intention of going to bed. 'This is the real life, my son! The sea, fishing, not that miserable office life you're inflicting on yourself. Listen carefully and you'll see: the two of us could found an empire together!' They sat in a café and Boulhas ordered two bowls of mushroom soup, some bread and coffee. For a few months Boulhas had been travelling regularly to Marrakech. 'Everyone thinks I'm crazy but I'm sure it's the place to be. A city where it's warm even in winter – that's the dream, don't you think? Believe me, if I do a good job, I'll build a better hotel than the Mamounia and everyone will want to stay there. The Spanish figured that out before we did. Franco said it: tourism is the future. He is giving work to his people and you should see the Andalusians who came to work here ten years ago, they're opening hotels now, filled with English and

German customers.' He belched softly, sucked his oil-covered fingertips, and led Mehdi into his factory, across from the café.

An infernal racket filled the vast warehouse. All the workers there were women. There were at least two hundred of them, maybe more. They worked standing up, dressed lightly despite the cold. Their feet, most of them shod only in rubber sandals, were ankle-deep in brackish water, mingled with fish guts and blood. Some of them carried babies or toddlers on their backs and kept them quiet by swaying from side to side or clicking their tongues. They scaled the fish at top speed while foremen yelled at them to go faster. Mehdi felt ridiculous standing there in his suit, his damp trouser hems tucked inside his boots. He was falling asleep and could not follow Boulhas's explanations. He fiddled nervously with his cufflinks and one of them fell from his wrist. He saw it gleaming among the fish heads that lay at the bottom of a plastic bin. He was about to bend down and retrieve the cufflink, which he had bought to celebrate getting his job at the tax office, when a white-coated foreman pushed past him and ordered the women to take out the dregs. Mehdi watched as one of the female workers leaned down and picked up the rubbish bin. She carried it to the back of the factory and Mehdi didn't dare ask for his silver cufflink.

Before letting Mehdi leave, Boulhas insisted that the young tax inspector go home with him. The sardine king lived in a large house outside town. He ushered Mehdi into a reception room furnished with benches in bright, brocaded nylon. Boulhas slipped away then and Mehdi was left alone in front of a table covered with food. Almond cakes, briouats slathered with honey, aniseed-flavoured biscuits like the ones he used to eat as a child. A maid walked through the room, lowering her head when she saw him. He felt as if he had been sitting there for hours and in the end he stretched out his legs and rested his head against a cushion. He was close to falling asleep when Maria came in. The young woman greeted him, then picked up a plate of patisseries and held it in front of his face. Mehdi took one of the cakes but did not bite into it. He just held it in his hand and looked at Maria's face, at the long braid of hair which snaked down over her breasts. He told her he had been feeling tired and apologised for lying down on the bench, his bare feet on the rug. 'Do you know when your father will be back?'

'My father has left,' she replied. 'He asked me to tell you that the chauffeur will take you back to Rabat later. He wants you to feel at home here. He says you should take your time.'

For a second Mehdi thought about getting up, thanking her for her hospitality and rushing to the door to find the chauffeur. But Maria was staring at him with her pleading eyes, her aubergine eyes, and he was fascinated by their violet gleam.

'Did you go fishing tonight?'

'Yes. Have you been on one of your father's boats before?'

'Oh no!' she said, laughing. 'Those boats are not for girls.'

Maria had no gift for conversation. She agreed with everything Mehdi said. He asked her if she was a student and she explained that she had finished school and was now helping her mother at home. He wanted to know what she liked. Music? Films? She shrugged. 'Do you like to read?' he asked. 'I don't know,' she answered. Finally Mehdi got to his feet and said goodbye. When he got in the car, he was still holding the uneaten piece of cake.

In the back seat he thought that it would not be unpleasant to be married to a woman like Maria. A girl who would take care of him. Their children would be beautiful. She would withdraw to the kitchen whenever they had guests. When they made love, she would moan softly and keep her eyes closed. She would take him back to his roots, and during Ramadan, half-asleep on a bench, he would hear her telling off the children and ordering them not to wake their father. It was as if Maria spoke an ancient tongue, a language Mehdi had once known, long ago, whose memory would be rekindled in his mind by her sweetness, her docility. And as he dozed in the car, Mehdi saw again the tall blonde woman standing by the side of the pool on Aïcha's farm. She looked at him. And she dived in.

At the end of June 1971 Mehdi received an invitation to the king's forty-second birthday party, to be held at his summer palace in Skhirat, by the ocean. His minister remarked upon His Majesty's concern for the country's young executives. He was insistent that all guests must come in casual attire, leaving their suits and tuxedos in their wardrobes. 'Even the ministers and generals have been told to dress down.'

Mehdi would never have dared admit this to anyone, particularly not his former university friends, but this invitation sent him into a state of nervous excitement. He had never been inside any of the king's official palaces before. He had never attended such a prestigious reception, with all the country's top diplomats, ministers, military officers and friends of the royal family. He felt as if he had made it. Or, rather, as if he was about to make it. On 10 July, the day of the king's birthday party, he would take his place among the great and the good of Morocco. What excited and worried him was not the magnificence of the palace, the arcane rules of protocol or the fact that he would not know anyone there. No, like a child about to meet a film star or a singer, what obsessed Mehdi was the idea of seeing the king up close. This is ridiculous, he kept telling himself: the king is just a man like any other; the power he possesses does not make him sacred or special. And yet now, whenever he walked past any of the dozens of portraits of Hassan II displayed in town, he would tell himself: 'I'm going to see him in real life, maybe even talk to him. And he will smile at me and say my name. That means my future is assured.' He was ashamed of these thoughts, which he knew to be base and unworthy, but he couldn't help rejoicing at the idea that he had been chosen, from among thousands of others. Singled out. In the most fashionable boutique in town he bought a pair of white trousers and a pale-pink short-sleeved shirt. He paid a fortune for a pair of leather moccasins and went to a barber to have his hair cut and his beard trimmed.

The night before the party, he could not fall asleep. The heat in his apartment was suffocating and he spent the night lying on his bed under the open windows, waiting for the morning breeze. At six o'clock he got up. The sky was overcast: it would be another baking day. By eight o'clock he had showered and dressed and he was pacing around his living room, incapable of reading, working or even just sitting still. He was afraid of falling asleep on the old bench and being late for the lunch. One of his colleagues had warned him: it was important to arrive neither too early (for fear of appearing impatient and ridiculous) nor too late (for fear of offending the king, who would inaugurate the meal). When the tension became unbearable, Mehdi grabbed the keys for the Simca and decided to set off. He would get a head start, in case the car broke down, and he could always stop off and see Henri, whose beach hut was on the way to the palace. Mehdi could not possibly consume alcohol in the king's residence, but he would ask Henri to give him a glass of white wine. He could drink it on the terrace and it would help him relax.

He drove to the centre of town then joined the coastal road towards Skhirat. As soon as he was out of Rabat he felt calmer, almost in a holiday mood, and he started thinking how good he looked in his outfit, how surprised Henri would be to see him dressed so elegantly. To the left of the road the town had given way to countryside. Farmers were selling vegetables in little wooden shacks by the roadside: sweet peppers, onions, tomatoes. Then the ocean appeared, glittering in the sunlight, and in the distance Mehdi could see the ochre ramparts of an old kasbah surrounded by palm trees. Below that were the rocks where waves crashed in flurries of foam and some young barefoot boys were fishing for cockles and crabs.

He parked the car outside Henri's beach hut. The front door hung ajar. The living room and the kitchen were empty. He called out but no one answered. Eventually he found Henri asleep on the terrace, lying on a canvas deckchair, a book open in his lap.

'Henri?'

The lecturer opened his eyes and a smile lit up his face when he recognised his former student. 'Mehdi? What a nice surprise!'

Mehdi looked down at his overpriced moccasins and decided he would not tell Henri about the king's birthday. Henri was too polite to criticise him or express his disapproval, but Mehdi felt certain he would be disappointed. Mehdi did not want to be thought of as a sell-out, a traitor, a bourgeois hypocrite.

'Well, well . . . You look very elegant. And I like your beard now. Less Karl Marx.'

Mehdi stroked his chin. 'Yeah. Well, we're all getting older, aren't we? Isn't Monette here?'

'No, but they shouldn't be long now. You're a little early.'

'Early?'

'Yeah, she's gone to the airport to pick up Aïcha. She's spending the summer here. Don't tell me you didn't know?'

Mehdi had arrived here feeling swollen with pride and self-confidence, but now, hearing this news, he felt as if he were melting, crumbling, liquefying. His outfit suddenly struck him as vulgar and embarrassing. Henri must think that it was for her, for Aïcha, that he had bought these too-tight trousers and this shirt which now felt as if it were choking him.

Henri clambered out of his deckchair. 'I'm sorry, I haven't even offered you a drink. I haven't been sleeping too well at night, so during the day all I have to do is open a book and I'm gone. Why don't we open a bottle of white wine?'

Mehdi nodded. His tongue was stuck to the roof of his mouth and he could not utter a single word. Aïcha was coming. In a few minutes, maybe in an hour, she would be standing here, in front of him. What message was fate trying to send him? He watched as Henri returned from the kitchen, bottle in hand. His former professor was saying something but Mehdi did not hear him. His head was too full of thoughts. I ought to leave now, he thought. If I don't, everything will be screwed. He wondered if anyone would notice his absence at the birthday party. Would the minister look for him among the other guests, to introduce him to the king as a young man with a bright future? No, Mehdi told himself, he would have bigger fish to fry.

'Hell of a time for her to arrive, isn't it?' Henri asked, laughing.

'What do you mean?' Mehdi stared at him, his face creased in an anxious frown.

'The king's birthday, in Skhirat. Monette was afraid she wouldn't be able to get to the airport with everything going on. I offered to go with her but she wanted to do it alone. You know what those two are like.'

No, Mehdi didn't know. He didn't know anything any more. He gulped down his glass of white wine. He could feel the cold liquid running down into his empty stomach. If he got drunk he wouldn't have to think any more. It would become impossible to back out then, to get in his car and introduce himself to the members of the Court. He looked at his watch. Almost eleven. For a few seconds he stared at the hands on that little round face. Then he gave his glass to Henri, who poured him another one.

'Nervous, huh?' Henri was amused by his friend's attitude, which he attributed to romantic feelings. Mehdi could not keep still. He sat in the deckchair then got up again. His trousers were digging into his belly and he stood there, glass in hand, his gaze switching from the front door to the ocean and back again. The sky was a very pale blue, almost white, and his shirt was drenched with sweat. It was so hot that the ocean itself looked like it was boiling. The huge waves crashed onto the beach with a sound like thunder.

'Could you lend me a pair of trunks?'

'You want to go swimming? Really?' Mehdi was already unbuttoning his shirt, there in the middle of the terrace, as though he were all alone in the world. 'Hang on, follow me. I have what you need.'

Mehdi wished he could tell him. He would have loved to have the courage to ask Henri for his advice. 'Will she be happy to see me? Will she think I'm setting a trap for her again? Tell me, Henri, is she still angry with me?' But he said nothing and locked himself in the bathroom. He got undressed, put on the trunks, which were a bit too big for him, and went down to the beach where the sand burned the soles of his feet. He started running and threw himself into the hollow of a wave that was coming towards him. Every time he lifted his head out of the water he had to dive down again to avoid being swept away. The waves kept coming, ever higher, full of foam and salt like the drool of a rabid dog. He tried to swim but it was not his arms or legs that carried him forward. His feet kicked in the void. He was pulled out by the current, further and further from shore. He opened his myopic eyes. The sand and the hut had disappeared and all he could see was the infinite black expanse of bubbling water. There was no point trying to resist so he let himself be rolled like a stone by the backwash. With one hand he held up his trunks, which were sliding down his thighs. He couldn't catch his breath but he wasn't afraid. He let his body be sucked into the depths. On his skin he could feel the bite and sting of sand and shells. He thought about the way Aïcha swam, her grace and tenacity. And, once again, he remembered the image of the tall blonde woman by the side of the pool, in her mauve swimsuit. Now and then he would manage to raise his head above the surface of the water, to suck in a mouthful of air, and then he was swallowed again, dragged down towards the bottom, flung around like a rag in a washing machine. But the ocean didn't want him. He was still holding on with one hand to his trunks when it spat him out onto the shore, his hair full of sand and stones. Henri was there and he helped him to his feet.

'You scared the shit out of me. I almost went in after you.'

'Everything's fine,' said Mehdi. 'The current was stronger than I realised, that's all.'

Henri wrapped him in a towel and they went back to the terrace. They finished the bottle of white wine and opened a second one. Mehdi chain-smoked cigarettes, squeezing the filter tightly between his thumb and his index finger. At the palace, now, they must already have served lunch. The king would be sitting at his table alone, as protocol dictated. Mehdi was drunk now. His eyelids were heavy, his thoughts hazy, and there was a satisfied smile on his face. It was the most beautiful day in the history of the world. Nothing could happen to him. Fate continued to make his decisions for him and all he had to do was submit, to abandon himself, to trust in destiny as he had trusted in the current that had brought him safely back to shore. He felt refreshed by his swim, his body relaxed. He looked at his watch. The hands were motionless. He had forgotten to take it off before he dived into the sea and now it wasn't working any more.

Then he heard a car engine. A woman's voice. It was Monette, calling Henri, asking him to help her carry the suitcase. Mehdi felt as if he was still somewhere deep in the ocean, and the sounds that reached him there were distant, muffled. He stayed sitting in his deckchair, with his back to the beach hut. He could not bring himself to stand up. He imagined that, the moment he saw her again, his heart would stop beating. Through all those months spent thinking about her, torturing himself, Aïcha had become almost unreal, like one of those mythological creatures who cannot be looked in the eye without the beholder being transformed into a pillar of salt. And yet here she was. Just in front of him. He held up his hand to shade himself from the blinding sun. Here she was, her long straight hair cascading down over her bare shoulders. She was wearing a black dress with thin straps and he stared up at her slender bust, her long neck, and lastly her face. He stood up so suddenly that his head started spinning. She kissed him on the cheek and in that instant, as she was leaning towards him, he had to force himself not to hug her. Not to yell 'I love you' and 'Please forgive me, I beg you.' Instead he said, simply, 'Hello', and smiled at her.

Monette set the table. 'So are we allowed to have some wine or have you drunk it all?' She had been afraid they weren't going to make it back. 'There was a roadblock just after the palace. Some military trucks had been parked sideways across the street. Apparently they were stopping all cars coming from Rabat. But they let us through. We must have made a good impression on them!'

Mehdi did not speak much during lunch. He gave peremptory replies to the questions Henri asked him about his job at the tax office and his new responsibilities. Aïcha asked if he was still writing and Mehdi got into a muddle. He concluded: 'As soon as I have time, I'll get back to it.' Occasionally she would look up at him and stare without smiling. She seemed less shy than she had before, more sure of herself. She ate and drank with gusto. Monette kept shooting her knowing looks and Mehdi thought they must be laughing at him. When Aïcha talked about Strasbourg, she kept going on about 'David this' and 'David that', as if that damned young man had become an essential part of her life. Not only that, but David was currently in Spain with his parents and it was not impossible that he would join her here, in August. 'We'd be very happy to have him to stay,' said Monette with an amused smile. 'Wouldn't we, Henri?' Henri nodded but said nothing. He was staring at Mehdi's hand, the fingers of which had been drumming on the wooden table for some time now.

Mehdi felt like he was about to explode. His drunkenness had turned to anger and he regretted having stayed, having waited for this woman who seemed to be enjoying his humiliation. He should have gone to the palace, continued along his own path, thought only of himself and his career. He would have met important people there and written down their names, addresses and telephone numbers in the little notebook that he always kept with him. His watch was broken and he had spent all that money on his clothes for nothing. What a mistake it had been to open himself up to this hurt. He was about to invent an excuse to leave when a man, one of their neighbours, came to the front door. Henri stood for a few minutes with him in the doorway and when he returned to the terrace Monette noticed he was looking very pale.

'What's going on?'

'That was Robert. He says something's happened in Skhirat. People have heard shots being fired and apparently he can smell gunpowder at his place. For the moment he thinks we should stay where we are. He'll let us know as soon as he hears something.' He went to fetch the radio from their bedroom and switched it on. He seemed relieved when he found the national radio station, which was playing an Egyptian love song. 'And we still don't have that damn telephone! It's intolerable, not knowing what's happening.'

The Egyptian song ended abruptly. And Henri recognised the notes of 'La Galette', a military march. All four of them were staring at the radio now, as if this object contained the answers to the questions that tormented them.

'What about my parents?' Aïcha said. 'They must be worried.'

They began guessing what might have happened. The Libyans had fomented an attack. The king was dead and would be replaced by a regent. All four of them felt a mixture of fear and excitement. They were aware that they were living through an important moment, a historical day that would be written about in books. Unable to keep still, they began pacing around the terrace, smoking. Two helicopters flew over the beach. Aïcha and Monette surrendered to panic: 'What's going to happen to us?' Henri started lecturing them about how it had been bound to happen, how he'd sensed the status quo could not be maintained much longer. Mehdi grew impassioned, talking about popular revolutions and guerrilla wars. He was so glad he hadn't gone to the birthday party. Not only because he was still alive, but because now he could pretend he had always been on the right side. He could say he had not rubbed shoulders with all those powerful people. Later, if anyone asked, he would explain that, yes, he had been invited but he had refused to go, wishing to signal his opposition to such an indecent display of luxury.

'I was supposed to be there,' he admitted.

'What are you talking about?' Henri asked.

'The king's birthday party. I was invited.'

'Ah, now I understand.'

'Understand what?'

'Your clothes, the way you were acting. You should thank Aïcha, then. I reckon you're much better off here than you would be there.'

225

He turned up the volume on the radio. 'Attention! Attention! The army has taken power. The monarchy has fallen. The people's army is in control. A new era is beginning.'

Throughout the afternoon and part of the evening, they believed that the king was dead and that Morocco had fallen into the hands of its generals. Aïcha thought about the portrait of Hassan II in her father's office. She remembered the jubilation that had greeted Mohammed V's return from exile. She could not imagine her country without a king. Were they really going to become one of those states run by soldiers? On the radio, the message from the army was played over and over on a loop, and Henri was being driven mad by the absence of news. 'Why hasn't Robert come back? We can't just stay here forever, waiting like idiots.'

'What else did you have in mind?' Monette asked him.

Night fell, plunging the beach into darkness. They had finished the wine and Henri went to fetch some beers from the fridge. Only a few cigarettes were left, so they shared them, passing each one from hand to hand like a joint. They fell silent. All four of them appeared to withdraw into themselves. In the face of the unknown it seemed pointless to talk about something they knew nothing about, to make speculations that would probably turn out to be false. They thought about their own futures. About the consequences this would have for each of them. In their secret hearts, they calculated what they might lose and what they could gain. What would happen to their careers, their ambitions, their happiness? They couldn't have said if this coup d'état was a good thing or a bad thing. If they should worry or rejoice. But they were all afraid.

The moon, as round and incandescent as a cigar end, was reflected in the big puddles that the ocean had left behind as it withdrew. From the terrace the beach looked like a ploughed field, and in the distance some vague shapes reminded Aïcha of the outlines of oxen. It was almost midnight by the time Robert returned. General Oufkir had spoken on the radio. The coup had failed and the king was alive. The loyalist army, deployed in the streets of the capital, had retaken the radio station and the Ministry of the Interior. In Rabat rumours spread like wildfire, passing from house to house, fuelled by the tales of those who had survived the coup and returned home and the lies of those who were jealous that they had not seen anything. Already the traitors' names were being whispered: General Medbouh, Colonel Chelouati and Lieutenant Colonel Ababou, director of the NCO training school in Ahermoumou, whose young soldiers had led the coup d'état. Robert had spent the evening on the phone, but he was incapable of answering Henri and the others, who assailed him with questions. What had motivated the coup? 'Too early to say.' How many people were dead? 'Dozens, maybe more. Someone told me that there were corpses floating in the swimming pool at the palace. They spanked a general and hunted the king to the toilets where he was hiding.'

'I'm going to bed,' Henri declared, and Monette followed him inside. Aïcha and Mehdi were left alone on the terrace.

'I was thinking about finishing my residency here in Rabat. It might not be such a bad idea.'

'So you'd abandon your David?'

'He's not my David.'

227

'Whatever.'

She got to her feet. She picked up the glasses that had been left on the table and the ashtray full of cigarette stubs.

'I suppose you're going to sleep here, then?'

'I don't have much choice, do I?'

'Let's go inside. It's cold.'

They were lying next to each other on the damp bench when Hassan II gave a speech on the radio, around one in the morning. She turned her back to him. She appeared to be sleeping. Mehdi thought he would never be able to fall asleep. He wanted her so desperately that he had to force himself not to cover her with kisses, hold her tight against him. He was thirsty and his breath smelled of wine and tobacco. He couldn't kiss her with a mouth like that. He would have to venture through the freezing house in his underpants. Drink a glass of water, come back, then kiss her skin. He would start with her back. Let his lips linger in the hollow at the base of her spine. Lick her belly. Wake her softly.

Meanwhile the king is still speaking. The king is not dead. And tomorrow the king will appear on television to describe the attack by soldiers who fired at his guests, who wanted to kill him – yes, him, their father, their protector, their guide. He will reveal, to a fascinated public, that he looked his young assailant in the eyes and that the soldier laid down his weapon. Together they prayed and the king left the room safe and sound, his reign unbroken.

Mehdi decided not to get up. He moved his tongue around inside his mouth and swallowed a few drops of saliva. He put his hand on Aïcha's breast. He could feel it, round and small, through the thin fabric of her nightshirt. He buried his face in her hair. This woman who had come back to him. She smelled of salt from the sea wind. She was cold and she was sleeping, her legs brought up against her torso. Hands joined, beseeching. How could she sleep? Couldn't she feel him there against her? The blood throbbed inside his erection. It wasn't painful, just annoying. Like an exasperation, a panic made worse by the sheets rubbing against him. A yell that wanted to spurt out. The suffocation of someone buried alive.

In the streets of Rabat the mutineers are being loaded into vans. Cadets, only nineteen or twenty years old, heads shaved, almost blue, faces marked by fatigue and shock. Their wrists and ankles have been tied together with leather straps. The king is not dead. Tomorrow he will say: 'I am more king today than I was yesterday.'

Aïcha stirred. She turned around and wrapped her leg around Mehdi. He could feel the soft warmth of her inner thighs. She kept her eyes closed. The night was not over. She abandoned herself to him and Mehdi kissed her in a way he had never before kissed a woman. Gently, he bit the edges of her lips. He devoured her cheeks, her neck, and she let him. Mehdi loved her and his love was located in a place more vast and mysterious than the heart. He thought: I should have died twice today.

In Rabat the journalists are phoning in their articles. 'Like Sardanapalus!' writes a French reporter. 'A Shakespearian tragedy.' 'A warning for the monarchy,' suggests another.

You are going to see what you are going to see.

The guilty are executed in public, among the crowds on Place de Grève. What would be the point in a firing squad or a guillotine if the people were not there to watch? If men did not go home in terror and vomit in the tiny bathrooms of their apartments and swear that they will always – yes, always – stay on the right side of the law? What would be the point of finding someone guilty at all if not to make an example of him? On execution days parents take their children to watch. Fathers carry them on their shoulders so that they can see the scaffold. They tell them to keep their eyes open, not to look down when the executioner moves forward. 'Look what happens to lawbreakers, criminals, naughty boys. Look what they do to those who defy the government. Open your eyes and look.' The fathers tell their sons: 'You have to be a man to see that. You have to be strong and not cry at the sight of blood.'

Decades later the children will remember the whistling of bullets, which they will imitate by vibrating their lips. The crowd will shout to drown out the sobs of the guilty, who have only seconds to live. What does it matter if the criminal has regrets now? What does it matter if he weeps, begs, is frightened? What does it matter if he prays to God or pisses himself? It is a spectacle for the whole family. The biggest and most impressive spectacle of all, which embeds itself at the back of your pupil and will, your whole life long, lurk within you and wake you in the middle of the night.

In 1962 the cafés of Rabat and Casablanca had been provided with television sets. 'It's free – a gift from the king!' they were told. Government officials encouraged the café owners to keep their televisions switched on, as often as possible, so that people would be exposed to the state propaganda urging them to vote for the new constitution. At first people had been wary of this cursed contraption, and the oldest among them had refused to even glance in its direction. Then they got used to it and televisions began to appear in bourgeois living rooms, in the apartments of those same government officials. Housewives would watch television while they peeled carrots or plucked chickens. It was no longer onions that made them cry, but the heartache of a young Egyptian woman abandoned by her lover. Some said that the king himself chose which programmes were shown. If Hassan II was unimpressed by a particular film, he would even call the head of the national broadcasting company to make him take it off the air. Any film that wasn't funny enough, that was too long or boring, would suddenly stop in the middle of the action. And the next day, in the town's markets, people would make bets. Had the film's heroes found each other again? Had that beautiful young woman with long brown hair received her father's permission to marry? In the secrecy of their living rooms, some of the king's subjects grew irritated: they did not share His Majesty's tastes.

But today – 13 July 1971 – the programme will be exceptional, something never seen on television before. Something that will give you goosebumps and make you cry. To start with it looks like a Western. The screen shows a vast expanse of windblown sand. In the distance some cliffs are visible and there is the sound of waves crashing against the rocks. It is a high-budget Hollywood production. Men in uniform emerge from ultra-modern half-tracks and the camera closes in on them. These are not just any men, they are A-list actors, giants wearing jackets weighed down with medals. Close-up shots of faces. Mathilde is sobbing so hard she can hardly breathe. Amine grows irritated. He wishes she would shut up, show some dignity, but he too is stunned by what he is watching and can't say a word. That man whose face, black and white and a little blurry, appears on the screen is someone they know. They have danced with him and his wife, a Frenchwoman, during evenings at the hacienda. That man, like Amine, went to war; he fought in France, in Italy, in Indochina. On the screen a soldier approaches the colonel, whose hands are tied behind his back. He tears off the colonel's stripes, removes his helmet, the badge of his rank. To judge from the look on Amine's face, you would think *he* were the one suffering this humiliation: he gives a little gasp and softly knocks his fists against his knees. The camera pans to the side and we see the face of another man, a general with bruised lips who looks away. The condemned man, his head tilted sideways, eyes half-closed, does not seem to understand what he is doing there. Amine thinks of Mourad. If he were here, the two of them would remember the courage it took to go to war. They would remember how much they had admired these men, their commanders, their superiors, whose orders they unthinkingly obeyed. Was it possible people had forgotten? That the memory of that war had vanished? Those men, Amine thinks sorrowfully, are ancient history. The wars we fought have passed into oblivion.

A man gets out of the back of a military truck, surrounded by three soldiers whose faces are partly hidden by their combat helmets. The traitor stares at the camera, as if praying or asking for something. His shirt is open, revealing his vest beneath. Amine tries to understand what the condemned man is saying but the image is too blurry for him to lip-read. Later the journalist present at the execution will claim that the prisoner shouted: 'I wasn't part of it. I'm innocent!' In a calm, reassuring voice, a journalist lists the names of the condemned men, like a football commentator presenting the teams' line-ups. It is the same voice he uses for royal ceremonies, inaugurations, religious holidays. Then his voice is silenced, as if swallowed up by the sound of boots and the wind whipping up clouds of ochre dust. The mutineers, the traitors, the criminals yell: 'Long live the king!', 'Long live Hassan II!' while they are led towards the posts that have been erected at this deserted firing range a few miles from Rabat. A cameraman runs, almost tripping over a rock. As they advance, the condemned men grow pale and some of them turn around to look behind them, their eyes wide with fear. A photographer moves closer to capture their terror in his lens. Tomorrow he will sell exclusive images, taken from the back of the half-track, to *Paris Match*.

How many people are watching all of this? In how many minds will these memories be engraved? There must be thousands watching as the soldiers drag an already dead body, its face unrecognisable, and tie it to one of the posts. It was not part of the script for the traitor to expire during torture, but death will not save him. He must die twice, and he must die publicly.

Amine keeps saying 'I don't believe it' and Mathilde, who can't stop sniffing, finally takes a handkerchief from her sleeve. How is it possible that people they know, people with whom they have danced and drunk and eaten, people they admired, how is it possible they are there, in that Wild West setting, in those gusts of wind, about to be shot by a firing squad? Mathilde's sobs grow louder. She is weeping now for the men's wives, who are perhaps watching, and she almost shouts when she thinks about the children whose fathers are going to die on television.

Amine was happy when they bought the television. He asked Mathilde to serve dinner in the living room so they could watch while they ate. Now their children have left home, he sees no reason to continue that ludicrous ceremony of meals at the dining room table. The soldiers flank the condemned men and push them towards the cliff edge. Amine shakes his head and thinks: This isn't real. Soon they will see John Wayne appear, or Indians on horseback, wearing feathered headdresses, fingers plucking a taut bow string. And they will realise that all of this is merely cinema, that it is fake, that it is taking place somewhere else, that it never happened. But no, this is not the Grand Canyon and John Wayne will not ride in to save the day. A man yells: 'Fire on my command!' and the ten soldiers shoot their bullets. Members of the army, the air force and the navy rush over to the lifeless bodies. They hawk up phlegm, turn the bodies over to check if the traitors can still see or hear, and they spit in their faces.

Mathilde sobs. 'Why are they showing us this? We know those men.' Amine balls his fists so tight that the knuckles turn white. He glares at her. 'How the hell could you expect to understand? You have no idea what power is.'

As she did every Sunday, Mathilde picked up her handbag, tied a scarf around her neck and asked Amine for the car keys. Her husband gave a long sigh and pretended not to hear before eventually handing them over. She drove to the boarding school where Sabah had been living for the past two years. On the back seat there was a box of cakes and a stack of women's magazines. They were old magazines that she had read many times, filled with photographs of film stars and members of European royal families. Counts and duchesses. Princesses and kings. Sabah liked to cut them out. Already, on the wall above her bed, there were images of Sophia Loren, Grace Kelly and Farah Pahlavi, the shah's wife, with a diamond tiara on her head. Sometimes Mathilde would give her clothes. But nothing new or expensive. Amine forbade that. He didn't like Mathilde going to visit her so often, didn't approve of his wife's closeness to that yellow-skinned girl, the mere sight of whom was enough to put him in a rage.

Mathilde parked outside the boarding school. Sabah was waiting for her on the steps. Together they walked through the streets of the European town. They sat on a terrace and Sabah ordered a glass of orange juice. Before letting her drink from it, Mathilde wiped the edges of the glass with a handkerchief. 'The waiter looked dirty.' She told Sabah about Aïcha's wedding, which was due to take place the following summer, and about her future husband, who had an important job in the capital. Opposite the café a young man perched on a donkey was selling oranges. He shouted out: 'Who wants my oranges? Good, juicy oranges!' Mathilde leaned down towards Sabah and whispered an Alsatian song into her ear. 'What does that mean?' the girl asked.

'Lift up the horse's tail, blow in his hole, and a green apple will pop out for you!' Mathilde burst out laughing. 'I taught that song to your mother when she was young. One day she sang it in front of your uncle Amine and he got really angry. He demanded to know who had taught her such obscenities. Your mother never told on me.'

Mathilde asked a few questions. The same questions as usual. Sabah answered her with lies. Yes, she was happy and her classmates were nice and the teachers were good at their jobs. Yes, she did her homework and she enjoyed learning and she would do everything she was told, without complaining, with all the gratitude expected of abandoned children. Sabah had pretty eyes but her eyebrows were so thick and bushy that no one ever noticed them. Her hair was never brushed and often greasy. There was something about her – a lethargy, a sickliness – that made you ill at ease. It was as if she had come down with one of those strange diseases that deform the body, making the sufferer look simultaneously like a child and an old person. Life had taught Sabah to lie, never to ask for anything. She concealed everything with a dexterity that the adults around her never suspected.

Once a month her mother would come to visit her. She would turn up in her sleek car, in her beautiful outfits, and Sabah would hide her rage. She said thank you for everything.

She didn't cry. She never let her mother catch a glimpse of her anger or her sadness. She was fifteen now, no longer a stupid, naive child. She understood what an odd couple Mourad and Selma must have been, and she sensed, without being able to explain it, that her birth must have been a tragedy for her mother. Sabah knew she was a burden. She realised she had been a mistake, an accident, even a sin. There was no point complaining or demanding anything. All she would get is another lecture: 'You don't realise how lucky you are to have an uncle who takes care of you.'

Whether you looked at it in terms of morality or propriety, whichever way you looked at it, everyone would have been better off had Sabah not existed. Nobody wanted her near them, nobody wanted her at all. When the adults thought about Sabah, it was to wonder where to put her, the way they might think about tidying away some old knick-knack that cannot be thrown out for obscure sentimental reasons. This was what Mathilde had said when Selma announced her intention to go and work in Rabat: 'So what are we going to do with Sabah?' But the best ally of an abandoned child is the very indifference they provoke in others. Nobody cares about them. They can lie without fear.

Mathilde took Sabah to the park. She told her she'd booked appointments for her at the dentist and the hairdresser. They would go together at the end of the month. 'Look through the magazines I brought you – you might find some ideas for a new hairstyle.' Sabah thanked her and left it there. She did not tell Mathilde what happened behind the walls of the boarding school. Did not tell her about those thick, high walls covered in flaking paint, which the girls liked to scratch off and use as eye shadow. About the corridors, which smelled of urine and garlic. Or how the caretaker and the gardener would fondle themselves when they watched the girls running to the showers in their beige slips. Not that they took showers very often. The headmistress was a thrifty woman. After all, they weren't princesses. 'That's obvious. If you were, you wouldn't be here.' The girls washed their uniforms only twice a month.

The previous Tuesday, Sabah had been reading under her beige blanket in the first-floor dormitory. She needed to pee but it was so cold that she couldn't bear to leave the comfort of her heavy woollen blanket. A gift from Mathilde. Then she noticed that her knickers were wet. She thought she had pissed herself and that everyone would laugh at her. She stuck her hand down her knickers and when she brought it out again she saw that her fingers were covered with a sort of blackish, sticky phlegm. She was not naive or ignorant; she knew that women bled. But she had never imagined it would look like that, like this nightmarish ooze, this viscous matter that gave her the impression she was rotting from inside. She had assumed a few drops of bright-red blood would flow from her vagina. Nice, healthy-looking blood.

In many ways it was a tragedy. A tragedy because she would have to go and see the matron, who would give her just one sanitary towel that Sabah would have to change and wash herself, who would shout at her if she stained her uniform. 'Blood doesn't wash out.' A tragedy because of the terrible pain, which would sometimes make the girls cry since they were not given anything to relieve it. 'This is your cross to bear. Spare a thought for men – they have to go to war.' A tragedy because of the stench of metal and fish that impregnated their clothes and wafted from between their thighs every time a pubescent girl had to uncross her legs. Yes, this was how women lost their childish smell, the sweet smell of innocence. And because of the way others looked at them – a disillusioned look, stripped of the indulgence they had enjoyed before, that indulgence from the time when they were still little girls – they turned into bitches. A strange fury took hold of them, a desire to writhe, to feel. They became dangerous, and from then on, whenever one of the girls invited another to join her in bed, you knew that they weren't just looking for a hug or a shoulder to cry on. Girls with dark hair on their upper lips slipped beneath the sheets. They slid their tongues between unclean labia, they poked their fingers with their too-long nails into their class-mates' vaginas. They scratched, they bit. After that, the girls complained that it stung when they urinated; they were left with shameful infections in which nobody seemed interested.

Sabah told her aunt none of this. Faced with Mathilde, whom she thought so beautiful with her blonde hair and her pale complexion, she behaved like a reasonable child who knows she cannot hope for more than she has. She thanked her for the magazines and said it didn't matter at all if the shoes that Mathilde gave her were too big. All she had to do was stuff them with cotton wool. Or perhaps, you never knew, one day her feet might grow.

* * *

On Friday evenings boys would begin hanging around outside the boarding school. They would park their mopeds under the dormitory windows and wait. They would smoke cigarettes, laugh and punch each other in the stomach while watching women walk by, the shapes of their buttocks visible under their djellabas. The headmistress did not seem unduly bothered by their presence. In fact, she had decided to try and take advantage of it. Hicham, the leader of the gang, would often give her packets of sugar, bouquets of mint, jars of smoked meat which he brought with him from Fes and which she adored. In exchange for these treats she agreed to turn a blind eye to the girls' activities. She thought they were all lost causes anyway.

Sabah was not the prettiest of them. And although she went outside with her classmates, she did so without enthusiasm. Just to pass the time. Even so, Hicham noticed her. He was only twenty and he wore blue jeans and immaculately clean shirts. He was always chewing something: a liquorice stick, a toothpick, an ear of wheat. The first time he saw Sabah, he went up to her and reached out to her forehead with one hand. He gently caressed the roots of her hair and the boys and girls around them all fell silent. Sabah had a long scar there, although she had no idea how she had got it because nobody had ever told her stories about her childhood. Hicham nodded and smiled at her. He patted her head with a tenderness that made her weak at the knees. She felt like she had just been adopted by him, like he recognised her.

It was not until a few weeks later, while they were leaning against a car, that Hicham explained things to Sabah. That scar, he told her, must have been caused by knitting needles or an iron rod, the kind of tools that women would sometimes use to get rid of an unwanted pregnancy. 'It damaged your forehead. But the fact that you're here proves that you're tough and that God didn't want you to die.' Sabah touched the scar with the tip of her index finger then covered it up with her hair. I will never tie my hair back again, she thought. She would have a fringe from now on, like some of the Frenchwomen she had seen in town. She burned with shame at the idea that everyone had seen that opprobrious mark, that they all knew she had survived an attempt to kill her.

Hicham, though, seemed even more interested in her. Every time he came back to see the boarders he had something for Sabah. He had noticed her love of food so he would always bring a cake or an ice cream. He watched her eat coffee-flavoured cream puffs and smiled like a satisfied father when she licked the cream from her fingers. The girls all fought to win Hicham's attention and some of them were upset that Sabah, who looked like such a virgin with her ridiculous little pout, could have become his favourite. One Saturday night he parked under the dormitory windows and honked his horn twice. The girls laughed and waved at him. Leaning against a wall of the boarding school, Hicham smoked a cigarette. He asked Sabah about her family and she answered evasively. She thought he felt sorry for her, that he understood where she had come from. He told her: 'I could be your brother, you know? You don't have a brother, right?' She did not reply but Selim's face appeared in her mind. She almost said: 'No, I don't have a brother but I have a cousin who's like a brother to me.' But this struck her as too complicated and a bit embarrassing. She did not want to have to explain, never mind share with this man, this stranger, the fact of Selim's existence. So she just nodded and he put his hand on her chin, forcing her to look into his eyes. 'Well, you do now, okay? You can be my little sister and I'll take care of you. But you're going to have to listen to me because a brother is there to protect his little sister, to stop her choosing the wrong path or getting mixed up in the wrong company.'

'She's a little sneak, that's what she is. You think I can't spot girls like that? Twenty years I've been running this boarding school and I know what I'm talking about. The caretaker found her on the street, in the middle of the night. We were all frantic with worry and she was there, on the boulevard, sitting on her suitcase and waiting for some criminals. She's a sneak and an idiot who swallows the lies of the first boy she meets and is ready to follow him anywhere. God protect us from that filthy mob! I am very disappointed, Madame Belhaj, and you must understand that I cannot continue sheltering such a scorpion in my school. Who knows what influence she might have over my other girls, what vile stories she might tell them. She might even be pregnant! If I were you, I would take her straight to the doctor. I bet that little pest still has some nasty surprises in store for you. This is a respectable institution and I have to protect my other boarders. Since she has already packed her suitcase, you can take her now. That girl needs to be punished. I'm sure her uncle can persuade her to stop trying to run away.'

Several times Mathilde tried to interrupt the old head-mistress as she was waving her hands in the air, the fingers deformed by arthritis. She tried offering her money – 'a considerable sum to pay for any damage caused and to continue supporting this venerable institution' – and she invoked the good Lord, whose mercy should be extended to all and especially to the youngest and most fragile among us. While Sabah sat there staring at the ground, Mathilde tried to plead her cause by reminding the headmistress that she was an orphan whose mother had abandoned her. But none of it did any good. Every time Mathilde uttered a word the headmistress shook her head frantically, put her hands in front of her face and, like a child who refuses to listen, began heaping abuse on Sabah, insulting her. 'I don't want to know,' she said with an air of finality. 'I don't want anything more to do with you.' Mathilde picked up her handbag, rose to her feet and headed towards the door of the office. She turned around and said in an emotionless voice: 'Are you coming?' The girl followed her through the corridor to the lobby, suitcase in hand, shuffling along in her shoes stuffed with cotton wool. The other boarders watched them leave and some of them blew kisses to Sabah. She understood that there was no affection in the gesture and that they were not going to miss her. What they felt, however, was a kind of admiration that she had found a way out of that place, accompanied by the tall blonde woman who spoke with an Alsatian accent that made them laugh.

Sabah sat in Mathilde's car, her head lowered. Her aunt got behind the steering wheel and sat motionless for a few minutes, eyes closed, trying to suppress the fury she could feel rising within her. Mathilde did not know who she was angriest with. The headmistress, who had been so contemptuous towards her, spurning her money and refusing to hear her excuses? Sabah, who, beneath her docile exterior, was just as slutty and sneaky as her mother? Or Amine, who had refused to let Sabah stay at the farm with them so that Mathilde could take care of her and educate her as if she were her own child? She started the engine, pressed down on the accelerator and turned suddenly onto the avenue, provoking a volley of honked horns from the other motorists. 'You're a public nuisance!' one of them shouted at her. She drove fast, staring straight ahead, and after half an hour Sabah realised they were not heading towards the farm. She wanted to ask: 'Where are you taking me?' but she was too frightened that Mathilde would yell at her.

Her aunt turned to look at her. 'I'm so disappointed in you,' she said. 'Never would I have believed you could be so stupid, so irresponsible. Is that the life you want for yourself? Is that the kind of girl you want to be? A little slut who goes with the first boy she meets and who believes all the lies he tells her? Where were you planning to go, exactly? What did that boy promise you?' Sabah kept her eyes lowered and Mathilde started to shout: 'Answer me! Where were you going?' But Sabah kept her mouth shut. 'Anyway, I don't care. It's none of my business any more. You're the most ungrateful wretch I've ever met. If you knew all I've done for you . . . You don't have the faintest idea how much you owe me. Thanks to you, thanks to your stupidity and your selfishness, I'm going to bear the brunt of your uncle's anger. What am I supposed to tell him? Huh? Tell me, what should I say? Nothing to say? Well, good. I don't want to hear you and I don't even want to see you any more. Your uncle was right, I should have listened to him. You're a pair of ingrates and scroungers. I wash my hands of you. You and your mother can deal with this between the two of you. Since you don't want our help, since you show contempt for everything we give you, you and your mother can learn to get by on your own.'

So that was where they were going. To her mother's house. Sabah's heart sank. She would have preferred anything at all – another boarding school, a slap from her uncle – to finding herself face to face with Selma again. The last time she had come to Rabat, to the little apartment on Avenue de Temara, she'd had the impression she was disturbing her mother. Selma kept spying on her, told her not to touch her make-up, her clothes; she started yelling when she caught her daughter opening a drawer filled with old photographs. 'Keep your nose out of other people's things,' she had scolded. On the Saturday, her mother had spent most of the afternoon locked in the bathroom. Sabah, bored, had sat alone in the living room and read magazines. Then Selma had appeared in the corridor and taken some cash from the pocket of her dressing gown. 'Here, go and have fun, and don't come back before two in the morning. I have friends coming over – you can't stay here.' And Sabah had ventured out into Rabat's dark and empty streets. She had sat in a café, ordered a glass of almond milk and prayed for time to pass quickly, for her to get home safe and sound. 'Your mother's a whore,' one of the girls at the boarding school had told her once. Sabah had attacked the girl, punching her in the face, but that evening, in the empty café in Rabat, sitting in front of her glass of milk, it was Selma that she imagined hitting, locking up, hiding from the world. She was ashamed of her mother and did not want to see her again. 'Mathilde, please, take me to the farm,' she begged now, but her aunt said nothing. For several miles she drove behind a truck transporting mules, the only parts of which she could see were their fat rumps. Mathilde, who liked to drive fast, began grumbling then honking her horn.

In a thin voice, Sabah sang: 'Lift up the horse's tail, blow in his—'

'Oh, shut up!'

* * *

'Selma isn't home. She went to the hammam.' Hocine looked at Sabah as she stood there in the middle of the avenue, suitcase in hand, and pinched her cheek. 'So you're her daughter? Yeah, I can see the resemblance. But you're too skinny. You need to eat more.' Mathilde, her arm firmly around Sabah, smiled hypocritically. 'Mademoiselle is watching her weight. But she has never lacked for anything and she's always had enough to eat, believe me.' Sabah sat down on the steps, her bag between her knees. Every time a woman crossed the street or a taxi stopped outside the apartment building, she jumped. What would she say to her mother? How would she react? Mathilde, who was pacing around on the pavement, bought a cigarette from a passing street vendor. She smoked it slowly, like a teenager who has not yet learned to inhale properly. Then Selma appeared. She was walking along the avenue, her wet hair rolled up in a beige headscarf, her face still red from the heat of the hammam. She was wearing a green gandoura with gold embroidery around the edges of the collar and the sleeves. Men turned to watch her walk past, and a motorist leaned on his horn.

She recognised Mathilde first. Even from a distance, even on a crowded street, she would have recognised her sister-in-law anywhere, with her blonde hair, her manly shoulders, her hideous legs swollen in the heat. Then she saw her daughter, slumped on the steps, head between her knees.

248

'What are you doing here?'

'We should go inside,' Mathilde said.

'Is there a problem? Did something happen?'

'Let's go to your apartment to talk about it. I have no desire to make a scene.'

They walked upstairs in silence and Sabah stared at her mother's slender ankles, her calves, which were exposed under the gandoura every time she climbed to the next step.

'Go to the bedroom and close the door,' Mathilde said in a stern voice.

Sabah did as she was told. Then she sat on the floor, ear pressed to the wall, and tried to hear what her mother and her aunt were saying. In the living room the two women talked in whispers. Now and again one of them would raise her voice, annoyed. 'It's always the same with you. You're completely irresponsible!' Mathilde shouted. 'All of this is your fault!' Selma retorted. Then their voices would grow quieter again and Sabah could make out nothing but their tense whispering. She turned to look at her mother's room. The large bed was covered with a thick pale-pink duvet. A handsome Venetian mirror hung on the wall and on the lemonwood dressing table there were necklaces, bottles of perfume, a teacup filled with make-up brushes. The open wardrobe overflowed with dresses, coats and high-heeled shoes. On the inside of the wardrobe door Selma had stuck a photograph and a postcard showing the Eiffel Tower, with the word 'PARIS' written in golden letters. Sabah pulled the photograph off the door. It was a portrait of Mouilala, in her white haik, her eyes heavily made up, and five-year-old Selma, who seemed amused by the idea of having her picture taken. On the back of the photograph were the handwritten words: 'Rabat, 1942'. Sabah stared at the little girl's face and thought: She doesn't look like her mother. Then Sabah crawled over to the bed and buried her face in the duvet. She sucked in deep breaths of Selma's smell, that musky smell she had always associated with her, and which remained on her skin for hours after her mother had kissed her.

'Come here!' Selma shouted, and Sabah slowly walked through the corridor and stood in front of the two women.

'Is it true? You tried to run away from the boarding school?'

Sabah did not reply.

'Don't try that with me, my girl. You're going to answer me, even if I have to beat it out of you. Understood?'

Sabah nodded.

'Where were you planning to go? What did that boy promise you?'

Sabah stammered something.

'We can't hear you. Look at me when you speak.'

Sabah noticed her suitcase in the entrance hall. She crouched down, unzipped it and took out a thick stack of letters, which she handed to her mother.

'What's this?'

'I wanted to find Selim. I haven't heard from him for weeks. I just wanted to make sure he was okay.'

Mathilde came up to Sabah and grabbed her by the shoulders.

'What are you talking about? What does my son have to do with all this?'

'Go back to the bedroom!' Selma yelled. 'Leave us.'

Mathilde reached out for the packet of letters but Selma held on to them tightly. 'Wait a minute.' She opened a small cupboard and took out a bottle of whisky. 'The glasses are behind you, on the shelf.' Mathilde grabbed two and they sat on the bench next to each other. After swallowing a mouthful of whisky, Selma divided the stack of letters in two. 'Here.' A photograph fell out onto the thick wool carpet. Selim, bare-chested on a beach, his blond hair hanging halfway down his back.

Neither of them understood and both were jealous. Both mother and lover wondered why he had written to Sabah instead of to them. Why had he chosen that boring girl, that secondary character in their lives? Looking through the letters, they realised that this was in fact what united Sabah and Selim. This feeling that they were living on the margins of life, never fully valued. Both of them had been abandoned by Selma. Both of them had, albeit in different ways, suffered the wrath of Amine. The two women looked at the letters lying in their laps and thought: I wish they'd been for me. I wish they'd been love letters. He would have written that he couldn't live without me, that my absence from his life was driving him mad with grief. He would have apologised for running away, and in heartbreakingly tender words he would have promised to come running back into my arms very soon. He would have signed the letter Selim who loves you with all his heart. Selim who cannot forget you. They were both disappointed. The first letters were from autumn 1969 and Selim merely described his life with Nilsa, Simon and Lalla Amina. Mathilde recognised her son's stuttering prose style. Selim wrote in short sentences. He did not use any punctuation and wrote things like: 'How are you I am fine' and 'So what about you tell me about the boarding school', just like he used to when he would write to his mother from the holiday camp where he'd spent his summers. Mathilde remembered his child's words: 'I miss you maman the canary laid an egg it's been raining for three days now.' Back then, she had been his everything. Whenever she spent longer than expected in town, he would wait for her at the entrance to their estate with tears rolling down his cheeks. If he watched her buckle her high-heeled shoes or try on a hat, he would exclaim: 'How beautiful you are, Maman!' The adoration of that little boy consoled her for all her sorrows. But in these letters, the letters to Sabah, Mathilde did not even appear. She kept turning the pages over, examining each sentence, but not once did she find any mention of herself, Amine or the farm. As if her son had forgotten her. As if he were indifferent to the pain his disappearance had caused her. 'Have you finished? Pass me yours,' she told her sister-in-law.

But Selma did not look up. She was reading a rather unhinged letter from early 1970 in which Selim talked about women's bodies, about the lust to which he had abandoned himself, and now Selma wanted to kill him. What was this 'free love'? With his vague, clumsy words, Selim tried to explain this new vision of a world where nobody belonged to anybody else. Where men did not possess women and there were no oaths of eternal fidelity. A world governed only by the whims of desire. Where you could reach out and draw a body towards you, where you could ride it in the coolness of the night. And all this love-less sex had hardened his heart. Everything he had believed in had been crushed and swept away like a sandcastle hit by a wave. Marriage, children, that life his parents had chosen, that childhood shaken by yells, curses, suppressed hate. 'I will never marry,' he wrote. 'Other people's bodies do not belong to us and I do not belong to my parents I do not belong to this country.' The little shit, thought Selma. So full of himself, claiming that women wanted him more than they wanted other men. Maybe because he didn't talk very much and unlike the other hippies wasn't always spouting off about the world. He didn't boast about reaching nirvana or pursuing a quest. He could sit for hours watching trees bend in the wind, and women were intrigued, charmed by his indolence. The little shit, daring to write such crazy things to a fifteen-year-old girl while decorating his letters with childish drawings of boats in the port. The little shit, swearing he had become a man. He knew what he wanted to do with his life: Selim, the ignorant, lazy, mediocre student, finally had a few ambitions. During the months spent with the hippies, he had listened avidly to their stories. Among them there were doctors, engineers, architects, intellectuals, whose vast knowledge he admired. 'Over there on the other side of the ocean there's America.' He wrote to Sabah about travel the way you might tell a slave about freedom, a world without fences. He had asked his friends to describe America for him. The hippies thought he would be disgusted by what they told him: 'It's the kingdom of money and violence, a country of vast vertical cities where girls sell their bodies and men dream of being rich and powerful.' After that, he was obsessed with New York. His most recent letters spoke of nothing else. He wrote about setting off soon for that distant land. He would find some money and leave behind this village of poverty and boredom where nobody did anything and the air was thick with the sickening smell of overripe tomatoes that emanated from Diabet's only shop.

Mathilde and Selma were drunk. 'He's a kid!' Selma said angrily.

'An ungrateful and irresponsible kid,' Mathilde added. Her tongue was so heavy, she found it hard to articulate.

'Maybe I was a lazy student, but at least I could spell. Do you remember? You made me work at it. Selim makes the kind of mistakes a five-year-old would make.'

Mathilde asked for a cigarette, then went out onto the little balcony to light it, blowing the smoke noisily from her mouth. Yes, of course she remembered the classes she'd given on spelling, history and geography in that damp house in Berrima. She remembered Selma as a child, insolent and capricious, but generous too. The little girl who would come back from school and copy out her Arabic lessons for her sister-in-law. Afterwards she would make Mathilde recite it and she wouldn't laugh when the Alsatian woman struggled to pronounce an R or a K.

'I'm sure he's on drugs.'

'Oh, stop,' said Selma. 'It's not that big a deal, believe me.'

'What do you know about it? Maybe that's why he's stopped writing to her. Something could have happened to him. I saw a television documentary the other day. It said they're all junkies, that they eat food from rubbish bins and some of them have died from overdoses.'

254

'I know your son. He's not like that. I could criticise you for many things, but you raised your children well.'

'It didn't stop him running away.'

'He'll come back. Trust me.' There was a small wooden box on the table. Selma opened it and said: 'You want to try some?'

'What is it?'

'Hashish.'

'You smoke that stuff?'

'No, not really. Someone left it here the other day. But we could try it.'

One night, lying on a bench in Selma's apartment, Omar listened to a radio programme that fascinated him. It told the story of a young Turkish actress at the start of the century who, because she was a Muslim, was not allowed to perform on stage. But this young woman was so talented and driven that she succeeded in joining a theatre company. Every night she would go on stage in the theatres of Istanbul. The audiences loved her and her fellow actors supported her. Sometimes the police, tipped off by an informer, would burst into the theatre, and the young actress would have to escape across the rooftops, aided by her accomplices, and the audience would jeer the policemen as they left empty-handed, glancing back angrily at the vacant stage.

This was what the town of Essaouira was like when Omar arrived there in February 1972: a stage set abandoned by a theatre company or a film crew who had, for some strange reason, been forced to pack up and leave in a rush, leaving behind a few worthless objects – a painted sunset, a fake living room that still showed the traces of a party. Omar was welcomed like some eminent government official. In the shabby police station of that abandoned town, the officers had washed their uniforms especially and had set out, on an old desk, a plate of cakes and a steaming teapot. 'Please sit, Chief!' The man who addressed him was called Ismaël. A detective in his early thirties who had never been beyond the confines of this backward region. A handsome young man with clear skin who slicked back his hair with argan oil and smelled of burnt hazelnut. He stared at Omar, smiling nervously, his eyes expressing an anxiety that the police chief found quite touching. 'It must make a change from Casablanca,' the detective added, raising the teapot into the air and pouring the hot, foaming liquid into two glasses. 'Nothing much happens here. Apart from the hippies . . .'

For the previous four years the authorities had turned a blind eye to the hippie camps in the forest. Pagan ceremonies. Half-naked dancing in the ruins of Dar Soltane. Fornication in sordid brothels where you could get a girl for less than ten dirhams and where Western men would beckon over young Moroccan boys and teach them to say 'cum' and 'hard-on' in French. Occasionally the police would raid the houses and hotels of Diabet to arrest a hippie whose visa had expired. Foreigners were permitted to stay in the country for only three months and the ones who were arrested were sent back home. For a long time such problems had been solved with a bit of cash or an imported object. After all, it was their business if they wanted to get high or live in filth.

But since the attempted coup in Skhirat, the government had decided to take matters into its own hands and halt the corruption of Morocco's youth. The drug dealing. The stolen passports, which drove the foreign consulates to distraction as filthy young foreigners descended upon them in tears to report the latest theft. In Tangier the authorities were told not to allow young men with long hair to enter the country. The customs officers became part-time hairdressers, threatening the arriving hippies with clippers. On television a reporter made them his favourite target: 'The hippies' time is over!' Morocco wanted real tourists now, wealthy and respectable people who would pay in cash for a camel ride and offer shameful sums for a Berber rug or a felt fez.

All colours had vanished from the town. The murals had been removed from the walls and the Hippie Café had been transformed. The owner now wore a suit bought at a flea market and he turned up the volume on the radio when a certain popular song came on, the chorus to which went: 'Hippie, we don't like you, go home.' 'Just last week some young guy died in Diabet,' Ismaël went on. 'Nobody in the village wants to talk about it, but according to our information he overdosed. All those hippies care about is getting high. They're as skinny and toothless as tramps.' Omar did not touch his glass of tea. He gazed at the wall and Ismaël found himself wondering what he was thinking about, this strange man with skin as red and blotchy as the fishermen on the coast. Abruptly Omar stood up and buttoned up his jacket.

'I'm looking for a boy,' he explained. 'A Moroccan who lived among them.' He took a photograph from his pocket showing a bare-chested young man with hair bleached almost white by the sun. His green eyes seemed to blaze even brighter in comparison.

'Him? He's a Moroccan?'

'He's as Moroccan as you and me. Have you seen him?'

'I don't know. Maybe. They all look the same, those hippies.'

'Send your men onto the beaches, into the forests, into the houses of the medina. Send them anywhere he might be hiding, you understand?'

The next day Omar was driven to Diabet. The wind was cold and wet, with a tang of salt, and Omar had to make a superhuman effort not to rip the buttons off his shirt and scratch himself until he bled. There was a rotting smell in the air, as if the ocean were merely an immense swamp. The villagers kept their shutters closed whenever the police arrived, and the men, when they were interrogated, gave only vague, fearful answers. They regretted having abetted such debauchery, having welcomed drug addicts and vagrants into their homes. One woman, in an old beige kaftan, began weeping in front of the police chief. She swore she had been cheated and humiliated and she asked if there was someone in Rabat who could investigate her case and pay her compensation. Surely Omar had friends in the ministry? Ismaël shoved the old peasant woman away.

Omar went to see the few remaining hippies. Four skinny, sickly boys lying at the back of a freezing room. One of them kept scratching himself, infested with stink bugs or scabies. Some of the others had caught hepatitis and went to relieve themselves behind a tree in the tamarisk forest. It was there, in the forest, that three of the hippies had been buried. Omar kept asking questions but was given no clear answers. Who were they? What had they looked like? Had one of them spoken Arabic? He wondered if the people here simply didn't care about him; they seemed strangely indifferent to the authority of the police. The villagers talked about voodoo ceremonies, trancelike states, foreigners found dead with bulging eyes and enigmatic smiles. 'Where did the drugs come from? Who sold them the drugs?' Omar yelled at a terrified peasant. A former postman explained that the hippies received letters soaked in LSD, which they cut into little pieces and ate. Others whispered about suicides – may God preserve us – and they talked in particular about a Moroccan girl, impregnated and abandoned by an American man. That was the real crime. That was the real betrayal. The hippies had lied when they promised to keep their distance from Moroccan women. They had converted a few of them to free love and artificial paradises. They had injected poison into those poor young souls.

Throughout the investigation Omar kept his arms down by his sides and his mouth tensed, as if afraid he might be infected by some virus circulating in the air. He asked to wash his hands and Ismaël, embarrassed, led him to a drinking fountain near where a donkey was grazing. Omar stood with his hands in the jet of water for a long time, his face suddenly relaxed.

'I was told about a certain Lalla Amina, who lives in the medina. I'm sure you know who that is.'

Ismaël smiled. For the first time since Omar's arrival, he was going to be able to satisfy him.

It wasn't difficult for Omar to reconstruct Selim's last days in Essaouira. He acted like a competent policeman, a meticulous detective, not like a worried uncle or jealous brother. First he paid a visit to Lalla Amina, who seemed unimpressed by his occupation and rank. As this tall, thin Black woman led him into the house, he wondered if she was feigning senile dementia or if she was, like the rest of the town, genuinely descending into madness. She would begin a sentence, stop halfway through it, then run her tongue over her gold teeth, which were now a copperish colour. She pointed with her bony fingers at a door. 'He slept in there!' The tiny bedroom contained only a bed, a wardrobe and a small wooden table on which stood a stack of books, their cardboard covers falling to pieces. Poetry collections, novels about travels in America and essays on the condition of Black people. Omar picked up one of them. He took off his glasses and lifted the book very close to his eyes. It was a short work on Buddha, a strange Indian god who, having given up everything, had reached nirvana. Inside this book were some photographs of Nepal and India, and of men with shaved heads, their bodies enveloped in orange fabric. He put it down on the bedside table. 'These books belong to you?' Lalla Amina howled with laughter. '*I* can't read! I looked at the pictures, though. They're pretty.'

Omar penetrated the mystery of the photographs and his investigation led him to Karim. He had the boy brought to the police station. Karim kept swallowing. He looked terrified. Ready to confess to anything in exchange for a little mercy. When Omar explained what he was looking for, Karim exhaled. He sat up in his chair and began talking, very quickly, about this funny blond Moroccan boy who had lived with his aunt for three years. He heaped insults on his former friend, presumably thinking this would please the half-blind police chief with his perfectly filed fingernails, like a woman's. He called Selim ungrateful, secretive, twisted. 'Who abandons his parents and never bothers telling them where he is?' he demanded indignantly. 'That kind of thing is okay for foreigners, but here, there's no greater shame.'

'So, do you think he went home?' Omar asked.

'I'd be surprised. All he ever talked about was going to America.'

261

'I see. But it's expensive, travelling to America. Do you have any idea where he might have found the money for such a trip?'

'An idea? Yeah, maybe.'

In Diabet everyone knew that Selim had a gun. 'He should have been more discreet,' Karim said. 'One day he took the pistol out of his bag and used it to threaten this gang of hippies who were completely off their heads. Apparently it was because of a girl. The Moroccan girl that some American man had got pregnant. Selim wanted to defend her honour. But girls like that don't have any honour to defend. Anyway, he always kept the gun on him. He put it under his pillow when he went to sleep. And one day he asked me if I knew anyone who might be interested in it. He wanted to sell the pistol, you understand?'

'It's not a pistol,' Omar interrupted.

'Oh yes, sir, it was, I can assure you of that. I saw it. He had a pistol—'

'I'm telling you, it's not a pistol. It's a revolver with central percussion. An eight-millimetre with a six-cartridge cylinder and walnut grips.'

* * *

'Walnut grips.' At the time, Omar had not had any idea what those words meant, but he thought they sounded beautiful and he would repeat them as if reciting a poem. Amine had returned from the front at the end of 1945 and one night, in the house in Berrima, he had pulled a revolver from its leather holster. There, in the darkness of the patio, lit only by a few candles, he had begun playing with the gun, spinning

262

it around his index finger, aiming at an upstairs window as if ready to fire. 'Here, take it, it's not loaded.' And Omar, still a teenager, had held that weapon of war in his hand. Amine told him how it worked. The cylinder, which opened to the right ('it's a cavalryman's gun'), the button you had to press to eject the cartridges, and the way you had to hold it to be sure of hitting your target. Emboldened, Omar had asked: 'Have you killed people with this?' And Amine had replied: 'What do you think? It's not a toy. Come on, give it back to me.' The years had passed and Omar had given it no further thought until the day he joined the police and was presented with his own gun. It had all started there, he realised then. His vocation as a policeman had begun in the garden in Berrima, at the precise moment when his brother had grabbed the gun from his hands, contemptuously returning him to his status as a child.

That night, Amine joined Mathilde in her bed. They had been sleeping apart for several years now. Amine said it was because he didn't want to disturb her with his snoring and the sound of the radio which he listened to until late at night. The truth was that he often came back late from his secret excursions, his clothes steeped in the scent of another woman, and he could not bear the thought of having to justify himself to his wife. But that night, that searingly hot night in July 1972, he quietly opened the door to Mathilde's bedroom. His wife was not asleep. She was lying naked in the darkness. Amine had always found it strange, this obsession she had with sleeping unclothed. He himself couldn't do it. She turned her face towards him. It was her husband – yes, just her husband – and yet she felt frightened. She was seized with anxiety, as if this were the first time he had seen her naked. As if, through the magic of that summer night, she had become a young, innocent virgin once again. He lay down beside her. She let him kiss her, stroke her hair. Amine's warm, strong hands held her by the hips. It was not unpleasant. He was not a brutal or clumsy lover. Even so she could not manage to feel anything at all. She was outside her own body, looking down at herself being taken, a limp rag doll stretched out on the bed. She even felt a sort of prudishness, thinking how ridiculous it was after thirty years of marriage, after two children. But that was the thing.

All that time spent together, all those habits, those secrets and her ageing body, it was all this that held her apart from him. She prayed. Please don't let him do anything embarrassing. If he tries to flip me over or put his tongue inside me, I will scream. From outside, she could hear the perpetual, infernal croaking of toads. Ever since they had had the swimming pool built the garden had been infested with toads, which made such a racket that it kept Amine and Mathilde awake at night. Perhaps, she thought, she should grab the rifle, as she used to do with the rats, and shoot at those ugly creatures. Their sticky bodies would explode in a hail of bullets. But no, what was she thinking? Her daughter was getting married the next day: everything was ready, and the last thing she needed was bloodstains all over the paving stones in the garden.

Amine kissed her neck. He said something and she pretended to smile. 'I love you more than anyone. You're everything to me.' She swallowed. This declaration was so strange, so out of character. Why now? And what would remain of this passion tomorrow, after the sun had risen? She wanted him to get off her now. She wanted him to finish up. Mathilde knew what she had to do to speed things up, to make him come at last. But she didn't want to have to start moaning or to slide her hands between Amine's thighs, to use all her old tricks. There was no spite or selfishness in this unwillingness, simply a feeling of shame. A fact that bewildered her. Nearly thirty years earlier she had felt ready to do anything with Amine, and her nudity itself had seemed like a liberation.

She had to get some sleep. Tomorrow she would look like shit; she would have dark rings under her eyes in the wedding photographs. But all the world's mothers have insomnia the

265

night before their daughter's wedding. There was no way around this. Oh well, she would just have to ask her hairdresser to tie her hair in a high bun, a chignon so extravagant that nobody would notice her drawn features, her pallid complexion. The anxiety had been gnawing at her for days. What if the guests were bored? What if the musical group from Casablanca she had hired did not turn up? What if the heat was so bad that it spoiled the mayonnaise she was planning to serve with the fish? What on earth had she been thinking, choosing all that fish and oysters and seafood for the banquet? There would never be enough ice and all the guests would end up getting sick. Years from now people would still be talking about that wedding at the Belhajes' where the guests had eaten rotten prawns and vomited in the bushes. And now, the night before the wedding, with all these fears tormenting her, Amine decided he wanted to make love! 'Oh Mathilde, I couldn't live without you!' What was going on? What could possibly have driven him to speak her name? And to say it like that, in that languorous voice? Was he expecting her to say something in reply? She repeated the phrase inside her head. She wanted to laugh. Amine was covered in sweat. Drops of the stuff were running down his neck and his forehead. The window was open but there was not even the hint of a breeze to cool them down. She was going to suffocate in this heat, her body crushed beneath her husband's. He frowned, his jaw tensed, he stared at the ceiling. He was about to groan. At last he came and Mathilde felt suddenly relieved, almost giddy. There, she had done her duty. The task was behind her and she felt pleased that she had managed to get through it without showing the reluctance she had felt. Tomorrow he would be in a wonderful mood. Nice and relaxed.

Mathilde woke at dawn, her legs hot and swollen. She got up without making any noise. Not daring to open a drawer, she put on a beige slip that she found lying across a chair. She had to get outside and breathe, to wash the night off her skin, to rid herself of this smell of sweat. She walked barefoot through the house and out to the garden. The clouds, pink in the first light, glided above Zerhoun, which looked in outline like a woman lying on the ground, her breasts pointing up at the sky. Mathilde loved the smell of morning, the smell of wet earth, of geraniums and oleanders. She walked down the steps into the swimming pool, feeling the cold water like a blessing. Her body was reborn, filled with vigour again after the night's heat had left it tumid and lethargic. She lay face down, legs straight, arms outstretched. Her blonde hair spread across the surface like seaweed in a Japanese pond. Even as a child she had loved holding her breath in the freezing Rhine, and when Selim had joined the sailing club she had taught him breath-holding exercises to improve his lung capacity. The first time, Selim had been so impressed by his mother that he'd applauded. He didn't have a stopwatch, but he could have sworn that she had stayed underwater for, what, a minute, maybe more, without coming up for air. Since he had gone away, since her son had disappeared, Mathilde had pushed herself to new limits. The most important thing was not to move. To be perfectly still, not even to think, to free yourself from anything that might weigh you down. To float like a water lily on the surface of this pool she had so desired. She surrendered to weightlessness. Eyes open, she observed her shadow at the bottom of the pool. She could keep going even longer. Jaw and fists clenched, she swore she would hold her breath as long as possible, beat her own record. Then she felt something grab hold of her foot. Frightened, she thought of the rats and grass snakes she had often seen swimming on the water's surface, and imagined it was some foul creature touching her ankle. She lifted her head and found herself staring into her daughter's face. Aïcha was in her wedding dress, waist-deep in the water.

'What the hell are you doing?' Mathilde yelled. 'Look at your dress!'

'What am I doing? I saw you lying there completely still in the water. I thought you were dead!'

'Get out of the pool! Out, right now! You'll ruin your dress.'

Mathilde helped her daughter out of the swimming pool and the two of them sat together in the grass.

'Who goes swimming in their slip at this time of day? Are you completely crazy or what?'

'Me? What about you? Why are you wearing your wedding dress?'

'I wanted to try it on. I was looking for you so you could help me button it up.'

'I'm sorry, I didn't mean to scare you. I do it because it relaxes me. I'm teaching myself to hold my breath.'

'Does Papa know you do that?'

'Why? Are you going to tell on me?'

The two women looked at each other and simultaneously burst out laughing. Mathilde laughed loudly, her mouth wide open, and she wrung out the hem of her slip. Aïcha, in her soaked dress, was shaken by silent spasms. She laughed at the hilarity of the situation, and even then the two of them were probably thinking delightedly of what a funny story they would have to tell the others. But they also laughed to chase away evil spirits, to drown their own fears in forgetting. What kind of omen did such an event signify? They sensed that there was, in this false death, a warning, a threat, whose exact nature they were unable to decipher.

'At least you didn't get your hair wet,' Mathilde said. She led her daughter into the house. The wedding dress slopped across the tiled floor, leaving a damp streak behind. They locked themselves in the bathroom and Mathilde undressed her daughter. Aïcha crossed her thin arms over her breasts and sat naked on the edge of the bathtub. While Mathilde rinsed the dress in fresh water – 'We can't have people saying that the bride smelled of chlorine!' – she remembered the day she had found Aïcha, still a little girl at the time, wrapped in a white sheet which she had folded over her head in lieu of a veil. Her daughter had been pacing around her bedroom, taking care not to trip over her train. Mathilde had laughed, then leaned down and asked: 'Are you pretending to be a bride?'

'No,' Aïcha had answered. 'I'm practising for my communion.'

Mathilde had lost her temper and ordered the little girl to get dressed again. 'You'd better forget that idea,' she'd said, 'because it's not going to happen.' If Amine had found out, he would have been furious. He had let his daughter go to the convent school and he had grudgingly accepted the crucifix she had hung on the wall of her room. But a communion? That would have killed him.

Never before had Amine earned as much money as he did that year. In Spain frost had destroyed the harvests, and the Belhaj domain had been buried under an avalanche of orders. Amine set aside that money for his daughter. He wanted everyone to know that she had succeeded: Aïcha was a doctor and she was marrying a man with a great future. Mathilde spent months writing down ideas for menus and decorations in little graph-paper notebooks. She followed Amine everywhere he went, asking him for his opinion. To everything he replied: 'Tell me how much it costs and I'll pay it.' Mathilde lost all sense of proportion. She cut photographs of society weddings out of magazines, and in the boutiques she visited she would show the saleswomen those images and say: 'That's what I want.' She bought ivory velvet ribbons by the yard and tied bows in the palm trees. From the branches of the other trees she hung strings of lights and Chinese lanterns. At a caterer's in Casablanca she ordered crockery and silver cutlery, which she had delivered by van the day before the wedding. She sent a vellum invitation to everyone in town, featuring a watercolour painting by a local artist of the cypresses on the Belhaj estate.

On the advice of a saleswoman who told her that it would 'bring out her eyes', Mathilde bought a green silk dress for the ceremony. She tore out pages from magazines lauding the unparalleled effectiveness of the latest crash diets. She refused to look like a whale in her outrageously expensive dress. She refused to have people making fun of her behind her back. 'What on earth has she been eating to put on so much weight?' In the weeks preceding the wedding she ate nothing but tomatoes and pineapples. Her stomach burned and she had constant diarrhoea, which left her pale and exhausted. She started doing gymnastics, and the farmworkers became used to seeing her run through the fields, making peculiar movements with her arms.

* * *

Now, at last, the big day was here. Mathilde oversaw the arrangement of the tables in the garden. She explained to the two boys who would be working behind the bar how they should behave, and insisted that they should never let a glass remain empty. 'Never!' In the kitchen Tamo was sulking. Strangers had taken over her territory and she was reduced to chopping garlic and parsley. She had to obey the orders of a fat woman from Casablanca with skin as black as the charcoal they used for grilling meat. All the same, she did her best to work hard. The party was for Aïcha, after all, and unlike these strangers Tamo had known the bride all her life. She had seen Aïcha grow up, transforming from a little savage to a woman of the world. She still couldn't get over the sight of that long, supple chestnut hair which hung down the middle of the bride's back.

At four o'clock in the afternoon the regiment of hairdressers and make-up artists arrived, armed with their vanity cases filled with bottles of varnish, hairpins and hot rollers. Aïcha and Monette stayed in the bedroom where, from time to time, Mathilde would burst in and eye the employees with a steely glare. She was annoyed about all the money she had spent. Then the waiters put on their white jackets and tied the black bow ties around their necks. They were each given a silver platter shining like a mirror and they took up their positions in the garden. The musical group turned up late and Mathilde told Amine: 'You should say something to them. If I do it they won't take me seriously.' So Amine went to see them. He found himself face to face with four long-haired Moroccan boys who were busy unpacking their instruments. The name of the group was emblazoned on the skin of the bass drum: The Strangers. They were laughing among themselves, glancing wryly around at the flashy decorations in the garden.

Two sweaty farmworkers guided guests to the car park and then towards the entrance. Mathilde had given them two of Amine's old jackets and the peasants, proud of their elegance, played their role with absolute seriousness. They ran along the dirt path waving their arms at the drivers, who went very slowly because they were afraid of damaging their cars' body-work. The farmworkers rushed over to open car doors to ladies who emerged holding up the hems of their dresses, perched on high heels which sank into the earth. The peasants had never seen such dresses before and they stared idiotically at the heavy jewellery hanging from the women's ears. One of them said: 'I bet they can hear the music all the way out in the douar.' The other one started laughing. He thought this music was a bit stupid.

Mathilde and Amine stood at the entrance for two hours, smiling and concentrated. At that moment they were unaware that there were three or four future ministers among their guests. How could they have imagined that the group's drummer would become a governor, or that the drunken boy hiding behind the big palm tree to smoke a joint would die a few months later in a secret torture centre? They shook hands. They graciously accepted compliments about the decoration of the garden and thanked the guests for praying for their children's future. Now and then they would turn and look at each other. Each knew what the other was thinking: about the pile of rocks that this farm had once been. About the dinners that Mathilde had made, almost out of thin air, when Aïcha was a child. About the patched clothes they had worn, the bills that used to give them nightmares, the howling of jackals on those pitch-black nights. It was with awe that they measured the scale of their achievements, and from the heights of their success, he in his tuxedo and she in her silk dress, their past humiliations and sorrows appeared to them more painful than ever. They looked at each other and neither of them could really believe it.

But tonight they had to forget all of that. And when the photographer came to find them so he could take a family portrait, they held hands and walked towards the swimming pool. 'Parents in the middle.' Flanking them stood Mehdi, in his white suit with bell-bottomed trousers, and Aïcha in her long-sleeved dress. Selma had come from Rabat and she placed her hand on her daughter's shoulder. Sabah, for her part, had a fringe so long that it covered her eyes. Omar stood behind them, in his dark suit. They had all agreed on an official version of events to be given regarding Selim. He was in Paris, where he had a good job, but his employers had refused to let him take the time off. And when a guest remarked that it was 'such a shame Selim couldn't be with us', every member of the Belhaj family would tilt their head to one side and give a sigh of vexation: 'Ah, those French! Clearly they don't have the same family values as we do.'

Amine proved himself to be a wonderful host. He went from one group to another, glass in hand, and the waiters followed him around to make sure he always had something to drink. He invited his daughter to dance with him and the guests formed a circle around them. The women smiled, their hands covering their mouths, and it was hard to tell if they were moved by a father's tenderness towards his daughter or if they envied Aïcha for the hands that held her by the waist. Amine laughed and Aïcha stared at his white teeth, surprised to discover that her father was an excellent dancer. At eleven o'clock dinner was served and the guests gathered around the buffet. They elbowed one another, knocking a spoon to the ground, asking for a little more mayonnaise. Amine, who stood apart from the crowd, noticed a movement in the bushes. He walked over and spotted a group of peasants behind the trees. They were watching the party. Women and children sat beneath the big rubber tree, staring open-mouthed at the dancers, stunned by such beauty. There was a look of wonder on their faces, as if they were seeing the ocean for the first time or marvelling at the workings of some sophisticated machine. Amine headed towards them. He recognised Achour from his limp and the dead right arm that had hung uselessly by his side ever since he'd had his stroke. In the darkness Amine could not distinguish his face, deformed by the paralysis, but he saw Rokia, his wife, and two of their sons leaning against a tree trunk. He couldn't have said how many there were altogether. Ten, perhaps? All of them wore dark clothes and the branches of the rubber tree hid them from view. They were betrayed only by the sound of their shoes in the dry grass and the whisperings of the children who were excited by the music. All Amine would have had to do was wave his arm or whistle loudly and they would have scattered like wild cats, but he didn't. He drew back. Although he couldn't have explained why, he saw in the peasants' discreet, respectful presence a vague menace that he was too fearful to confront. He went to find Mathilde. 'There are people watching us.' She reassured him: 'Don't worry, it's all in hand. We're going to give them something – so they can enjoy the party too.'

A dark and burning anguish took hold of Amine. He turned to the house. The silhouettes of his guests were reflected in the glass doors, giving the illusion of a vast, endless crowd. He looked at those people, listened to the music, the English words pronounced with a Moroccan accent, and he thought that something was not quite right. All these young people were speaking French, drinking whisky with ice cubes and swinging girls between their legs while they danced. Mathilde hadn't wanted a traditional Moroccan group. 'I hate that kind of music – it gives me a headache.' Amine was suffocating. He ran a finger around the inside of his collar and struggled to follow the conversations of his guests. Idle chatter irritated him. Smiling, he said: 'Back in a minute', before slipping away. He felt ridiculous, as if he had been forced to wear someone else's clothes and shoes, and they were too small for him. A cloud passed overhead, veiling the silvery glitter of the stars. Beneath the trees the farmworkers were still sitting and watching. Mathilde had sent them plates of chicken and bottles of Coca-Cola. Amine wondered if they had ever tasted oysters or prawns. If they even knew what such creatures were. Was it possible they suspected that their severe and silent boss had himself been married in church to a woman dressed in white, that he had knelt before a priest? The photographs of that wedding were hidden in a box under Mathilde's bed. And they must never get out. Amine had forbidden her to show them to anyone, never mind to frame one and put it on the pedestal table in the dining room. Even the children had never seen them.

A waiter came over to fill his glass, but Amine brusquely refused. He had to keep a clear head. He had to protect his family. He did not take his eyes off the peasants sitting in the grass, eating chicken with their hands. The children bit into the wings and sucked their fingers. Amine imagined that something bad might happen to him. A misfortune. An attack. The farmworkers, maddened by this exhibition of wealth, would charge into the middle of the party. They would throw themselves at that extravagant buffet, smashing the bottles of alcohol and spitting at the bourgeois women who had so much time and money to waste. They would call them whores, kiss them on their mouths and necks. And it would excite them, the smell of perfume, the taste of imported lipstick. They would tear the white velvet bows off the palm trees and use the ribbons to lynch the guests. Their bodies would hang from the tree branches like marionettes, figures in tuxedos and embroidered kaftans. The peasants would stuff their pockets with necklaces and earrings, which they would sell in town on market day. They would roll around laughing on the sofas. Then the most violent among them, the heads of families, would round up the troops. They would send men to fetch weapons – pitchforks, rakes, spades, sticks – and soon the swimming pool would fill with blood. Even the waiters would have their throats slit.

In a panic, Amine grabbed his wife by the arm. He pointed out the peasants. 'They have to go. I don't want them watching us.' Mathilde stroked his hand. 'Most of them have already left, can't you see?' And it was true: only a few children remained under the rubber tree, holding big glass bottles of soda in both hands and blowing into the necks to make noises. Their parents were visible in the distance, heading back to the douar. One man had his arm draped around his wife's waist. Amine slowly nodded, like a child waking up after a nightmare. Mathilde understood then that her husband had spent his whole life terrified that everything he had acquired might one day be torn away from him. For him, happiness was unbearable because he felt he had stolen it from others.

Amine had advanced, step by step, slow as a tortoise, a dignified and hard-working creature. He had advanced towards an apparently modest goal – a house, a wife, children – but he had not understood that this goal, once he had reached it, would transform him. As long as he was struggling, menaced by other people, by nature, by his own despondency, he felt strong. But an easy life, a life of success and abundance, frightened him. His body was corrupted by a poison, swollen by bourgeois self-importance. He felt like a piece of fruit that had macerated in its own juices too long and had lost its firm roundness. People thought he was rich. People thought he was lucky and they wanted him to share what he had. To make up for the carelessness and injustice of fate.

How could they have been so happy? Thirty years after his wedding, sitting in a prison cell in Salé, this question would haunt Mehdi. He would think back to his early years married to Aïcha with a mixture of nostalgia and shame. Such happiness would strike him then as inexplicable. He would regret all the time that had passed and would be filled with remorse that he hadn't suffered, hadn't fought, hadn't risen up against the dark forces that were taking possession of the country.

Most of the prisoners in his cell were younger than him; they had not lived through that period. They could not understand. Nor could they possibly have suspected that what obsessed this discreet gentleman, dressed in a suit, smoking cigarette after cigarette as he sat behind bars, was not so much his future as his past. Mehdi, leaning back against the mould-covered wall, ran through his trial in his head. He was simultaneously the judge and the accused, and the crime that he was investigating bore no relation to the one that had landed him in this prison cell. It was a far greater and more terrible crime. A crime that was hard to define. For mitigating circumstances he could plead youth, recklessness, ambition, the desire to do the right thing. They had all acted the same way, he told himself, but the self-justification was hypocritical and he did not really believe it. It was true, all the same: he knew because he had seen them. He had shared with them those years of happiness and frivolity, of work and fun. The New Year's Eve celebrations on the beach. The sack races in the countryside. The hunting parties and boat trips. The second homes, from a simple hut to a luxury villa. That damned elite that everyone had always harped on about. For years he had told himself stories. Always the same stories, as fragile and unsound as a house of cards. He had told himself that he was caught between the devil and the deep blue sea, between the predators and the sheep. There were those who stole and those who were robbed, and he stood between them like a sheep dog, his task to guard the herd, to protect the power of his masters. Up to a certain point this compromise had struck him as acceptable. But the question kept returning, like a throbbing pain, a pulse in his temples, a punch in the stomach: how could you have been so happy? Happy despite the assassinations, the arrests, the deportations to secret labour camps? Happy despite the injustice, the fear, the whispers, the threats of public disgrace? Blissfully happy with that woman whose face came back to him now in dreams. Her smile, which he had photographed so many times. Her dark eyes, as determined as a soldier's. The vast expanse of her smile. The infinite grace of her hands.

He should have chosen another life. A life in which he would have been content to teach and to write. Ah, if only he had written, in the secrecy of his room, everything that had flowed through his heart! Tears rose to his eyes at the thought that he had betrayed his dream, that his soul had been impure, his heart false. He had raised his children in the cult of discretion and truthfulness. He had told them what his own father had told him: 'The makhzen is like a camel: it crushes what is under its hooves and stares always at the horizon. Keep your distance from it.' In the final months of his existence Mehdi would feel nostalgic for a life he had never led. Not the life of a hero, but of a simple man. Deep down, he would think, perhaps we didn't deserve to be free. At almost sixty years old, reduced to the company of rapists, drug dealers and murderers, he would make a strange observation. Age was not enough to rid one of illusions. Everything would have been so much easier if ideals truly died. If time could permanently erase them, expunge them from the depths of your conscience. But the illusions remained there, lurking somewhere inside. Damaged, withered. Like a regret or an old wound that flares up in cold weather. You can never be free of it, you can only pretend you don't care any more. All those years he had been condemned to a sort of inner exile. Inside him there survived a clandestine personality, silent and immobile now, which he would allow to escape only on rare occasions. All his life he had been wary, less of others than of himself.

How was it possible to live like a coward? To wake up like a coward, to get dressed like a coward, to eat like a coward and to love a woman while knowing, always, in your innermost heart and mind, that you were a coward? How was it possible to live with that knowledge? And to be happy?

Mehdi and Aïcha moved into a two-storey house in the hills of Rabat. From their bedroom they could look down on the Bou Regreg valley and, on clear days, the small town of Salé. To furnish it they went to the joutiya – the local flea market – and bought an old leather sofa, a long wooden table with sculpted feet, and a bookcase for Mehdi's books. They weren't rich but that didn't matter. They spent most of their time working and, as far as their leisure time was concerned, their salaries were sufficient for them to have parties with friends and to organise a few trips to the mountains or the seaside. The future did not worry them. They knew they were on the right side.

After months of hesitation Aïcha decided to specialise in gynaecology and obstetrics. Perhaps this choice owed something to the example of Dr Dragan Palosi, who had, when she was a child, helped her quench her thirst for knowledge. Or perhaps it was the memory of the woman whose stillborn baby she had delivered in the douar years earlier. Mehdi tried to dissuade her. He said he was concerned about the onerous work hours and the late-night emergency calls. The truth was that he did not think this specialty sufficiently noble. He was revolted by the idea of his wife always having her head between other women's legs, stuffing her fingers into their vaginas. All those years of study to do something that illiterate women had been doing for centuries: bringing children into the world.

On the day they moved to their new house, Mehdi gave her a copy of *Doctor Zhivago*. She didn't really like it when he gave her books. She felt he was trying to educate her, to fill the gaps in her culture, and these presents, instead of bringing her pleasure, left her feeling hurt. One evening, when she came home from the hospital, he asked her if she'd had time to do any reading. She apologised: it wasn't that she hadn't wanted to, but it was exhausting being on call, and, besides, this book was so difficult. All those characters with their complicated Russian names and all those stories of war and revolution left her bewildered. She kept having to go back to the previous chapter to remind herself what was happening. 'Ah,' Mehdi sighed, 'I thought you'd be interested in that book. The main character is a doctor, after all.' Aïcha was not swayed by this argument, and Mehdi was left to reflect on just how stubborn and tough-minded his wife could be. Nothing could make her deviate from the path she had chosen.

Dr Zhivago was a poet, and so was Aïcha's department head, Dr Ari Benkemoun. In Rabat it was said that he had delivered half of the city, and Aïcha thought how strange it must be to keep passing people in the street to whom you could truthfully say: 'I was the first person to see your face.' He welcomed Aïcha with an enthusiasm that took her by surprise. On her first day he gripped her shoulder and guided her through the department at top speed, talking constantly. He was midway through an anecdote about his student years in Paris when he stopped to greet a nurse. 'She's the real boss here – never forget that,' he told Aïcha, who nodded. They went into a room and for ten minutes Dr Benkemoun held a patient's hand between his own large, hairy hands. 'Thank

you, Doctor,' the woman said to him. 'I'll never forget you.'
He asked Aïcha to have lunch with him: 'You have so much
to learn and I have so much to impart!' And, while eating
marinated anchovies with his fingers, he told her about his
memories of one extraordinary birth ('The woman swore
she was as virginal as Jesus's mother!') before assuming a
more serious expression to warn Aïcha about septicaemia and
the tubal infections that often killed their patients. 'All over
the city we face dangerous, insidious competitors: chouafas,
butchers, unscrupulous midwives who carve women up. By
the time they come to us it is often too late. Maternity is a
mysterious thing, mademoiselle. Nothing is stronger than a
woman's determination to have a child. Well, nothing except a
woman's determination to get rid of a child she doesn't want.
You will see patients with burned thighs from melted lead
because someone has convinced them that their vagina has
been colonised by a djinn. You'll see women who have drunk
the blood of a cockerel or touched a dead man's penis.' Aïcha's
eyes widened. Benkemoun licked oil from the corner of his
lips. 'Don't look so shocked, mademoiselle! Our colleagues
too, however well qualified they might be, sometimes resort
to brutal practices. Have you never seen a clumsy curettage
that has caused an infection?' Aïcha nodded, remembering
the face of a twenty-year-old woman who had come to the
hospital in Strasbourg late one night. She had been a political
science student, dressed in a blue silk blouse and brass bracelets. To judge from her wounds, the doctor who had treated
her had wanted to punish her in the place where she had
sinned. Yes, Benkemoun was a poet who did not look down
upon the numerous legends surrounding the mysterious

act of procreation. To bear the pain of labour and to protect their baby, some women would cut up little pieces of paper on which they wrote verses from the Quran and then eat them during their contractions. Being a doctor, he explained to Aïcha, also meant facing up to the irrational, to this idea that women were connected to the cycles of the moon and that everything they imagined or fantasised during their pregnancy would have consequences for the well-being of their child.

During Aïcha's first weeks at the hospital Dr Benkemoun behaved as if possessed by an urgent need to teach. As if he were about to die from some terminal illness and had to pass on all his knowledge to his heir before expiring. In reality Dr Benkemoun had only one thought in mind: retirement. He wanted to move as far away from this little town as he could, away from all his patients, all the children he had brought into the world. He'd had all he could stand of simpering as young women told him ecstatically: 'You delivered my mother and one day you will deliver my daughter too!' Dr Benkemoun would rather die, frankly. He was so sick of the screaming of women in labour, of their never-ending contractions, of those telephone calls in the middle of the night. Wherever he went he feared the ringing of that cursed device. 'Dr Benkemoun!' would shout some maid or maître d'. 'They need you at the hospital!' How many card games had been interrupted by that sound? How many meals ruined by his inability to drink more than a single glass of wine, his departure before the desserts were served?

In Aïcha he had found his successor. He liked her, and not only because of her brilliant academic record or her somewhat old-fashioned politeness towards him. He watched her with the patients and was impressed by the aura of authority she emitted for one so young. To women whose husbands had forbidden them to take the pill she would say: 'Just do it anyway – he doesn't have to know.' One Friday evening he told her that he had to go out of town and he was leaving her in charge of the department until Monday morning. 'And when I get back I only want to hear good news. Understood?' That weekend, six children were born.

It wasn't easy living with a woman. There were certain things – in Aïcha's physical presence, in the reality of sharing a house with her – that disgusted Mehdi. The hair products she used and the peculiar smell, like furniture polish, with which they filled the bathroom. Her bedtime ritual of pulling her hair to one side, pinning it in place, then tightly knotting a scarf around her head. The boxes of sanitary towels which she no longer even bothered to hide from him, and all the pills she would take even before she was ill, 'because I can tell I'm about to get a migraine'. He didn't want to know about any of that, just as he had no desire to get involved in housework. He obstinately refused to accompany her to the shops, because what if he saw someone he knew? What would they think of him, walking around carrying a basket of vegetables? He rarely entered the kitchen and when he did it was only to ask her to bring him a drink. Try as she might to stare meaningfully at the fridge and invite him to help himself, he pretended not to understand.

He soon realised that he did not understand women at all. And what Aïcha told him when she came home from the hospital struck him not merely as uninteresting but positively repugnant. All his life he had been told what girls were allowed and forbidden to do, the rules for a virtuous existence, and he felt perfectly justified in being repulsed by women who talked too loudly or flirted with other men. As for everything connected with the mysteries of the female body, it revolted him to his very core. All this, he thought, was the fault of Cyd Charisse and those other actresses who had haunted his dreams as a child.

Aïcha was often absent but Mehdi did not criticise her. As the chief of staff for the Minister of Industry, he worked all week, often late into the night. On weekends he would spend hours at the golf course in Dar Es Salam, opened with great pomp a few years earlier. Important decisions regarding the country's future were made on the green, and anyone who wanted the ear of the king and his Court needed to know how to handle his woods and irons. In Rabat everyone dreamed of being a golf champion. Mehdi bought himself a traditional English golfing outfit: tartan plus-fours, plum leather shoes with metal studs, and a woollen cap that made him itch whenever he sweated. To all those who asked him for a favour or a discreet chat he would answer: 'Come and find me at the golf course on Sunday morning.' And the petitioner would walk down the fairways alongside him, hardly daring to speak as Mehdi addressed the ball and stared into the distance to calculate his shot. With his friends, his colleagues and sometimes even with Aïcha, he would talk about swings and bunkers, and he would buy books in which the great champions gave their advice on the game. Occasionally Aïcha would find him in the bathroom or the living room, legs apart, hands joined, swinging his arms back before striking an imaginary ball.

One evening they attended a reception organised by the king's chamberlain. Mehdi kept telling his wife: 'There will be some very important people there.' The inhabitants of Rabat always did that. They informed you about people ('She is the minister's mistress. He is a very influential man'), and they advised you to pay attention to what you said, the way you behaved, how much alcohol you consumed. They did it in an easy-going, casual way, but it changed everything. Aïcha wore a black dress with a velvet bow on the right shoulder. She tied her hair into a chignon at the back of her neck. Mehdi liked it when she tied back her hair. 'Don't tell everyone you're a gynaecologist. It makes people uncomfortable. Just tell them you're a doctor.'

That evening Aïcha stayed close to Mehdi, who seemed happy, at ease, as if all these people were old friends of his. They sat on the terrace. Mehdi ordered a whisky from a waiter in a Western-style jacket. He pontificated about travelling, his childhood, the importance of education in building the Moroccan of the future. He himself was the perfect example of this, having come from nothing, having – he claimed – lived in the direst poverty and extricated himself from it through sheer hard work and determination. Aïcha let him lie. She did not contradict him. She did not highlight the inconsistencies in his account or question his version of events. At one point he turned to her and asked: 'Do you remember?' and she bore witness to an imaginary scene. She said that she had been there, that she had seen it with her own eyes, and she laughed, as if this memory invented by him was as true as her love for him. She thought that was what loving someone was. Being loyal. Letting the other person reinvent and reconstruct his own life, not opposing his desire to turn himself into a fictional character. It would have been petty of her, she thought, to force him to smell the putrid stench of reality. It was not for others that Mehdi made up these stories – stories of distant voyages, comical encounters, heroic bar-room fights; it was not because he wanted to win anyone over or impress them. He himself was the only person he wanted to impress. He wanted his existence to be larger than life. He imagined himself a giant and he expected Aïcha to take part in the creation of his personal epic.

It was true that Mehdi invented stories, but – to Aïcha's great regret – he was not a writer. He expressed himself not with the words of a poet, but with the clumsy, complacent, self-congratulatory words of a bourgeois man. Those words that crush everything in their path, that have no meaning other than to dominate the world. Among these people, sitting beside her husband whose eloquence was dazzling them all, she thought back to the silent dinners of her childhood, to the fragmented, limping conversations between her parents. Mehdi used grandiose expressions. He said: 'It's a fundamental principle.' When he began to speak he sat back in his chair and, sure of his audience's attention, started his speech with 'the first point' before moving on to the second point. What Aïcha loved were the words of peasants, the frightened, inarticulate words of her patients. Poor words that tasted of ruin and a draught of air. Timid words that did not claim to understand the world, that offered no answers.

Aïcha stood up. She made a discreet signal to her husband and went back into the living room. She walked silently among the guests, the champagne in her glass slowly going flat. Mehdi told people: 'She's shy', and he said it in a tone of disappointment. He must have thought shyness a handicap, a defect that prevented you from living life to the full. He imagined that she must be sad, discouraged, frustrated not to be at ease with other people. 'You don't know how to put yourself forward,' he said regretfully, and Aïcha shrugged. Her shyness did not bother her. On the contrary, it seemed to her that this self-effacement, this absence of desire to be seen and heard, had enabled her to develop a sort of gift. A presence with others of which Mehdi knew nothing. First of all, she liked watching people, and even during long receptions when she didn't say a word she was never bored. She stared at the other guests and noted all the little details that nobody else could see. A scratch, a few centimetres long, at the base of the neck. A scar behind an ear. The young minister's bitten fingernails. A shaking hand. A callused heel in a shiny stiletto. She took up so little space, demanded so little time to express herself, that people confided in her with a freedom that had long ago ceased to surprise her. That night, sitting at the table opposite the king's chamberlain, she kept her eyes lowered to her plate as the woman beside her told her about losing a child, years earlier. 'It's something I never talk about. I don't know why I'm telling you all this.'

At work this gift of Aïcha's got her into trouble with the nurses. They were furious because her consultations lasted forever and every working day would go hours over schedule. Lying naked on an examination table, legs spread, her patients would talk about their lives. They would reveal secrets they had never spoken aloud before. They would tell her about their loneliness, their sorrows, their husband's harshness, their mother's indifference, their children's ingratitude. They would talk about their lovers, their money problems, and it was as if they'd forgotten the presence of the doctor in the white coat sitting between their thighs. Sometimes, leaving Aïcha's office, these women would wonder what had got into them and blush at having unburdened themselves like that. Was it because they were nervous, ashamed at having to strip off in front of another woman? Or was it the way the doctor had looked at them that had bewitched them somehow? Mehdi would often express surprise that Aïcha knew so much about people. In the street, when her patients recognised her, they would throw themselves at her, hug her tightly, then say to the husband or children who stood beside them: 'This is the doctor I told you about.' Mehdi, on the other hand, was so occupied with his own affairs that he forgot names and faces. Often he would turn to his wife and say: 'Who is she again?'

When she was a child, Aïcha used to play the 'Ladies' game with her brother. In the afternoon, when Amine was out in the fields and Mathilde in her clinic, they would open the wardrobes and borrow their mother's dresses, hats and high-heeled shoes. Selim would sometimes climb onto his mother's white dressing table so that he could reach the hat shelf. For the little boy, the excitement of dressing up in his mother's clothes was intensified by the fear of being caught in the act by his father. He would smear his face with make-up, weigh down his neck and wrists with jewellery and prance around on high heels, giggling. 'That's not how you're supposed to do it,' Aïcha would scold him, annoyed that he wasn't taking the game seriously. For her it wasn't a fancy-dress party or a source of ridicule, it was about becoming a real woman. The kind of woman who wears woollen coats and gloves, who slips a stack of banknotes into her bra – a gesture that struck her as horrifyingly coarse, but fascinated her. She imitated the mannerisms of neighbours, strangers, her mother, clutching her handbag to her chest, spinning a bunch of keys around her index finger. She held her doll in one arm and told it off for not being good. She pretended to smoke and shouted orders at an imaginary maid.

Now she was a lady, a real one. Her handbag was not filled with sweets and the keys she carried were used to open a real car, to lock the door of a real house. But what she wanted more than anything was to know how to be a good wife to her husband, to know how to 'keep house' and receive guests. She was hardly ever there, she couldn't cook, and they mostly survived on sandwiches and pizzas. Her mother, by contrast, was the queen of her castle. In March every year Mathilde would embark upon what she called her 'big spring clean'. All the drawers were lined with fabric. For years she had provided three meals a day to her indifferent children and continually asked them: 'What would make you happy?' She knew recipes by heart and when Aïcha asked her about how much butter or cumin to use, Mathilde would reply: 'I don't know – that kind of thing is a question of feel.' Mathilde could sit in silence with other women and recite condolences in Arabic. She could hug poor, sick people without feeling disgusted by their filthiness or their symptoms. Not once had Aïcha thought of her mother as submissive. On the contrary, Mathilde seemed to her a sort of fairy to whose will human beings, animals and inanimate objects were all obedient. And now that she was a lady herself, she kept thinking enviously about her indefatigable mother who ran around the house, a duster draped over her shoulder, humming Alsatian songs.

One day Aïcha suggested to Mehdi that they organise a dinner party for some of his colleagues from the ministry. 'I know it's important for you. You need to nurture those relationships.' Mehdi hesitated. He was preoccupied with a speech he had to write and deliver in front of the Council of Ministers and His Majesty. A speech in classical Arabic that was giving him cold sweats. At the colonial school he had never learned to write in his own language and now, at almost thirty, he was secretly studying the alphabet and verb conjugation. His friend Ahmed had advised him to transcribe his speech phonetically, and now he spent all his evenings practising his pronunciation. 'You wouldn't have to do anything,' Aïcha reassured him. 'I'll take care of it all.'

While she examined her patients she thought about the menu she would serve to their guests. Once, she wrote 'salmon mousse' on a prescription instead of a particular brand of pills. And when the patient, perplexed, asked her what it meant, she became bogged down in absurd explanations: 'You should eat more salmon,' Aïcha stammered. 'It's good for your hormones.' She considered preparing some Moroccan specialties but she was afraid of making a fool of herself in front of these men, most of them Fassis, whose mothers were all excellent cooks and who had passed on their own mothers' impressively sophisticated recipes to their children. Then she remembered the success she had encountered during her first summer at Monette's beach hut by serving Alsatian charcuterie. In fact, Mehdi's colleagues often called her the Alsatian. They told her about their university years in Paris and the little brasserie in the Latin Quarter where they could drink pints of beer and eat *saucisses-frites* for only a few centimes. I know! Aïcha thought. I'll make them sauerkraut.

Aïcha went to the Porcelet Gourmand, the best charcuterie in town, which was run by a tall, severe Frenchwoman with skin as rough as a gherkin. Her assistant was a young, balding Moroccan man who had trouble pronouncing the words 'ham' and 'saveloy'. Aïcha queued for fifteen minutes behind Frenchwomen, visiting lecturers and chauffeurs for rich people.

She stared at the young man's hands as he sliced lard and *saucisson* with astonishing dexterity. 'Next.'

All afternoon she slaved away in her kitchen. The potatoes were overcooked. The cabbage, despite the wine and the spices, was somewhat bland. But the charcuterie looked excellent and she could already imagine her guests dipping their frankfurters into the mustard, going into ecstasies over the pork knuckle that melted in the mouth. She waited for a long time, sitting at the kitchen table, vainly swatting away midges from the plate of fresh fruit. Twice she called the ministry and Mehdi's secretary explained, in a sympathetic voice, that the meeting still hadn't ended. When she finally heard the car entering the garage she smoothed down her skirt, straightened her hair and furtively lifted the lid from the cooking pot. Everything was ready. Aïcha, whose teachers had always praised her for her calmness and composure, was a hive of anxiety. She was afraid of making a faux pas, saying the wrong thing.

The guests – all of them men – took their seats in the living room. Aïcha began moving back and forth between the kitchen and the living room. She opened a bottle of champagne. 'There's whisky too, if you prefer.' She passed around a plate of little *gougères*, insisting that everyone take second helpings until a look from Mehdi informed her that it was time to back off. 'Dinner is served,' she announced, and the men headed towards the dining room. Aïcha put the dish of sauerkraut in the middle of the table and ceremoniously removed the lid from the pot. She stuck a fork in a sausage and brandished it in the air. 'Sauerkraut from Alsace. A typical dish from my homeland.' Later, she wondered if it had been that little phrase that had shocked people, even more than the fact that she was serving them a pot full of pig meat. 'A dish from my home-land,' she had said, and it was as if she had forgotten where she was, who she was, who her husband was. She had grown up in Morocco, just as all her guests had. Her name was Aïcha, she was the daughter of a local farmer, and yet she had said 'a dish from my homeland' while waving a sausage in their faces. One of the guests brought his napkin to his mouth as if he wanted to wipe away a blemish. Then he raised his hand and said softly, apologetically: 'That's very kind, but not for me. I've had sauerkraut before and it's very nice. But I've just come back from Mecca, so . . .' Still holding the fork with the pinkish frankfurter hanging from its tines, Aïcha turned her gaze on another guest. 'Would you like to taste it?'

'I'll take some cabbage. You cooked them separately, right?'

The meal seemed to last forever. They chewed the mari-nated cabbage in silence and Aïcha found herself glaring at the pot with its lid firmly in place. She was afraid of how Mehdi would react once his guests had left. She imagined him in a rage, and his image became blurred with memories of Amine, whose yelling had terrorised her as a child. She wished she could beg for forgiveness, admit she'd been stupid, that she'd acted unthinkingly. But Mehdi didn't yell. He closed the door behind the last guest and joined his wife in the kitchen. He did not offer to help her wash up. He just lifted the lid from the pot, took out a sausage, and bit into it.

When Aïcha told Mathilde about her misadventure, her mother advised her to hire a maid. Everyone had a maid, it really wasn't a big deal, but Aïcha – who paid a woman to come and clean her house twice a week – had never wanted to hire anyone on a full-time basis. She hated the idea of another person living in her home, someone who would watch her living, being happy, getting drunk, someone who would spy on her, perhaps, her husband and herself, when they had sex. All her life Aïcha had heard women talking about their maids. It was an inexhaustible subject of conversation, a breeding ground for sordid or comical anecdotes. 'You'll never guess what my maid did!' a woman would say over tea. Then another desperate housewife would ask: 'Would you happen to know of a good maid? I've just fired mine.'

Aïcha began her quest. She asked friends, colleagues, the nurses at the hospital. She even asked her neighbour, who employed two maids, a chauffeur and a caretaker. And for weeks she would listen to these women who, like an ancient chorus, warned her of the dangers to which she was exposing herself by allowing a servant to enter her home. Maids are thieves, maids are horny little minxes. You're bringing a virgin into your house, after all; it's hardly surprising if she ends up becoming hysterical, violent, jealous. Maids are sexually frustrated, so they make advances to the man of the house, and you can hardly blame the husband if the girls end up pregnant and jobless, can you?

The local watchman went even further. Aïcha was a young, naive woman. She mustn't be too soft with them. 'Maids are liars and deceivers,' he told her. 'If they don't look you in the eye, it's not out of respect or fear, believe me. They're ungrateful, never content, even when you spoil them, and even after years or decades living under your roof they will betray you and let you down.' Aïcha talked to her friends about the issue. They were lawyers, doctors, university lecturers, who understood her consternation and who, like her, did not have the time to stir the tajine sauce, change the baby's nappy, iron the husband's shirts, chop olives and coriander. To do all that, they told her, you had to train a maid. According to Ronit it was better to hire a young girl. 'The old ones think they know it all when the truth is they're just as ignorant as all the others.' She would have to teach the maid to do everything: set a table, stop acting like a savage, get used to the morality of civilised people. Make a bed, follow the rules of hygiene, know when her apron has become so dirty she needs to change it. Maids wore specially designed blue or pink uniforms that could be bought from shops in the city centre or even at the main market. Aïcha went into one of these shops and also bought some woollen blankets – 'maids adore blankets'. Maids did not eat at the same table as their employers and were only allowed to eat certain brands of yoghurt. They ate leftovers in the kitchen. All they cared about was bread and sauce anyway, so what did it matter if their employers had eaten all the meat? The problem, her hairdresser remarked, was that maids couldn't read, and that complicated everything. You couldn't ask them to follow a recipe, you couldn't leave a note on the kitchen table with instructions for the day. They were creatures of instinct. You had to show them everything, and then all of them – from the most gifted to the stupidest – were capable of reproducing the correct actions. Women would also sometimes say things like: 'I tell you, that maid isn't stupid, it's a shame' or 'What a waste – a girl like that could have made something of herself.' But nobody liked intelligent maids. They were the least trustworthy, the most recalcitrant of all.

Selma worried: 'Where will she sleep?' Some employers made their maids sleep on the kitchen floor but Mehdi didn't like that idea. He said it wasn't seemly. 'These days, in all the most fashionable houses, the maids have a building for themselves at the bottom of the garden, or a basement,' Aïcha's aunt explained.

The chief nurse assured Aïcha she could find her a young Black girl, a Touarga, raised among the slaves in the palace, who was a divine cook. The local watchman suggested his cousin but she had back problems and couldn't lift anything. And then, one day, Fatima entered her life.

Fatima arrived one Monday morning, dressed in a dark djellaba, her feet shod in worn old slippers. Her hair was tied in a bun and covered with a headscarf. Aïcha ushered her inside. She felt ill at ease. What was she supposed to say? Should she invite the young woman to sit down? Offer her something to drink? She decided to show her around the house, without meeting Fatima's eye. The girl remained silent, content simply to nod. Two living rooms. There were two living rooms in this house. Two living rooms, each bigger than the biggest shack in the shanty town. She stared at the floor. It would take time to clean all those tiles. And it must be slippery, a floor like that. She kept sticking her hand under her headscarf and scratching at her scalp with long, dirty fingernails. Aïcha asked her questions. Did she know how to cook? Fatima shrugged and Aïcha said: 'I'll teach you. We don't eat at home very often anyway.' Fatima's room was next to the laundry room, beneath the kitchen. As she showed the maid her new quarters, Aïcha hesitated. The room was big, the bed brand new, but the air there was stifling because of the boiler and the noisy old fridge. 'You need to air it,' she said. 'You won't forget, will you?' She put a white uniform on Fatima's bed, with a pocket on the right breast, and a pretty blue apron wrapped in plastic packaging. 'This is your uniform. Whenever it gets dirty, take it off and put on a clean one. There are two others in the wardrobe.'

Later she told Mehdi how uncomfortable she had felt during that first afternoon with Fatima. He was barely even listening. He did not want to get involved. But she had no reason to feel guilty. They were giving the girl a job and they would do everything they could to make sure she was fine. Then, one evening, Aïcha started scratching her head. She thought the itching must have been caused by the product she was using to straighten her hair. But one day at work, as she was scratching hard behind her ear, she felt something burst under her nail. On the tip of her index finger she saw a huge head louse and a small drop of blood. On her way back from the hospital she stopped at a pharmacy. When she got home she went down to Fatima's room and made the girl sit on a chair. Aïcha put on rubber gloves, draped a towel over the maid's shoulders and asked her to untie her headscarf. Fatima refused, reacted ridiculously in fact, crying like a lamb about to be slaughtered. 'Why are you being such a baby about this?' Aïcha demanded. 'I'm not going to hurt you. I'm going to use the same stuff on my hair, you know. I've got nits, thanks to you.' In the end Fatima calmed down. She untied the scarf, and for the first time Aïcha saw the maid's hair. It was auburn, dirty and tied up in a turban. Grimacing, Aïcha took out the dozens of pins that were holding it in place. The maid's hair fell down her back, all the way to the base of her spine. 'How long has it been since you washed your hair?' Aïcha asked in what Mehdi called her 'doctor's voice' – a clear, curt, authoritative voice; a voice without malice, a voice that did not judge; a voice that healed. Fatima was incapable of responding. She kept snivelling, as if her employer had stripped her naked and mocked her. Aïcha poured out the entire contents of the bottle onto the maid's head. 'If I'd known you had this much hair I'd have bought more.' After that, she wrapped Fatima's hair in a white sheet, as Mathilde used to do when they were children. 'And now we wait.'

Fatima sat on the chair to wait. She didn't dare move. She stared at the wall facing her, at the mould stain that made the whole basement smell bad. Aïcha came back. She removed the towel, dropped it on the floor and gave a cry of disgust. There were so many lice that the white towel appeared almost black. 'We're never going to get them all like this. We'll have to cut your hair.' Fatima stood up and screamed. She did not want her hair cut. She refused to let Aïcha touch it. She ran into the bathroom, shut the door and locked it. Aïcha hammered on the door. She begged the maid to be reasonable. 'It'll grow back, you know, it's not the end of the world.' But Fatima did not reply. She stayed there all evening and refused to open the door when Aïcha brought her some dinner. Mehdi was obliged to intervene. He ordered the maid to leave the bathroom. 'You're not a child – stop acting like one!' He threatened to call the police if she did not obey him. Finally the maid appeared, her eyes swollen from hours of weeping. She sat on the chair and watched as long strands of her hair fell to the floor.

Once a month Fatima went home to the shanty town. As soon as she opened the door of the shack, her mother demanded money and Fatima handed over her wages. The mother licked the tip of her index finger and counted the notes in silence. She couldn't read, but she certainly knew how to count. She arranged the banknotes into little piles, folded them in four and stuffed them in her bra. Once, Fatima asked her what each pile was for and her mother replied: 'None of your business. Just concentrate on working.' In the shanty town nothing changed: nothing in the landscape, nothing in the houses, nothing even in people's conversations and habits. They brooded over the same problems, they suffered always with the same pains. Fatima understood then that this was what poverty was: a world that does not change. When wealthy, bourgeois, educated people met each other, they would always discuss what was new in their lives. Their daily existence could surprise them. They talked about the future and even revolution. They believed that change was possible.

Sometimes Fatima's mother would ask her about her employers' house. What it looked like, what they ate. She wanted descriptions of their car, their bathroom. But the maid was incapable of describing anything in detail. What intrigued her were not furnishings, household appliances or the bookcase overflowing with books. No, what she found strange, what frightened her, was the silence. That graveyard-like silence unbroken by the shrieking of children or the sound of rain on the corrugated-iron roof or women yelling insults at their neighbours. During the day, when her employers went out to work, Fatima found herself alone in the house. In that silence everything felt ominous. She had never realised before just how loud her life was. The sounds of her own body disturbed her. She startled at the smallest of noises. The rush of water in the onyx sink, the gurgling of the pipes, the roar of the imported refrigerator. The house was located in a chic residential neighbourhood. Nobody walked in the surrounding streets. The only noise was the rumble of passing cars – big, beautiful cars – in which chauffeurs drove children to the French school. That silence tortured Fatima. On Sundays, Aïcha would lie down on the living room sofa, her feet resting in her husband's lap, and the two of them would read. They didn't even look at each other. Occasionally they would summon Fatima with a little bell that Mathilde had given them, and ask her to bring them refreshments. And Fatima would always wonder why reading made them so thirsty.

Her employers always spoke French to each other, so Fatima did not understand anything they said. She tried to remember certain words: 'quickly', 'spoon', 'goodbye'. She did not speak their language, but she was the first one to realise that Aïcha was pregnant. Her employer no longer ate anything at breakfast and sometimes she would leave work in the middle of the afternoon to come home for a nap. She started buying gherkins, which she would eat while standing in the kitchen, and she changed her brand of cigarettes. Fatima thought she would like looking after a baby. She would like it much more than she liked cleaning toilets and washing the paving stones in the garden. She would no longer have to spend her afternoons alone, moping in front of the television, listening to the king's speech on the national broadcasting service without understanding a word he said. The king, too, spoke French sometimes. Fatima started dropping hints. One day she told Aïcha that she had two little brothers and a little sister and she had looked after them when they were babies. 'I know how to raise children,' she boasted. But Aïcha wasn't listening. 'I can't stay in the kitchen,' she told the maid. 'The smell of meat makes me feel ill.'

After three months Fatima thought perhaps she had been mistaken. What did she know about the lives of these people, after all? All that stuff about gherkins and cigarettes was none of her business. No matter how hard she stared at Aïcha's belly, it remained as flat as ever. Her employer was on call at the hospital again, she no longer refused to accompany Mehdi to parties, and she was wearing the same clothes as before. Perhaps the baby is asleep, the maid thought. She remembered the old legend she'd heard so many times, about how the foetus, inside the mother's belly, could be put to sleep by a magic spell. For months, even years, it would keep still, being born only when the mother felt ready to welcome it into the world. Fatima wished desperately she could talk to Aïcha about this. She would beg her: 'Wake it up and I'll help you look after it. You wouldn't have to do a thing. You could go to work, and your husband too. I'd look after that child like it was my own.'

When Amine gets out of bed, the sun is not yet up. The sky is barely light and on the grass a layer of frost crackles under his feet. Throughout the winter of 1974 he has suffered from insomnia. The country's troubled situation has thrown him into a state of constant anxiety. In August 1972, one month after Aïcha's wedding, there was another attempt to assassinate Hassan II. His Boeing was attacked in mid-air, but somehow the king survived. 'A chance in a billion' was the judgement of the computer analysts after they had examined the bullet holes in the aircraft's body. The king had survived odds of a billion to one. It was a miracle.

Since then Amine has not been able to sleep. The simple act of lying down, resting his head on a pillow, puts him into a state of extreme nervousness. He has to do something. Produce. Invent. So he puts on a jacket, tugs a fur ushanka over his head and walks along the dirt path towards the orchard. The farm is deserted and he is suddenly overcome with a desire to crouch down on the frozen ground and roar like an animal. A yell to bring the panicked peasants running from their homes. 'Get to work!' he would shout, and the women would rush towards the humid heat of the greenhouses, scarves in hand, their uncovered hair blowing behind them. The men, still barefoot, would pull on their boots while hopping forwards.

He has used several different foremen since Mourad's death, but none of them have impressed him as being sufficiently hard-working or competent. They do not understand Amine's ambition, or when they do understand, their eyes take on a shifty, envious gleam and Amine gets rid of them. I can do it all myself. I don't need anyone else, he thinks, pacing up and down the rows of mandarin trees; the boss should always work harder and be better than his employees, if he wants to deserve what he harvests. He picks a mandarin from a branch, peels the fruit, then methodically eats it, one segment after another. He takes a small notebook from his pocket in which he notes, for each fruit, the number of pips he spits into the palm of his hand. It doesn't matter that he hasn't eaten anything else since the night before and that the mandarin's acidity gives him stomach ache. If he wants to improve the variety, to one day produce seedless fruit, he has to keep doing this. Amine raises his jacket collar. He rubs his eyes. He's sleeping so little that he's started having visions. He talks with the dead and the missing. His son Selim, whose voice he heard on the telephone the previous spring. The boy called for Mathilde's birthday, but it was Amine who answered the phone. And he just stood there, silent, petrified, despite his son's desperate shouts on the other end of the line: 'Hello? Hello? Can you hear me? Hello?' By some strange irony, his son lives in America now, in the country that was once a source of inspiration to Amine. He had wanted to turn his own territory into a new California, he remembers. He also talks with Mourad, whose ghost glides over the estate and whose memory weighs on his heart with all the heaviness of remorse. Amine begs him for forgiveness, just as he begs forgiveness from his father, Kadour, who left him this land and who never got to see these trees in bloom. Amine walks across the field of almond trees, goes around the big warehouse and comes to the whitewashed walls behind which are buried his brother Jalil and his mother Mouilala. He points his torch beam at his mother's gravestone and, even though it is not a surprise, even though he has seen it several times before, his heart speeds up as he makes out the silhouette of a palm tree in the darkness. The tree has grown there, at the foot of the tomb, facing Mecca, and there is nothing, other than a miracle, to explain its presence. Amine moves closer, puts his arms around the trunk and kisses the bark with his dry lips. It is the visible that is most mysterious, he thinks. Not ghosts and spirits and djinns, but trees and morning frost. Perhaps Mathilde was right. Perhaps he is going mad.

More than ever he feels attached to this earth. His dead are buried in it and his own corpse, one day, will rot here. He is from here and he feels a fierce attachment to this domain, this country. Amine inherited it from his father and he would like his own son to inherit it from him, but he cannot compete with the vast world that has snatched his children away from him. Selim in New York, Aïcha in the capital. Can he blame them for wanting an easier life? When they were young, the few times when they didn't want to do their homework, Mathilde would tell them: 'You have to work if you want to succeed, if you don't want to end up a farmer.' The nightmare of ruin and debt was followed by the nightmare of having no heir to take over the farm. The pain of that still gnaws at him. When he is dead and buried, another man will tread this earth, a stranger of whom he knows nothing and who will perhaps destroy it all. These thoughts obsess him and he does not understand what he has done to deserve such ingratitude. Sometimes he has the feeling that this land is cursed, that instead of welcoming and protecting those who live here, it forces them to flee. What did he do wrong? He committed so many sins. Worst of all, perhaps, his pride led him not to love those around him as well as he could have. When Selim was a little boy, they would sometimes arm-wrestle on the kitchen table and not once did Amine let him win. And yet he knew that winning would have filled his son with joy, that he would have jumped on top of his chair and yelled: 'I beat Papa!' But Amine could never bring himself to let it happen. It was beyond his control. A son, he thought, must be toughened up, must learn to lose.

How long does he stay there, standing in front of his mother's grave? It is daytime and his torch is still on when he decides to make his way back to the house. The first farmworkers are arriving from the douar and he beckons a few of them over with a brusque wave of his hand. Here, there's a hole in the plastic sheeting of a greenhouse. There, the crates have not been put near the plants to be delivered. There is so much to do. His brain is buzzing.

He sits at his desk and puts his hand on the teapot that Tamo has left for him. It is barely even warm. Through the window he can see the Christmas tablecloths that Mathilde has washed and hung from a line. Opposite the big palm tree, little Alsatian girls in wooden clogs are holding hands, and fat white geese are lifting their beaks up to heaven. He goes back to reading an article that Aïcha sent him, describing the research of a certain Ancel Keys on the benefits of olive oil. He is absorbed by his reading when Achour knocks on the glass door, making him jump. Since his stroke, Achour has found it difficult to speak. Using his left arm, the only one that still works, he gestures at Amine to come outside. Achour tells him that during the night some men built a large wooden stage on the other side of the road. This morning they arranged chairs, planted flags and spread vast carpets in shimmering colours over the ground. 'You know what that means?' Amine nods. 'The king is coming.' The king, who never walks on bare earth, on wet grass, city streets or sandy beaches. The king who, since the attempts on his life, is no longer merely their guide and protector but God's chosen one, saved by the grace of fate. Every day brings its litany of good news. The king wishes to give bread to the people, develop the road network, raise salaries, subsidise sugar, build dams, inaugurate a new holiday. On 19 September 1972, in a speech broadcast on television, the king announced the launch of an agrarian revolution and the nationalisation of colonised territories. And today, here and elsewhere across the country, a ceremony is being prepared to celebrate the handover of property deeds to landless peasants.

Amine leaves his office and strides along the dirt path, followed by Achour. 'Go back to work,' Amine tells him. 'And make sure the others are where they should be.' He walks to the front gate and crosses the road. Dozens of cars are parked below, and journalists, wielding notebooks and cameras, are taking their seats in the audience. Some of the European journalists have raised their jacket collars and are blowing into their hands, surprised by the bitter cold of December here, which slips through their layers of clothing and makes them shiver. They know nothing of this country, Amine thinks; they imagine Morocco is a hot country. A Moroccan television crew is setting up a camera between the rows of seats. Amine recognises the presenter, a specialist in royal visits who is mocked all over the country for his ability to speak endlessly without saying anything, his words filling the long silences while waiting for the king's arrival.

The wind blows and they all look up at the dozens of flags that line the side of the road. The bright-red fabric billows, making a flapping noise, and the green five-pointed star appears then vanishes. To the right of the stage a group of musicians in white djellabas, their shaved heads covered by turbans, are tuning their instruments. Amine climbs on top of the wall that encircles his property. From here he can see a truck arriving from El Hajeb. The sound of the engine sends the crowd into a state of chaotic agitation. The members of the orchestra stand straight, ready to play the first notes of the national anthem. They expect to see the king, but in fact it is only some peasants, who get out of the truck one by one in their new djellabas, their faces and hands scrubbed clean. Policemen escort them to their places, telling them in stern voices what they should say, what they should do, how they should behave. A journalist heads over to the group of peasants; he wants to interview them, but is told that this is not the time. The king might arrive at any moment, so he must remain in his position. There will be plenty of time afterwards to ask questions.

Amine does not take his eyes off these men. They shoot each other knowing looks; some of them laugh and kiss one another on the cheeks. They are lined up in front of an immense portrait of the king and his son, the crown prince. Hassan II, in a beige djellaba and a fez, a proud peasant among peasants. This picture bears no resemblance to the one that hangs in Amine's office. Gone are the double-breasted suit, the silk pocket handkerchief and the flannel jacket. Gone is the thousand-yard stare, like the models from Studio Harcourt. No, this portrait is very different and it reminds Amine of images from his childhood. The photograph of his own father, Kadour Belhaj, taken at a studio in the city centre. The fez, the woollen djellaba, the hard gaze of a man used to commanding others.

Someone gives the order and the musicians pick up their lutes and drums and strike up an ugly, nagging tune, one of those soulless songs that are played constantly on the radio. Amine realises that the king will not come and he is about to head back to work when he hears some journalists cry out in surprise. In the distance, in a cloud of dust, a dozen horsemen can be seen arriving, dressed as if in the time of the Sultan Moulay Ismail. Fine leather boots, red and green turbans. They raise their muskets and fire into the air as the crowd roars excitedly. The Europeans can't believe their eyes. For a moment they forget that they are here to work, that they have articles to write, and they behave like children at a fairground. Images of a long-gone age appear before their eyes. The great ancestral Morocco, which the people here are always harping on about, is not dead after all. The riders steer their horses in rapid circles, the front hooves rearing up at the last moment. The peasants applaud, smiling proudly at the thought that all this pomp is just for them.

Two Mercedes advance along the roadside and some men get out. Amine recognises the pasha and, beside him, a man he thinks is probably a minister, though he isn't sure about that. He pulls his woollen socks up over his calves and stands on top of the narrow wall. This way he has a better view of the pasha, who climbs onto the stage and sits in the smaller of the two chairs. The throne, with its golden frame, remains unoccupied. The audience understands that the king will not come and an immense wave of weariness seems to overwhelm them. Ingrates, Amine thinks. Don't you think he has better things to do?

The pasha taps the microphone. It doesn't work. A thin young man in a grey suit starts frantically running around in all directions. At last the microphone is fixed and the pasha speaks. Amine can't hear his words very well but he recognises the tone. He has heard it before from children who have been to the msid, the Quranic school, and who have been forced to learn verses by heart. The pasha pays tribute to the king, glorified by God, and to the agrarian reform His Majesty has called for. 'The Moroccan agricultural revolution has begun! His Majesty, may God give strength to his reign, knows that it is the peasants who are responsible for this country's greatness and prosperity. And soon, with his dam-building policy, we will be able to irrigate every acre of land. We are going to give you back what is yours. We are going to enrich the poor without impoverishing the rich.' The young man in the grey suit hands the pasha a piece of paper. The pasha shouts out a name. A fellah steps forward as the crowd applauds. For the first time in his life, he walks onto a stage and people look at him, film him, cheer him. Tomorrow, perhaps, he will be on television, so the fellah turns to the camera and smiles. He has only two teeth. The pasha claps. 'Look how happy this man is!' And he presents the fellah with his property deed. Flashbulbs pop. The peasant kisses the piece of paper, then kisses the pasha's shoulder. Ululations rise from the audience, cries of joy, shouts of 'Long live the king!' and 'Long live the people!'

Amine knows how this will end. Once the property deeds have been handed out, they will rise in unison and swarm like grasshoppers over the buffet of couscous and grilled meat. Having no desire to see this, he steps along the top of the wall like a tightrope walker before jumping off the other side. He passes the rows of mandarin trees and sees the bright-orange fruit shining in the cold winter sunlight. It promises to be a good harvest. He should be happy: tomorrow there will be even more money, more success, more power. Of course, anything can happen. Frost, a storm, parasites that take over the plants and reduce his work to nothing. The farmer is always in God's hands. This is what he repeats to Mathilde, but she does not understand. She says he looks ill. That he should see a doctor. That his insomnia is taking a toll on his health. She has even insinuated that he is crazy, paranoid, as his brother Jalil used to be.

Outside the door of the farmhouse some peasant women are waiting, their heads and shoulders protected by large woollen blankets. Some of them are holding sugar loaves or young rabbits, which they will offer to Mathilde in exchange for her knowledge. In the courtyard the tablecloths have dried and it is easier to make out the colours in the dresses of the young Alsatian girls, the bright-yellow beaks of the geese. Amine goes over to the peasant women. Intimidated by the master's presence, they pull the blankets a little lower over their faces, speak in quieter voices, pat their babies' backs to stop them whining. The women move away from the door to let him pass, but Amine does not go inside. No, he just stands there, motionless, frozen, his feet rooted to the ground as if he has no intention of ever leaving. The women look at one another but say nothing. What is wrong with him? Why is he acting like this? Is he sick too? His eyes are red from lack of sleep and his hands shake slightly. Amine presses his forehead to the glass door. He watches Mathilde, who is sitting on a chair, slowly bandaging a young man's calf. She looks up at him and a smile illuminates her face. She jumps to her feet so quickly that the patient cries out in pain. Amine sees her coming towards him and he thinks she is capable, with that smile, with that boyish gait, of bringing him back to reason. And his lips articulate: 'Home.' Mathilde comes out into the courtyard and a woman rushes over to offer her blanket, but Mathilde waves her away. 'I'm not cold,' she says, taking her husband's frozen hands in her own. 'Mehdi called. Our granddaughter was born this morning.' Later the women in the douar will describe how they saw Amine draw his wife close to him, so close that the peasant women thought he was holding on to her to stop himself falling. And there, under the high palm trees, they began swaying from foot to foot, despite the icy December wind, despite the whispers of the incredulous watching women. They danced, and some of the spectators claimed that they could see tears rolling down the master's face and that they heard Mathilde say in Arabic: 'You are happy, aren't you?'

Acknowledgements

This book owes its existence to the precious testimonies of people who lived through this period of history in Morocco or who studied it. They were a great help to me. Thank you to Zakya Daoud for her generosity, her sense of humour, her frankness and open-mindedness. Thank you to Kenza Sefrioui for her precious advice, and to Driss el-Yazami for his unfailing humanity and integrity. All my gratitude goes to Tahar Ben Jelloun, who is forever teaching me about my history. I owe a great deal to Mohamed Tozy, who has been enlightening me for years, enabling me, through his colossal work, to better understand my country. Hamid Barrada, my eternal friend, was once again an exceptional source of aid, as was Perla Servan-Schreiber, who agreed to travel back into the past for me. And so too was Pierre Vermeren, my former teacher. Thank you to Dominic Rousseau, who has written about the hippies in Morocco and who very generously agreed to enlighten me on that surprising period in Essaouira. I must also thank Françoise Autin for her affection and for the methodical research she carried out on my behalf. Fatna El Bouih, for whom I feel great admiration, kindly agreed to answer my questions. Thank you to Souad Balafrej for her trust and friendship. I would like to thank my father's friends who came forward while I was writing this book and who, with great modesty and tenderness, recounted their youthful years in his company. I would also like to pay tribute here to all those who had the courage to testify to the Equity and Reconciliation Commission about crimes committed during the 'years of lead' in Morocco. The report that emerged from the commission was a priceless source for me, and those who helped compile it have all my admiration.